MW00490862

the
forgotten
wife

BOOKS BY EMMA ROBINSON

The Undercover Mother
Happily Never After
One Way Ticket to Paris
My Silent Daughter

the forgotten wife

emma robinson

Bookouture

Published by Bookouture in 2020

An imprint of Storyfire Ltd.
Carmelite House
50 Victoria Embankment
London EC4Y 0DZ

www.bookouture.com

Copyright © Emma Robinson, 2020

Emma Robinson has asserted her right to be identified
as the author of this work.

All rights reserved. No part of this publication may be reproduced,
stored in any retrieval system, or transmitted, in any form or by
any means, electronic, mechanical, photocopying, recording or
otherwise, without the prior written permission of the publishers.

ISBN: 978-1-83888-110-8
eBook ISBN: 978-1-83888-109-2

This book is a work of fiction. Names, characters, businesses,
organizations, places and events other than those clearly in the
public domain, are either the product of the author's imagination
or are used fictitiously. Any resemblance to actual persons, living or
dead, events or locales is entirely coincidental.

For my sister Caroline
With love x

CHAPTER ONE

Shelley

The removal men had only been gone for about an hour when they returned to the house, so the new neighbours couldn't have come from far. Shelley prised open the wooden blinds with two fingers: who was moving in?

It was inevitable, of course. There was only so long the house next door could remain vacant. Still, it had been an unwelcome surprise that morning when the large, square van had squeaked to a halt outside and two burly men had swung themselves out of the front cab, unrolled the shutter at the back with a clatter and started to unload furniture. Modern, expensive furniture. Was it too much to hope for that her new neighbours would be quiet, keep themselves to themselves and rarely be at home?

It was beyond pathetic that a woman in her mid-thirties had nothing better to do than spy out the window on a sunny Saturday, but there it was. She didn't have long to wait. A small red car drew up behind the van, and a man around her age jumped out and scooted onto the pavement to open the passenger door. He helped someone out of the car, obscuring them from Shelley's line of vision, then just stood there. Were they kissing? When he stood back, he had his arm across a woman's shoulders; they both looked up at the house, her hands on her stomach. Beautiful, in love and pregnant. Shelley came away from the window; she'd seen enough.

It wasn't until two hours later, when she was taking some rubbish out, that they first met. She jumped at the sound of a confident female voice.

'Hi.' The neighbour was standing in her own front doorway, hands resting once again on the top of her stomach in the way that all pregnant women seemed to stand. 'Sorry, I was just getting used to the view. I'm Lara. My husband and I have just moved in. It looks like we've chosen a lovely street.'

Shelley glanced down the ordinary road lined with 1960s brick-built semi-detached houses. Was it lovely? Maybe she'd thought so too when they'd first moved here over a decade ago, but she hadn't paid it much attention lately, apart from the two seconds it took her to get into her car for work in the morning and back out again in the evening. When she looked back, Lara was in front of her, the other side of the low wall separating their front gardens. Leaning across, she took Lara's outstretched hand for a surprisingly firm handshake.

'Nice to meet you. I'm Shelley. Hope you'll be very happy here.' As Shelley spoke, she could almost hear Mrs Williams' voice saying the exact same thing to her and Greg when they'd moved in. And they had been. Until he'd gone and ruined it, of course. Hopefully, now she and Lara had met and introduced themselves, she could disappear indoors and – like old Mrs Williams before them – keep neighbourly relations to a nod in the morning and signing for each other's postal deliveries.

However, Lara seemed keen on getting to know her better. She spoke with an eagerness and speed as if to keep Shelley there with her words. 'Matt, that's my husband, has gone to get some food shopping. He doesn't want me to start unpacking anything else until he gets back. I can't even make a cup of tea because I have no idea which box the kettle is in.' She paused, her brown eyes hungry as if waiting for a response.

Was she waiting for an invitation? Shelley's stomach tightened; this was the last thing she wanted but it would be rude to leave her standing there. The least she could do was offer her a drink. 'Would you like to come in to mine for a coffee?'

Lara's eyes widened. Dammit, Shelley had read her wrong. She didn't want to come in at all. But now she'd feel obliged in return. Sure enough, she recomposed her face and smiled. 'Oh, er, thanks. That's very kind of you. I don't drink coffee anymore, but I've got some special tea in my bag.' She waved her thumb in the direction of her lounge and disappeared inside, leaving the front door open. Shelley wanted to kick herself. Why had she taken the rubbish out at that precise moment? Ten minutes later and she could have avoided even saying hello. Now this Lara was coming in for at least as long as it took to make and drink a cup of 'special' tea. Whatever the hell that was.

Lara reappeared with a box of suspiciously healthful-looking tea bags. 'Is it okay to just step over the wall?'

Shelley felt mean. This woman was probably perfectly nice: dressed in leggings and a T-shirt, dark blond hair pulled back in a ponytail, smile wide and easy. If only they'd moved in last year, Shelley would have been excited to have a couple the same age next door. Maybe she should warn her straight away that she came as a single these days. Although that would open up another can of worms. This was only a quick drink. 'Of course.'

Lara followed her inside the house and into the kitchen. 'These tea bags taste like crap but apparently they are good for me. Feel free to have one but I wouldn't recommend it. I brought biscuits to disguise the taste.'

Did she always talk this much? It was a good thing that she'd brought her own biscuits, though, because Shelley had nothing in the house to offer her. Now Greg wasn't there to add cookies and chocolate to the shopping list, she rarely bought that kind of food. Or indeed any kind of food that couldn't be stabbed with a fork and stuck in the microwave. 'I think I'll pass. I've got coffee. Go and grab a seat in the lounge. I'll make the drinks and bring them through.'

At least she could be confident that the room was presentable because she'd spent the morning cleaning, vacuuming and dusting. It hadn't taken long enough, so she'd even taken the steam cleaner to the curtains.

Now Lara was jigging from one foot to the other. 'This is a bit embarrassing, but would you mind if I just used your bathroom? This kid is sitting on my bladder right now and I am getting the sudden urge to wee at the most inconvenient moments.'

An anxiety prickled in Shelley's stomach. Which was ridiculous. 'Of course. Top of the stairs, first on the right.'

One of the many superfluous gadgets Greg had insisted on when they'd redone the kitchen two years ago was an instant boiling water tap, so there was no need to boil a kettle. She'd had a fear of scalding herself, but he'd argued that it was much more practical and economical for only two cups of tea. Even more economical these days now that she was only making one. Had he already thought of that back then? As he'd shown her, she waited for the initial hiss as she turned the tap on, then held a cup of coffee granules beneath it. Just as the boiling water hit Lara's beige, lumpy and foul-smelling tea bag, there was a loud crash from upstairs. She took the stairs two at a time.

Lara was standing at the doorway to the box room, rubbing her head. 'I'm so sorry. I clearly opened the wrong door.' She held up a silver frame. 'I got hit on the head by this.'

Just inside the door was a pile of cardboard boxes; the frame must have been balanced on the top. The prickling feeling in

Shelley's chest spread further; she needed to move Lara out of there. 'Are you okay? This room is full of old rubbish. Sorry.'

Lara smiled. 'No harm done. It was my fault for not listening properly.' She held up the frame, with the front facing outwards; Shelley couldn't avoid looking at it. 'What a lovely photo. I love wedding pics – your hair is *gorgeous* piled up like that. So, this is obviously your husband?'

Shelley's hand went to her long dark hair, which hadn't seen a brush that morning. It was too much effort when there was no one here to see her.

She hadn't looked at that frame in months. Twelve months to be precise, which was when she'd thrown it in there with the rest of the crap. Even at an angle, she could see her frothy white dress and Greg's smile as he looked at her. *The look of love*, her mum had called it when they'd got the pictures back. At the time, she'd preferred these candid snaps to the staged group shots; now their hopeful expressions felt like mockery. Her heart twisted in her chest and she pressed her fist into her breastbone. 'Was. Was my husband. It's just me here, now.'

Shelley pressed her lips together. The words had left her mouth before she'd considered them. This wasn't a conversation she wanted to have with a stranger. It was private. Although maybe it was for the best. A bitter, single woman was a much less attractive proposition than a happy couple; she'd learned that the hard way when the dinner invitations from their shared friends had stopped coming. Lara would probably keep her politely at arm's length now she'd told her. It was easier that way.

Lara blushed. 'Oh, I'm sorry. I shouldn't have assumed. My sister's husband did the same to her a couple of years ago. Just left out of the blue. Some men are so selfish, aren't they?'

It was exhausting telling people; they wanted to discuss it, get the graphic details. Especially if they'd already heard half the story. But she wasn't going to explain. What she wanted to do was snatch the frame from Lara's hands and slam the door closed. She never looked in there except to throw things in. Most of his stuff had gone, but her memories were in those boxes. And she still wasn't up to dealing with them. Doing all the paperwork, communicating with the lawyer – that had been bad enough. She needed to get better at just shutting these conversations down. 'I'd rather not talk about it.'

Lara looked mortified. 'Of course. Sorry. I'll just…' And she shuffled past Shelley and out into the hallway.

Looking at the room through Lara's eyes, she could see it was a complete mess. On the floor, plastic storage boxes full of old shoes and paperwork jostled for space with piles of books, magazines and box files labelled with their contents. Reaching for the handle, she pulled the door closed and nodded to the one opposite. 'The bathroom is over there.'

Back downstairs she finished filling Lara's mug and brought it through to the lounge just as Lara got to the bottom of the stairs. 'Your home is so lovely.'

'Thank you.' It really was a lovely home. Neutral colours had not been her first choice but she appreciated them now. They were restful. Comforting. Safe.

Lara lowered herself onto the sofa. It was a three-seater: large and well-made. 'This sofa is impressive. You have very good taste in furniture.'

Shelley couldn't take the credit. It was Greg who'd spent six months researching sofas and giving her options before deciding this one was perfect for them. They'd waited nearly four months to have it delivered from Italy. Despite it being a constant reminder of happier times, she'd been glad of it the last few months, having spent many nights on it after falling asleep in front of the TV.

Time to turn the conversation away from herself. 'I bet you'll be glad when your furniture is all organised.'

Lara sipped at her tea before nodding enthusiastically. 'Definitely. Getting the mattress onto the bed was my first priority. Some afternoons I just need to crash out. And today has really taken it out of me. I'm shattered.'

She didn't look shattered. In fact, Shelley was the one who was starting to feel worn out by Lara's constant chatter and positivity. Still, it must be tiring being that pregnant. Not that Shelley would know, of course. 'It'll be all right once you get it sorted. I know the box room you've just been in might not show it, but I like to have everything straight too.' She had no reason to be embarrassed about the state of that room, but she was. 'It used to be more organised. I've just had a lot of sorting out to do and everything got chucked in there. A load of it belongs to Greg. I will get to it at some point. Maybe even this weekend.' Why was she trying to justify herself? As if Lara cared whether she was tidy or not – it was likely to be the one and only time she set foot through the door.

Lara, who had been nodding along as Shelley spoke, folded her arms over her bump. 'I'm the opposite – Matt says I leave a trail of destruction wherever I go. But we had a huge cull of our belongings before the move and it's a lot easier to stay tidy when you've got half as much stuff. I've got a fantastic book that takes you through the process. I'll lend it to you. It's a life-changer.'

Shelley hid her face behind her large mug by taking a long gulp. As if she hadn't had enough life changes this year, adjusting to being a single woman again. A familiar flash of anger heated her face. Greg had left her, after all those years together. Starting over wasn't something *she* had wanted, but he'd given her no choice. She did have a choice about who she let in her life from this point on though, and borrowing this book from Lara would only encourage a friendship she didn't have the energy for. 'Thanks, but I'm sure I can get it done on my own.'

*

Once Lara had returned next door, Shelley didn't have the urge to take the steam cleaner up to the bathroom and attack the tiles like she'd planned. Lara had only stayed for an hour but her absence made the house seem lonelier than before she'd come. That was the other problem with letting people in: the void they left behind. Before her mind wandered down the path to self-pity, Shelley reached for the remote control and sank down into the space Lara had vacated on the sofa; it was still warm.

Mindless TV was a saviour when she didn't want to think. Whichever soap she was watching right now – they all morphed into each other, really – had a young woman giving her friend a real talking to about her boyfriend. *Just leave 'im*, she was saying. *He ain't wurf it.*

Shelley had no idea what the boyfriend was supposed to have done, but she could tell the well-meaning friend why this straggly-haired woman might not want to leave him: because then she would be on her own. She would be sitting at home all alone, watching TV. And the well-meaning friends wouldn't be around anymore because they all had their own lives, and she couldn't bear their well-meant pity if they did come.

Anyway, in her experience, it was the men who did the leaving and the women who were left behind to pick up the pieces of their lives.

CHAPTER TWO

Lara

Brighter rectangles where frames had been removed from the magnolia walls; a floral carpet with a path worn from the door to the opposite side where the sofa must have been; a mahogany mantelpiece above an electric fire with fake coals. This room was the polar opposite of the lounge in Matt and Lara's old house. Their angular leather sofa and glass-topped coffee table looked like visitors from another century. As Lara unpacked the surviving books onto the shelving unit Matt had wrestled into place before he'd left for the supermarket, she tried not to mind. It was only decorative. They could change it to their taste. Eventually.

She hadn't meant to introduce herself to the neighbour so soon either. Matt would be keen, she knew, but she had never been the type to drop in and have a cup of tea with someone just because they lived next door. When she'd still been working, she'd barely spoken to their neighbours, although a detached house had meant that they were more remote to start with. Now they were sharing a wall with this Shelley.

Not that she'd got off to a good start with her anyway; what had she been thinking, commenting on her wedding photo? Of all people, she should know not to make assumptions about someone's status, both professionally and privately.

A key scraped in the lock and the stiff front door pushed open. Matt's voice echoed down the empty hallway. 'Are you there, Lar?'

That was quick. Better step away from the shelves: she'd promised him she wouldn't touch anything until he got back. 'In the lounge, love.'

Matt appeared in the doorway, a full bag of shopping in one hand and a paper bag in the other, which he waved in the air. 'I found a nice fish and chip shop on the way back from the supermarket. Crack out the crockery.'

She frowned. What about the list of ingredients she'd given him for the carbonara? 'But I said I'd cook for us.'

Matt looked a sight in his moth-eaten rugby shirt and old jeans. How had those clothes managed to survive the clear-out? 'I know. But this way you don't have to. It's been a long day. A long, emotional day. You need to relax.'

Cooking *was* relaxing. And it would've given her something to do other than watch him unpacking their belongings. How could she make him understand that it was better when she was *doing* something? Anything. She sighed. 'I'll get the plates.'

He shook his head. 'No, no. You sit down. I'll bring it out to you.'

As he disappeared into the kitchen, Lara sank onto the sofa. It was easier to give in: she didn't have the energy for an argument. Next door, chatting to Shelley, she'd felt like her old self for a short while. Back inside this new house, with Matt fussing over her, just drained her enthusiasm. He was right about the long day, though. It had been more upsetting than she'd anticipated leaving their old house, and no matter how many times Matt tried to persuade her that they would make this place their own, after seeing Shelley's beautiful living room and kitchen, this house felt like an old folk's home.

Matt reappeared with a tray, a plate of fish and chips and a tea towel over his left arm. He bowed slightly. 'Your food, madam.'

If one thing saved their marriage, it was his ability to make her smile, even when things were really tough. She took the plate and smiled at him. 'Thanks. I'm not sure how much I can eat but I'll do my best.'

'That's all I can ask.' Matt winked at her before going to retrieve his own plate from the kitchen.

She picked up a chip and nibbled at the end. 'I met our neighbour while you were gone. She's about our age. Divorced. Or separated. She said her husband left her a year ago.' Although, the way Shelley had reacted to the wedding photograph, she clearly hadn't moved on much in that year. Her husband must have hurt her pretty badly.

'Oh, yes?' Matt sat down beside her on the sofa and began to tuck in. 'I'm glad you've made a friend. I'll feel much happier if I have to do an overnight with work if you've got someone nearby to go to.'

For goodness' sake, he made her sound about fourteen. 'I keep telling you that I don't need looking after. Anyway, I'm not sure she's that keen on being best buddies. I practically invited myself in.' Lara had left with the distinct impression that Shelley was relieved to see her go; she couldn't see her popping round with a basket of muffins anytime soon. To be honest, they were probably too different to be friends anyway. Lara liked her friends a bit warmer and livelier. Well, she had.

Matt pointed at her with a forkful of fish. 'I'm sure you'll win her over. I've never known you not to achieve something you've set your mind to.'

Lara put her chip down. That wasn't quite true. But they'd agreed to start looking forwards, not back. That's what the book said. Which reminded her... 'Her house is lovely, really modern and bright. But she has a room upstairs which is full of crap. And I mean *full*.'

Matt shrugged. 'Some people like to keep their stuff. My dad used to have a shed which my mum was banned from. He had broken tools and sawn-off pieces of curtain rail and a ton of other crap my mum nagged him to throw away. He liked it.'

What he had probably liked about the shed was a respite from Matt's mum's moaning; a list of her ailments was practically her way of saying hello. 'It doesn't make sense, though, because she lives there on her own. The rest of the house is immaculate. There isn't any clutter and everything is coordinated. Actually, I wish we'd bought her house rather than this one.' She looked at him mournfully.

Matt slid his empty plate onto the coffee table, having practically inhaled his food. 'That one sounds like it would have cost us a lot more than this one. You know this was the right thing to do.'

She didn't need reminding of their reduced circumstances, but she couldn't shake the sadness of leaving their old house this morning. Maybe it was hormones. 'I know. I just miss our home.'

Tears started in her eyes and Matt pulled her towards him. 'Hey. This is our home now. And we can make this nice too. Let's go and choose some paint tomorrow and I can start next weekend.'

She pulled away from him slightly and gave a watery smile. It was ridiculous how quickly she cried these days. 'You? Paint?' Matt worked hard but he was not a fan of DIY. They'd always paid workmen in the past if they'd needed anything doing. Their old house had really high ceilings and huge glass windows. Any decoration was a mammoth task.

Matt pretended to be offended. 'You don't think I can do it?'

She laughed again, looked into his bright, kind eyes. Even if he was a little overzealous about it at times, he'd do anything for her; she knew he would. 'I'm sure you can. I've just never seen it in action. Do you even own a paintbrush?'

'Well, that was the old Matt. This one is going to learn to do it. Looking forwards, right? What's the name of that book of yours? *Chuck Out All Your Stuff and Cheer Up*? Isn't that what you've been telling me?'

She picked up a cushion and threw it at him. 'You know full well it's called *Make Way for Joy*.' Matt was teasing, but he was right. Maybe she should get the book out and reread it. She thought again of that cluttered room next door. Shelley had hustled her out of it pretty sharpish, obviously embarrassed by how untidy it was. How satisfying would it be to get in there and sort it all out for her? Lara's sister had been through the same thing with her awful ex-husband. Even after they'd split, he'd used their flat as some kind of free storage facility. Her sister had needed quite a few nudges, but even she admitted how much better she felt after making him come and collect all his junk. It was liberating to get rid of unnecessary belongings. Detritus from a life you no longer lived. Lara knew that first-hand. And she would explain it all to Shelley. Might as well give in and get to know her neighbour for once; if only to stop herself going mad with boredom. 'I'm going to give it another go with Shelley next door. Invite her over for a drink. Show her the book. She looks as if she could do with some joy in her life.'

Matt started to pick at the chips on her plate. 'Sounds like she's going to become one of your projects. I feel as if I should warn her.'

Lara smacked his hand as he reached for another chip. 'Make your mind up. I thought you were keen on me making friends with the neighbours.' Matt worked in medical equipment sales. Most of his clients were within a couple of hours' drive away, but some were further afield and necessitated a night in a hotel. He hated leaving her alone.

Matt stood and stretched, picked up his plate. 'I am. I am. I'm also keen on getting the bedsheets on before I'm too tired to do it.' He put up a hand to stop her as she made to put her plate down. 'No, you eat your dinner. I can do it.'

She gritted her teeth and let him go up alone. At some point he was going to have to let her do something. That was probably why she didn't fancy her dinner, because she'd done nothing to work up any kind of appetite. Instead, once Matt was out of the room, she picked up her well-thumbed copy of *Make Way for Joy* from the bookshelf and flicked to one of the case studies she remembered. *Client E: Recently divorced.* That was the one. *Client E came to me feeling tired and apathetic.* That was exactly how Shelley had looked. And anxious. Lara skim-read the rest of the page: ... *needed to cleanse her life... let go of the belongings which stored bad memories... Forgive... Let go... Find space...*

Yes. Although she'd just met her, Lara could sense that this was exactly what Shelley needed. Matt could call it one of her 'projects' if he liked, but Lara had decided now. She would persuade Shelley to let her help sort out that box room. If nothing else, it would give Lara something to think about other than being pregnant. Because Matt wasn't letting her think about anything else right now, and she was finding it more difficult by the day.

CHAPTER THREE

Shelley

'So, you have new neighbours?'

Her colleague Flora had rolled her chair over as close to Shelley as she could stretch the lead on her earphones. It had been a slow morning for incoming calls and Flora had decided they had time for an unofficial break.

Shelley nodded. 'Yes. Lara and Matt. I met her on Saturday. She seems nice.'

Lara *had* seemed nice, if a little pushy. But the whole time she'd been there, Shelley had felt uncomfortable. It had been bad enough when she'd gone upstairs – no one except Shelley and her mum had been up there for months – without having her poking about in that damn room. And then the falling photograph had meant she'd been forced to tell her that Greg had left. The woman was a whirlwind. Best to be avoided.

Flora took a chocolate from the box on Shelley's desk, a gift from one of her clients, who had left his glasses on the Eurostar. Sometimes her job was less travel consultant and more amateur detective. Still, it was nice when someone said thank you.

The pale blue walls and oak effect desks in the office were as familiar as Shelley's own lounge. Last year, when everything had imploded, it was coming here that had pulled her through. As part of this team, she was needed, appreciated, valued. Whatever was going on at home, coming to work was a refuge. Sitting at this desk, she wasn't Greg's former wife – she was Shelley Thomas: Travel Consultant. And she was good at her job.

'Ugh. Turkish delight.' Flora threw the remaining half of the chocolate in the bin. 'Well, I think it's great you've got someone new next door. It's good to make new friends. Maybe she'll do a better job than me of persuading you out of the house.'

Shelley ignored what was obviously Flora encouraging her to get out more and scanned the emails on her screen. There were messages waiting to be dealt with in twelve of her fifteen different inboxes, one for each of the clients she was responsible for.

Checking the list for any marked urgent, she found a flight to Munich that needed booking for tomorrow, a hotel reservation in Glasgow for next week and a cry for help from a new sales executive who was stranded in Belgium after their flight home had been cancelled. Best deal with that one first. She pointed at a flashing light on Flora's phone, prompting her to spin herself back round, plaster on a smile and press the button to pick up. 'Flora speaking, how can I help?'

Monday mornings were always busy: a relief after a near-silent weekend. Other than their conversation on Saturday, she hadn't seen her new neighbour again. Maybe Lara didn't want to fraternise with her now she knew she didn't come as a pair, probably preferring to make friends with the family of four on the other side. It had been a revelation how inconvenient she'd become as a single. Messing up the even number at dinner or – even worse – having someone's dodgy brother-in-law foisted on your right-hand side. Had she been that tactless when she and Greg were one of the happily marrieds?

Flora had finished on the phone and was checking her email too. She clapped her hands and called back over her shoulder, 'There's a couple of travel agent events coming up next month. One at that new hotel on the A3. Why don't we go together?'

Flora was fun. Working with her was a definite bonus, if only she would stop trying to make Shelley socialise. It was more than a little irritating when people suggested she should 'get back out there'. Her life hadn't stopped after Greg left; she was doing fine. If she chose to spend her evenings indoors with a TV remote and an electric blanket, what business was it of theirs?

'I think I'll pass.'

Flora folded her arms and shook her head. 'You never come. You always used to say you were already booked to go to some fancy event with Greg. But now...' Flora tailed off. 'You need to get out more.'

Shelley gritted her teeth. Why wouldn't she take no for an answer? There was an email from their boss in her inbox. That would help to change the subject. 'Have you seen this email from Steve? He's coming in to do a whole staff briefing. What's that about?'

Flora grimaced. 'I'm not sure you want to hear it.' She leaned forwards and lowered her voice. 'Rumour has it we are going to be bought out by Travel Express.'

Fear clutched at Shelley's stomach. Takeovers were common in their industry, and she knew how it worked. Larger companies absorbed smaller ones to grow their client base. What would happen to their team if Travel Express took over and decided to close this office? Would she lose her job? Be forced to move? After eight years here, the thought of being uprooted and going somewhere unknown was... unthinkable. This place was all that was keeping her putting one foot in front of the other right now. 'I really hope it's just a rumour.'

'Me too.' Flora was next to her again, scrutinising the map for the chocolate box. 'I guess we'll find out when Steve graces us with his presence.'

Shelley scanned the email to find out when he was coming. Wednesday. Two days for her to have the fear of more upheaval winding its way around her brain. More change that she'd be forced to accept and absorb and assimilate. And the worst part of it? The worst part was that the person she most needed to talk to about it was Greg. But he'd taken that option away. She had no one.

The phone rang again, but this time Flora's smile dropped almost immediately. Putting the call on hold, she raised an eyebrow at Shelley. 'It's Dee. Shall I do the usual?'

Shelley's stomach flipped as it always did now at the mention of that name. When was she going to give up? How many calls and unsolicited visits and stupid cards with kittens on them was it going to take for Dee to get it into her skull that Shelley didn't want to hear her apologies or make peace? She nodded once at Flora. 'Yes, please.'

Flora pressed a button to release the call. 'I'm very sorry, but the other Ms Thomas isn't available right now. Can I take a message?'

Shelley didn't need to read the handwritten note that Flora passed her to know what it would say. *Please call me.*

CHAPTER FOUR

Lara

Gardening was not Lara's forte – and Matt was going to moan at her for doing it – but she couldn't sit inside the house for another minute. On hectic days at Hoskins Legal Services she'd fantasised about a life of leisure in which she wouldn't have to wake up to a 6.30 a.m. alarm and have people asking questions of her all day long. And now? Be careful what you wish for.

The handkerchief-sized front garden comprised a small lawn surrounded by overgrown flower beds. With no knowledge of plants, Lara hacked at what she hoped were weeds with a pair of garden shears she'd found in the shed. Once the tangled greenery was cleared away, she could try and work out what was underneath. It wasn't difficult or strenuous but, crikey, it was boring.

That's why when she heard Shelley slam her car door and open the gate, she almost jumped on her. *Human contact at last.* 'Hey. How was your day? I envy you going to work. I'm going a little stir-crazy being at home all day. I'm not used to it. Who would have thought I'd miss slaving away at a hot computer?'

It wasn't surprising that Shelley jumped; Lara sounded as if she was trying to fit a whole day's conversation into one breath. Shelley hid her shock under a polite smile. 'Sorry, I didn't see you down there. Mind on other things. Are you on maternity leave already, then?'

Lara stretched and rubbed at her lower back with the palms of her hands. Maybe she *had* overdone it. 'Kind of. I was a solicitor, working in a legal services company. It could get pretty intense. Then there were some complications with my pregnancy so I'm on extended medical leave. Hence the move. Our old house was huge and we couldn't afford the mortgage on our other place on Matt's salary and the pittance I'm getting while I'm off.'

For goodness' sake, she needed to stop talking. This was the first time she'd opened her mouth all day apart from when Matt had called to check on her. Now she had verbal diarrhoea. Not only had she opened the pregnancy can of worms, she was also practically boasting about the size of her old house. Especially insensitive when her new one was the exact same size as Shelley's. *Say something nice. Quick.* 'Look, do you want to come in for a drink and some banana loaf? I made it this morning. I'm not exactly Mary Berry, so if it's inedible, I've got an M&S sponge cake on standby. And I won't make you drink my sludgy tea; I have coffee, I promise.'

Poor Shelley looked as if Lara had run her over with a steam roller. Matt often said that she overwhelmed people. Lara braced herself for a polite refusal and was surprised when Shelley reinstated her smile and accepted. 'Okay. Thanks.'

Lara pointed the way into the lounge – unnecessary seeing as the house layout was the mirror image of Shelley's – and saw Shelley flick her eyes around the room, which contained a sofa, a bookshelf and a coffee table. Nothing else. On the shelves were about twenty books.

'When is the rest of your stuff coming?'

Lara held her hands out to encompass the room. 'This is it. Downsizing was the perfect opportunity to clear out a load of our stuff. I told you about the book, didn't I?' She took it from the shelf and passed it to Shelley.

On the cover of the book was a smiling woman with her arms outstretched. '*Make Way for Joy*,' read Shelley. She looked up at Lara. 'Who is Joy?'

Lara laughed and took the book from her. 'No. *Joy*. Being joyful.' She flicked to the start and read aloud. 'Possessions can suck your energy. Only those which give you joy deserve a place in your home.'

Shelley's doubting expression was much the same as the look Matt had given Lara when she'd first introduced him to the idea. 'I'm not sure how much joy I get from my toaster. I need it though. What about the things you *need*?'

Lara returned the book to Shelley and grinned. 'Speaking of toasters, take a seat and I'll put the kettle on.'

Shelley put the book down on the coffee table. 'I'll follow you.'

Lara wished she wouldn't. The kitchen was particularly shabby and decorated in more shades of brown than she'd known existed. Matt had promised they would get it done before the baby came but there wasn't a lot of spare cash. She'd been browsing online for ideas to freshen it up on a budget.

'It's clean in here, but you might want to shield your eyes from the dodgy seventies tiling. It's not sleek and modern like yours. Anyway, how was your day at work? What is it that you do?'

Lara held up a tin of instant coffee as she spoke and Shelley nodded. 'Yes, please. White, no sugar. I'm a travel consultant. We make travel arrangements for corporate clients. Well, I am at the moment. There are rumours of a takeover, which might mean office closures.'

Lara filled the kettle and switched it on. 'Oh no, that sucks. Are you in the firing line?'

Shelley rubbed at her temples. 'I don't know yet. Often in these situations they will try and find jobs for employees somewhere, but the new company is based in central London. It would mean a much longer commute, which I don't fancy.'

Lara shuffled through the different tea bags in the tin without much enthusiasm. They really were disgusting. Matt had bought several boxes of different varieties from one of his pharmaceutical clients who had a sideline in complementary therapies and had made her promise to give them a fair try. Picking the least offensive-looking one, she dropped it into her mug. 'Would it be worth commuting for? Do you like it? Your current job, I mean.'

Shelley tucked her hair behind her ears, pausing as if considering how to phrase a response. 'Yes. I do. I mean, it's not always the most exciting job in the world. But I'm good at it. I like the people I work with too. I really can't imagine going anywhere else.'

Shelley's hesitant words didn't come across as overwhelming enthusiasm. In fact, she sounded just like the case study in the book about someone changing their job. Lara put her hands on the kitchen table and leaned forward. 'This isn't necessarily a disaster, it could be an opportunity. A change could be a really good thing. You *have* to read the joy book. Take it home with you. A dull job is like a bad possession. You need to rid yourself and find a job that brings you *joy*.' Lara had loved her job. Guiding people through difficult documents, ensuring they protected themselves, leading them through the processes involved in some of the most pivotal decisions in their lives. Being a solicitor was hard work but it was definitely rewarding.

Shelley shrugged. 'I'm not particularly ambitious. Never have been. My job has always suited me; it fit into our life…' She hesitated. 'Greg always used to talk about how full on it is, being a trader in the City. I wouldn't want a job like that.'

She clearly hadn't explained herself properly. When they went back through to the lounge, she'd show Shelley the chapter. 'It doesn't have to be a career; it just needs to make you *happy*. And not steal your energy. It should revitalise you, not diminish you. Honestly, I know it sounds like a lot of hippie hokum, but that book has changed my life.'

The kettle clicked off and she turned to pour. It did sound exactly like a lot of hippie hokum. If someone had introduced it to her two years ago, she would have laughed it off. But she'd been a different person two years ago.

Shelley looked interested. 'Changed your life how?'

Well, that was going to be a little tricky to explain. 'Let's go sit on a comfy seat.'

In the lounge, the woman on the cover still beamed at them from the coffee table, and Lara picked up the book with the reverence due to a religious text. 'The whole premise of the book is that we litter our lives with possessions and tasks and people that actually prevent us from becoming the person we are destined to be. We hold onto things because we think we should or because we're afraid of what we will do without them. Like your box room with the aggressive photo frames and the stuff your ex left behind. Do you really need to keep all those things? Do they bring you *joy*? Why doesn't he come and collect them anyway?'

'He doesn't want them. Doesn't need them, I guess.' Shelley's shoulders rose and she drummed her fingers on the side of her mug. Was she annoyed? Maybe Lara had been too forceful? But then Shelley's shoulders dropped and her face drained of energy. 'It just seems like a lot of effort to sort it all out, to be honest.'

That sounded more promising. Maybe she was persuadable? Lara shuffled forwards eagerly. 'Well, I could help you. I love a project and I have three months to kill before my life is apparently going to be "irrevocably changed", according to my mother.' She motioned to her burgeoning belly. 'Please let me help you sort it out.'

Shelley looked uncertain; she was losing her. 'I don't know.'

God, she wanted to shake her. How could she be this indecisive? They were roughly the same age but Shelley seemed to move in slow motion. Her ex-husband was off enjoying his new life, and there she was next door, going through the motions of a life. What she needed was someone to take her by the hand and help her move on, and even if they weren't destined to become best buddies, Lara could do that. In fact, she was feeling more and more excited by the idea of the two of them sorting out that catastrophic room. Definitely better than gardening alone. 'Come on, let me. It'll give me something to occupy myself. We can do it together.' Could she push her a little harder? Should she? 'Plus, if you do lose your job, you'll have a lovely tidy spare room to offer to a lodger.'

Shelley blanched. Had Lara gone too fast and scared her off? But then she seemed to consider it. 'Maybe.'

Maybe. Possibly. Perhaps. Plenty of her clients over the years had been just like Shelley. Sometimes people just needed a gentle push to do what was needed. Though they'd barely spent any time together, Lara had noticed a shadow fall across Shelley's face whenever Lara talked about the stuff in that room. Many of the women she'd helped in difficult circumstances had had the same haunted look that she saw in Shelley's face. Whatever her ex-husband had done to her, it must have been pretty bad.

CHAPTER FIVE

Shelley

Today Shelley was a new level of tired. Having woken up on the sofa at 4 a.m. – never a good time to be awake – she had struggled to get back to sleep. Although it was early June, it was still cold downstairs at that time of night, but there was no way she wanted to take herself upstairs to an even colder bed. Thoughts and memories and fears had battled for her attention for the next hour until light had seeped in through the blinds and she'd given up. Even BBC News 24 with its repetitive ticker tape across the bottom of the screen was preferable to spending time inside her own brain.

Now she had her face propped up on her palm as she flicked through emails; she just couldn't focus on anything. Flora put a cup of coffee down on her desk and she smiled up gratefully. 'Thanks.'

'You looked like you needed it. Not really full of the joys of spring this morning, eh?'

That reminded her. She leaned down under her desk and rooted around in her handbag to find the book that Lara had insisted she take. She really hadn't intended on seeing her again so soon, but the offer of cake – and company – had caught her on the hop and she hadn't wanted to appear rude. Unfortunately, it had also given Lara the opportunity to suggest, once again, an assault on her box room. Pulling the book out, she held it up to Flora. 'Have you heard anything about this?'

Flora peered at it – too vain to wear reading glasses unless forced to by the tiny print on some travel documents. '*Make Way for Joy*. Who is Joy?'

Flora was a complete tonic, she really was. Shelley smiled. 'That's exactly what I said. It's a book my neighbour gave me.'

Flora flipped it over and read the blurb. 'If we allow our homes and our hearts to become cluttered, it becomes difficult to see the joy in our everyday lives.' She looked over at her desk, which was covered with tissues, pens, half a packet of liquorice toffees and an uncountable number of paperclips. 'That might explain a lot.'

'I think I might be my neighbour's new project.' Shelley held out her hand for the book. She still hadn't decided whether to let Lara help her sort out her mess. 'What time is Steve due in?'

'Four. Do you think he's going to tell us the office is closing?'

Shelley's stomach plummeted. 'I really don't know.'

Dressed in a slim-fitting navy suit, Italian leather shoes and dark pink tie, Steve arrived in reception at exactly 4 p.m. He asked the staff to assemble in the conference room, an optimistic euphemism for a rectangular room with a round table and six chairs. The six chairs were filled, and the other members of staff – twenty-three in total – stood or leaned against the wall. Steve took the seat in front of the window, his fingers interlaced, elbows on the table, smile overly reassuring. It was going to be bad.

'Thanks for all being here so promptly. I know you're busy. In fact, it's due to that and the excellent work that you've been doing that we've had interest in what we're doing here from Travel Express.'

That was it then. They were being taken over by a bigger company. Shelley was barely listening as Steve evangelised about the opportunities within a bigger organisation, the facilities at their main office, the fact that there would potentially be roles for all of them if they wished to apply. A hot rage began to boil in her stomach. *Why now? Why me?*

A few people asked questions about timeframes and roles and other logistics, and Shelley had to fight the urge to scream. Life was so bloody unfair. She had done everything right at work, been on time, worked hard, put in extra hours when they needed it. Just like she'd been a good wife. And where had that got her? Dumped by the wayside. Her fingers clenched and she pressed her fingernails into the palms of her hands. *Don't listen. Just let the words wash over you.*

Once Steve had drawn the meeting to a close, she tried to get out as quickly as she could, but he called her back. 'Shelley, can I have a quick word?'

Oh no. What was he going to say? Had he picked up on her anger? If he had, he'd probably be surprised. She was a conscientious employee, and he'd never had cause to speak to her about her work, except in glowing terms. It wasn't his fault that the company was being sold, so her anger at him was irrational. Was it because he reminded her of Greg? They didn't look alike – Steve was blond and slim, not dark and broad like Greg – but they both dressed in expensive suits, were both ambitious, were both able to get what they wanted through their charm. Was that why she felt so flustered speaking to him?

Steve leaned back so that he was almost sitting on the table, crossed his arms and tilted his head. 'So, big news, eh?'

Confrontation wasn't Shelley's style, but she wasn't about to pretend everything was fine. 'You could say that.'

He nodded slowly, seemed to be choosing his words. 'I wanted to talk to you on your own because there's an opportunity for a—'

A buzzing in his jacket interrupted him. He slid out his phone and squinted at the number. 'Sorry – I just need to quickly take this.'

Great. Now she was stuck here trying not to listen to a personal call. 'Hi, Mia… Yes, of course, as soon as I can… Look, Mia, I'll call you back in ten minutes, okay?'

He sighed as he ended the call. 'Sorry about that.' He leaned forwards. 'Look, I can tell you're in shock. That's why I've come to see you myself. You've had enough to deal with lately.'

This again. She wasn't an invalid. 'Thanks.'

Steve nodded. 'And also because there will be a more senior position available when the takeover is finalised, and I really think you should go for it. You're ready for the step up to a management role.'

Management role? Career progression had been the last thing on her mind lately. But now she was on her own, maybe she should think about a position with higher pay? 'I don't know.'

'Just think about it. There will be more information coming out in the next few days about the roles that are available.' He stood to leave. 'I have to shoot off now, I've got a client the other side of Guilford who I need to see.' He paused with his hand on the door handle. 'You really do seem as if you're in shock. It's mid-afternoon, why don't you head home early?'

He looked at her so intently, she felt a blush creeping up her cheeks. Why was he being so nice to her? Leaving early was a good idea, though; she wasn't sure she would be able to turn her mind to work, and it had been really quiet this afternoon. 'Actually, I might do that. Thanks.'

He smiled, gave her a mock salute and strode across the office, calling goodbye to everyone as he left, probably heading off to ring that Mia girl back.

Flora was on the phone when Shelley came back to her seat, so she scrawled a quick note to say she had to leave early, grabbed her bag and left.

Leaving early meant her journey home was even quicker than normal and she was home just after five with the evening stretching in front of her like an abyss. There was no housework to do and her stomach was too knotted up to eat so it was pointless making dinner. She needed to do something though. Call her mother? No, she wouldn't be able to keep her voice upbeat, and then her mum would insist on scheduling a visit and – much as she loved her – she couldn't face that at the moment.

The remote control was on the coffee table so she picked it up and flicked on the TV. There was nothing on. Nothing she wanted to watch, anyway. They'd barely watched normal TV when Greg had lived here, preferring to work their way through shows on box sets. She needed to stop thinking about Greg.

She flicked off the TV. Was it too early for a glass of wine? That was something else she'd never done before the last twelve months: drunk alcohol alone. In fact, she'd never drunk much during the week at all. They would sometimes open a bottle of wine with their dinner, but she would only ever have one glass during the week. She pushed the memory of their evening mealtimes from her head. That was *not* going to help.

There was a nice bottle of red wine in the cupboard so she poured herself a glass and then returned to the sitting room. It was ridiculous, sitting there in silence staring at the wall. What about some music? There was a remote for the DAB radio too. Greg was always one for top quality electronics. She flicked it on to Radio 2. Adele singing about how sometimes love lasts and sometimes it hurts. It took several progressively aggressive attempts before she managed to turn it off.

Sitting still in the silence, fear and anxiety hardened in her gut and the anger which was never far away used them as steps to climb into her brain. She thought again of Steve, how unsettled she'd felt listening to the plans for the takeover. Why does everything have to change? She gulped at the wine, even though it hurt to swallow, barely tasting it. When it was finished, she thought about pouring another glass. No. That was dangerous. But she couldn't sit here like this, she needed to do something.

This must be what it was like for Lara every day, trying to find stuff to fill her time. Shelley didn't know if Lara had friends who she saw in the daytime – they hadn't had any visitors to the house that Shelley had noticed, but she wasn't here during the day. At least Lara had something to look forward to in the evening: her husband would come home and they would have the evening together. Whereas Shelley had no one and nothing. In the early days, she'd tried to go to bed by 9 p.m. so that the next day – and work – could come sooner, but it was fruitless. Her brain needed to be utterly exhausted in order to go to sleep.

Slipping her hands up the back of her shirt, she unclipped her bra then pulled the strap from her left shoulder so that she could pull the bra out of her right sleeve. The first time she'd done that in front of Greg, he'd been amazed. She hadn't liked to tell him that most girls can do that by the time they're fourteen. Catching herself smiling at the memory, anger rolled over her again. Why was he still in her head? It had been a year. Even the reams of paperwork had been finalised months ago. But the memories still had the power to knock her over, and that was why she hadn't been able to sort out that room on her own.

Before she could think twice about it, she left the house and knocked on Lara's door, arms crossed over her chest to hide her lack of bra.

Lara answered quickly then looked surprised. 'Sorry, I thought you were Matt. He's due home any minute.'

Was that her way of saying that she didn't want to invite Shelley in? Greg used to get annoyed if people dropped by unannounced. Unless it was Dee. 'I won't keep you long. I just wanted to say yes. Yes, please, I'd like you to help me sort out that box room. I'll start reading the book tonight.'

A smile spread across Lara's face. 'That's great. How about I come over this Saturday?'

CHAPTER SIX

Lara

When Lara knocked on Shelley's door on Saturday morning, dressed in a man's shirt that was three sizes too big and a pair of black leggings, Matt was still lecturing her. He had started earlier in the week when she'd first told him her plan to help Shelley sort out the room and he hadn't really stopped. *You're overdoing it. You should rest. Don't you dare lift anything.* Did he think she was a complete idiot?

She was calling back at him as Shelley opened the door. 'I won't lift boxes. I won't breathe in any dust. I won't perform any impromptu backflips.' She turned to face Shelley and rolled her eyes. 'Matt is worried I am going to overdo it.'

Shelley leaned out the front door and looked to her right, where a scowling Matt was facing her. It was the first time they'd actually met. 'Hi. I'm Shelley.'

He came out of his doorway, stepped over the low wall and held out his hand. He was tall, with a shock of red hair and the shoulders of a rugby player. His face was not a happy one. 'Hi. Matt. Lara's husband.'

Lara nudged him. 'I think she worked that one out for herself.'

'Ah, yes.' Matt shuffled from foot to foot. 'Look, I don't want to sound like a tyrant, but she is six months pregnant.'

Speaking about her like this, he sounded more like a father than a husband: it was embarrassing. What was Shelley going to think of them? 'Matt! We're sorting through some boxes, not redecorating. I'll be fine.'

Shelley smiled. 'I promise I won't let her lift anything. She is here for supervision and moral support only.'

Thank goodness Shelley wasn't offended, but Matt still wouldn't let it go. 'It's just, I know what she's like. She can't stop herself from getting involved.'

What was it going to take to convince him? Lara opened her mouth but Shelley got there first. 'Well, I can be very authoritative when the mood takes me. If she gives me any trouble, I'll knock on the wall three times.'

Shelley's face was a picture of seriousness but she was clearly mocking him. Lara watched with amusement as Matt looked at Shelley with suspicion. Then back at Lara. She gave him a little wave and he returned to their house, shaking his head and muttering about no one ever listening to him.

Lara followed Shelley through to the kitchen, another prick of envy at the sleek cabinets and granite worktop. 'Thanks for that. He's driving me crackers at the moment.' Matt had taken to following her around the house. Not like a puppy, but if she was in another room alone for too long, he would find an excuse to come in and get something. Did he not realise how obvious it was that he was checking up on her? It was getting to be too much. Suffocating.

'No problem. It's quite sweet that he looks out for you.' Shelley smiled as Lara pretended to stick her fingers down her throat. 'Tea?'

Lara could smell a delaying tactic. If they didn't start immediately, they'd end up sitting on the sofa and nothing would get done. 'No, I'm fine. Let's get going. If I start drinking tea, I'll be popping to the loo every five minutes.'

She knew she'd been right when Shelley took a deep breath. 'Okay. Let's do it.'

*

Once the door was open and they were confronted with the piles of stuff, Shelley tried to delay it again. 'Are you sure you want to do this today?'

This was obviously going to be hard for her but Lara wasn't going to help matters by letting her off the hook. 'Nice try. Come on. Get the book out. What does she say?'

Shelley opened the book and pretended to read. 'Close the door and forget that any of it is in there.'

Cracking a joke? Along with her deadpan mockery of Matt on the doorstep, this humour was a side to Shelley that Lara hadn't expected. Maybe this would be fun? Lara held out her hand. 'Stop it. Give it to me.'

Shelley's smile faded. 'I'm not sure if—'

Lara held up a hand for silence and read from the beginning of the book, remembering clearly how she had felt when she'd first started out. 'You will want to give up. It will all feel too much. Just take your time and breathe.' She paused and raised an eyebrow at Shelley, leaving her finger on the page.

Shelley sighed. 'Breathing I can do. What next?'

Lara's eyes went back to the words above her finger. 'Start small. One box. One album. One suitcase. Something achievable that will give you confidence.' Lara glanced around the floor and spotted a cardboard box. She nudged it towards Shelley with her foot. 'Off you go.'

Shelley held her knuckle against the wall. 'Push another box and I will knock for your husband.' She grinned but her smile faded again when she tilted her head. Lara watched her read the black handwriting on the side of the box: PHOTOS. She took another deep breath. 'Can we start with something easier?'

There was that look on her face again. It was as if she'd closed down somehow. But photographs were emotional for anyone, let alone someone whose marriage had recently ended. Lara could let her off that one for now. 'Okay. There's a box here that says "shoes". Want to start with that?'

'Okay.' Shelley shuffled towards the box on her knees. The packing tape had started to peel away at one end and she flicked at it with her fingernails, trying to scuff up enough to get hold of.

Lara started to do the same at the other end. It was oddly soothing. 'So, how long have you lived in the street?'

Shelley continued to pick at the tape. 'Eleven years. We moved here soon after we got married.' She didn't look up.

'Eleven years? Wow. You were quite young then?'

Shelley shrugged, still not looking up. 'Twenty-two. Almost twenty-three. Greg was twenty-eight.'

Lara managed to get hold of the edge of the packing tape with her thumb and forefinger. It made a satisfying tearing noise as she pulled it across the box. She really wanted to ask more about the ex-husband but she didn't want to be tactless. Still, Shelley had been the one to mention his name. 'How did you meet?'

'We grew up in the same area; had mutual friends. We got chatting in a local bar one night and he asked me out for dinner.' Shelley pulled the horizontal piece of tape free from the box and opened the flap. 'We're in.'

'Well done. What have you got inside?' Lara peered in. She loved shoes, and in her old house, she'd had a whole cupboard for all the pairs she'd treated herself to over the years.

There was a tangle of straps and heels, and a multitude of colours and fabrics. But they all had one thing in common: high heels.

'These are fab!' Lara pulled out a pair of navy stilettos with a bird motif. She stroked them lovingly. 'I miss heels. I used to wear beautiful shoes to work but Matt wouldn't let me anywhere near them after I started to show.'

Shelley pulled out a pair of gold strappy sandals; they were scarily high. She held them up by the straps, between her finger and thumb, as if they were something nasty she had pulled from a plughole. 'These instruments of torture were Greg's absolute favourites. He said I looked like a movie star when I wore these.'

Clearly not a fan of the gold shoes then. 'You didn't like them?'

Shelley shook her head. 'I didn't like any of them. These…' She pulled out a red patent peep-toe. It would have gone beautifully with a navy trouser suit that Lara used to have. But Shelley held it by the heel and waved it around like a weapon. 'These he bought for me after our first date. We saw them in a window and he *surprised* me with them the next week.'

She spat the word *surprised* and her eyes flashed. Being surprised with a pair of shoes didn't sound like a crime. Lara couldn't imagine Matt having any clue what shoes she might like. Or even what size she was. 'And you didn't want them?'

'No.' Shelley tossed the shoe to one side and then started pulling them all out and flinging them to the floor. Lara had to bite her lip to stop from yelping. The poor, beautiful shoes. 'I didn't want any of them. Do you know how much some of these things cost? It wasn't so bad when he bought them on the high street, but once he started to earn more money, he wanted me to have designer ones. Louboutins and Jimmy Choos and other ridiculous names.'

Lara slid her hands across the floor and started to pull a few random shoes closer to her. Maybe she could rescue a few pairs before Shelley started damaging them. They looked brand new; it would be a crime to wreck them now. 'So, you haven't even worn these?'

Shelley paused and looked at her. 'Oh, I wore them. And I wore the Michael Kors dresses and Valentino coats even though I would never choose them for myself. Because *he* said I looked amazing in them. Ridiculous, isn't it?'

She looked as if she might get upset. This was exactly how Lara's sister had been. Hating her ex one minute, crying over him the next. Lara reached out and took a navy kitten heel from her. 'We're probably all guilty of that a bit. Especially at the beginning of a relationship. Don't be so hard on yourself.'

Much as it pained Lara to say it, she knew what *Make Way for Joy* would say about these shoes. 'I think I know the answer to this question, but… do they bring you joy?' She reached out and squeezed Shelley's hand to show that she was joking.

'No.' Shelley was emphatic. 'Whatever the polar opposite of joy is, that's what these bloody shoes make me feel.'

'Well, then. That's an easy one. I would take them off your hands, but if I go home with a pair of heels that high, I think Matt will ban me from ever seeing you again.' She held up a handful of shoes. 'So, they can go?'

Shelley looked at the pile of shoes in front of her, then up at Lara. 'They can all go. I'll sort them into pairs and take them to the charity shop tomorrow.'

Lara began the pairing job for her, placing them side by side. 'That's incredibly generous of you, but why don't you sell them? That way you can use the money to buy yourself some shoes you *do* like.' Much as Lara agreed with charitable giving, she thought Shelley might need the cash if she was paying her mortgage alone now. And she'd already mentioned how worried she was about losing her job. 'There's a tabletop sale at the local school in a couple of weeks. I saw a banner as I drove past. Why don't we do that? I'm sure the yummy mummies would lap up your Louboutins.'

Shelley frowned. 'Tabletop sale? No, I don't think so.'

'Oh, come on, it'll be fun. You and me, plying our wares.' She held up a pair of shoes and waved them either side of her head.

'I'm not sure Matt will be keen on me taking you out to work. And don't they start at the crack of dawn or something?'

'Not a local school sale, I don't think. Anyway, I'm waking up annoyingly early at the moment, so I might as well do something useful, and it'll get me out of the house.'

The face was back. 'Maybe.'

Lara was beginning to realise that when Shelley said 'maybe', she actually meant no. She'd work on her again later, but for the next few minutes she wanted to play with these shoes and remember a simpler time when she'd had a collection of her own.

As she pulled out a mustard-yellow mule, a photo strip fluttered to the floor and she picked it up. She turned it towards Shelley. There were four photos of a young Shelley and another girl of the same age. From top to bottom, the photos were serious, then tongues out, then blown-out cheeks, and in the fourth photo, both girls in rapturous laughter. 'You look beautiful here. How old were you?'

Shelley reached out and took it from her. 'About seventeen I would think. I do look good, don't I? How come you never realise that when you're young?'

'Ain't that the truth.' Lara groaned. 'If only I was as "fat" now as I thought I was at sixteen. Who's the other girl?'

Shelley ran her finger down the photo strip. 'That's Dee. She used to be my best friend.'

CHAPTER SEVEN

Shelley

Before

Secondary school. Shelley had been preparing for this day all summer, ever since the day after her eleventh birthday when she found out that she'd passed the entrance exam for St Mary's, but her stomach clenched as she walked the path to the gates. Her mother had offered to take the morning off work and drive her there, but she'd said she was fine catching the bus. Better to get it over with. Now she yearned for the familiarity of her small primary school and the friends she'd known for six years who would right now be hanging out in the playground of the local secondary school. Was this a bad idea? Too late now.

Thanks to the compulsory uniform, everyone looked pretty similar at least. Neat ponytails, blazers with growing room, regulation-length pleated skirts. Shelley's socks had been straight from the packet that morning, and they were so white, they almost gleamed.

It was completely by chance that she sat next to Dee in Mrs McFarlane's form group. 'Hi. I'm Dione. But everyone calls me Dee. What's your name?'

That's how she was: upfront, direct, honest. She knew who she was and she wasn't afraid to show it. No way would Dee have spent the morning terrified about her first day. She knew her way around and all of their teachers' names by the end of the first day. By the end of the first week, she had worked out which of the dinner ladies gave the biggest portions, which after-school clubs were the most interesting and who on the staff you could have a joke with and who you definitely couldn't.

To Dee, life was an adventure waiting for her to live it. Luckily for Shelley, she wanted to take her along for the ride. They made other friends at school, but she and Dee were inseparable for the whole seven years. Shelley was an only child, and Dee – with an older brother at boarding school – was effectively in the same boat. They were more like sisters than friends.

It wasn't until her first visit to Dee's home that Shelley realised how different their out-of-school lives were. Shelley's mum had raised her eyebrows when she'd given her the address – one of the big houses on Pilgrims Way. *Don't forget your pleases and thank yous while you're there*, was all she'd said, but the way she'd fiddled with the collar of her work tabard had made Shelley nervous. What would Dee's parents be like?

Her mother's reaction made a lot more sense when she got to the address that Dee had scribbled out for her. Their house was another world. The space in every room made Shelley catch her breath. The small two-bedroom flat she shared with her mum could have fit in the sitting room and conservatory.

'It's called an *orangerie*,' Dee's mum had corrected her.

Shelley remembered her mother's instruction. 'Thank you.'

Dee rolled her eyes and pulled Shelley up to her bedroom.

When Dee opened her bedroom door, Shelley just avoided gasping like Charlie Bucket at the chocolate factory. Where should she look first? It was amazing.

For a start, her bedroom was twice the size of Shelley's lounge. There were two single beds – one for sleepovers – and a dressing table with an oval mirror. Along one wall was a row of high wardrobes which seemed to contain enough clothes, shoes and toys for three eleven-year-old girls. On the other wall, Gary Barlow and Robbie Williams smiled down at her.

Dee spun around and flipped onto one of the beds, disturbing a pile of magazines. She picked up a copy of *Sugar*. 'Have you read this one yet? You can have this if you like. I've read it.'

Despite her family's wealth, Dee was never showy or arrogant. She was kind and generous and fun. It gave her confidence. A knowledge about who she was and the self-belief to present herself to the world. Shelley envied her this more than her flat-screen TV and designer clothes. Dee was always the first with her hand up in class, the first to volunteer for school events or to apply to be a prefect, then head girl. Nothing intimidated her.

Even when they weren't in school, they were together. Sometimes Dee would come over to Shelley's flat to play but most of the time they were at Dee's house. Often, they would spend an afternoon in her room, listening to music and putting together outfit combinations from Dee's wardrobe. Crop tops and tartan trousers. Morgan de Toi and Naf Naf. Reebok trainers and Kickers. Then they would do each other's hair and make-up. Dee always dressed Shelley in something she would never choose to wear, but every time she got it right. Invariably, Dee would tell her to 'borrow' it. When Shelley tried to refuse – she knew her mother would not approve of her accepting clothes, and Dee's mother probably wouldn't be hugely keen on it either – Dee wouldn't take no for an answer or she'd stuff it in her bag when she wasn't looking.

In sixth form, they both opted for English A levels, although Dee combined hers with art and media whereas Shelley opted for history and politics. It was Dee's insistence that Shelley apply to go to university. No one in her family had been, and she had no idea how to go about it. But in her usual style, Dee made appointments for them both with the careers officer, and before she knew what was happening, Shelley was sitting with a UCAS university application form and a pile of prospectuses.

Dee dropped the one she was reading. 'I think we should apply to the same universities so that we can stay together. Or at least ones that are close. Let's make a list of the ones we like the look of and then find them on the map.'

Shelley was completely lost when she was flicking through the different schools. 'How can we choose?'

Dee raised an eyebrow. 'Well, for a start, we can look at the male-to-female ratios.'

Shelley was nervous at the thought of going too far from home, but Dee was horrified when she suggested she might choose a London university and commute. 'What's the point of that? We'll have our parents popping in every day. No. We need to go further away.'

In the end, she practically let Dee choose for her. It was that or stick a pin in a map. Their careers officer at school hadn't been a great deal of help either.

Dee even came to the open day at Warwick with her because Shelley's mum couldn't get the day off work. 'You can tell me all about it when you come home,' her mum had said, kissing her on the top of the head. 'I'm really proud of you, you know.'

Shelley got a warm feeling at the thought of making her mum proud. She was even prouder when Shelley's offer from Warwick came through. It was hard to tell who was more excited, her mum or Dee, who had also received an acceptance to Manchester. They held hands and jumped around the bedroom together. 'We are going to have so much fun!'

That's why it was so difficult to tell Dee when she decided to drop out after the first term. And why that might well have been the beginning of their problems.

CHAPTER EIGHT

Lara

The house was so tidy that Lara was nostalgic for the pre-*Make Way for Joy* days when there would always be a pile of papers, a cupboard or a drawer that needed a sort-out. Matt had worked like a Trojan to get everything in its place and now there was nothing for her to do.

Nothing.

She hadn't even had to make breakfast. Matt had insisted she stay in bed and relax while he made her tea and toast before he went to work. 'There's no need for you to get up early. Make the most of it.'

Lying there, she'd listened to him moving about downstairs: the clatter of crockery as he emptied the dishwasher, cupboard doors opening and closing as he put plates and cups away, the rumble of the kettle for her tea. Making up for working late tonight – and time away from home wining and dining with his boss tomorrow evening – by ensuring that she didn't have to lift a finger around the house. It wasn't worth even trying to tell him that he didn't need to. 'It's not as if you're out enjoying yourself. It's your job, Matt. You don't need to feel guilty.' He wouldn't listen. And she couldn't seem to make him understand that leaving her with nothing to do at all was worse; boredom made her miserable.

He nudged open the bedroom door with his knee, put the mug of tea on the bedside table and waited for her to shuffle up into a sitting position and take the plate of toast. 'You shouldn't be cleaning the house anyway. Why don't you do something else? You could call Natalie and invite her over here. She's still on maternity leave, isn't she?'

Inviting her old friend over was the last thing she wanted to do. Something else she had tried to explain to no avail. 'She's probably busy. A new baby and a toddler must be hard work.' Her voice sounded bitter; she hadn't meant it to.

He watched her as she picked up a triangle of toast and nibbled at the crust. 'Still, she'd love to see you. Actually, Chris texted me to check all was okay. It sounded like he'd been prompted by Natalie.'

That was pretty certain. Chris and Matt weren't particularly friends. Lara could imagine Natalie prodding her husband into asking Matt why Lara wasn't returning her calls. 'I'll send her a message later.'

He glanced at the display on the alarm clock. 'What about your new friend next door, Shelley? What time does she get home from work?'

Lara took a deep breath and held it. When was he going to stop with this? If she wanted to call or see people, she would. She wasn't a child. 'I'm not sure. And I don't want to keep pushing myself on her.' It had been okay sorting through the shoes but Shelley hadn't been overly enthusiastic about getting together again. *Maybe I should just let it go?*

Finally, he gave in and took a shower. Lara slid the half-eaten toast next to the mug of tea and wriggled onto her back, waiting for the reassuring tumble in her stomach. The baby always moved most in the mornings; even the slightest shift in her position could make the fluttering stop, so she would lay as still as possible, palms and fingertips splayed on her stomach. Which part of the baby was moving? Was that a hand or a foot? An elbow or a heel?

Closing her eyes, trying to imagine an actual baby somersaulting around inside her; it was impossible. Even seeing the evidence on the sonographer's screen didn't make it any easier to comprehend. How was there an actual baby in there? Mind-blowing.

When Matt reappeared from the shower, still towelling his hair dry, she beckoned him over with her fingertips, keeping her voice low. 'He's kicking around again. Come and put your hand here. I'm sure you'll be able to feel him this time.'

He dropped his towel on the end of the bed. 'I'd love to, but I've just realised the time. I need to get a move on if I'm going to make it in for the Monday briefing meeting.'

If he was in such a rush, why had he spent so long sorting out the kitchen? Or checking that she was eating her breakfast? 'It will only take a minute. Just lean over. Put your hand here, where mine is.'

He sighed and sat on the edge of the bed, let her take his palm and place it on the side of her stomach. As usual, the baby stopped moving. He raised his eyebrows. 'I can't feel anything.'

'You need to give it a bit longer.' She was speaking to his back now as he dropped the towel from his waist and pulled on a pair of trunks. 'Come back and try again. Just give it two minutes.'

Matt slid the wardrobe door open and pulled out a pair of trousers. 'You know I can never feel it anyway. You just enjoy it. I've really got to go.'

She hoped the 'it' referred to the movement rather than the baby. They didn't know the sex but she'd taken to referring to the baby as 'he' because 'it' felt so impersonal.

'Matt, please.' If he could just feel the baby move, she knew he'd feel better. More connected. But every time she asked him to try, the baby stopped moving, which made it worse.

He sat down again. Tried the other side of her stomach. She could practically see him counting the seconds in his head. 'Sorry, love. Still can't feel anything. And I've got to go.'

He left the room and she let her head fall back onto her pillows. She knew it was hard for him, but it wasn't easy for her either and she needed him on board. How could he be so focused on her – was she eating, drinking, resting? – but barely want to talk about the baby?

Twenty seconds later he reappeared. 'Sorry, I forgot to do this.' He came over and kissed her. 'See you later tonight.' She knew that he loved her and worried about her, but she wanted him to show that love to the baby too. Was she being unreasonable?

The front door slammed and she pulled the duvet over her head. Now what was she going to do?

Even after a really long bath, painting her nails and straightening her hair, it was still only 10 a.m.. A walk would kill some more time but the sky was threatening rain so she'd be better off leaving that until later.

It was impossible to shake off the feeling of disappointment from this morning. Feeling the baby kick was a highlight in her day, and she wanted to share it with Matt. If he felt the baby move, it would seem more real to him, she knew it would. He was such a great husband and he would make a wonderful dad. He would. She knew it.

Downstairs, she picked up the Kindle that he'd bought her to replace the ousted paperbacks, but she couldn't settle her mind to the thriller she'd been half-reading, always losing the thread of who was who and what was going on. She'd given *Make Way for Joy* to Shelley so she couldn't even flick through that.

It was a shame Shelley was at work, really. Despite not wanting to push herself onto Shelley if she wasn't wanted, Lara had quite enjoyed starting to sort out that room: feeling useful and productive. And those shoes! It was such a waste keeping them in that box – shoes like that needed to be seen and admired. Although, Shelley obviously hadn't felt like that.

Her reaction to them had been very odd. *Instruments of torture*, she'd called them. But in the next breath she'd said that she'd worn them anyway. What was all that about? Wanting to please her husband?

And what had he been like? In the wedding photograph which had hit Lara on the head that first day, he'd been handsome and happy, looking at Shelley as if he couldn't believe his luck. How did you get from that to divorce? What were the steps that took you from 'I do' to 'goodbye'?

Judging by Shelley's reaction every time his name was mentioned, Lara could only assume that Greg had hurt her pretty badly. Was it an affair? She thought again of the 'torturous' shoes. Could he have been abusive? Maybe it was the thriller she was halfway through sort of reading that was leading her mind to the worst conclusions, but there definitely seemed to be more to the story. Matt called her nosy, but she preferred to say she was interested in people. In her old law firm, she'd witnessed the aftermath of a full range of human behaviour: it would make you a cynic if you let it. Damaged women weren't likely to be effusive about making new friendships. Was she being unfair expecting Shelley to be enthusiastic about spending time together?

Maybe she would risk going for a walk; a few spots of rain wouldn't kill her. Staring around this bare lounge was making her maudlin. It had been the right thing to do to clear stuff out and 'make way for joy', but she'd been a little envious of Shelley's front room with its coordinated cushions and artistic – if empty – vases. It was strange that someone so tidy wouldn't have sorted out that box room before now. What had stopped her?

She sat on the bottom step of the stairs to pull on her trainers. Thought again of those beautiful shoes. What other treasures did Shelley have stored up in that room? Lara was itching to see what else was hidden. If Shelley had been hurt, she might be afraid to reach out to someone she hardly knew. Lara would have to take the initiative. She tore a page from the notebook Matt had left on the table by the stairs for her to list any jobs she thought needed doing around the house. She would scribble her mobile number on it and post it through Shelley's door on the way out. Maybe they could get together tomorrow night when Matt was out with his boss, and she could get to know Shelley – and her story – a little better.

CHAPTER NINE

Shelley

Sometimes it was the smallest chance conversation that could send Shelley into the pit. Tuesday, it was a phone call from some utility company about her electricity supply.

'Good evening, Mrs Thomas. I'm Justin and I'm calling to see if you're happy with your energy supplier.'

The *Mrs* was the first problem. The *Thomas* was the second. Could she still call herself that? For how long? 'Er, I guess so.'

'Because we have some excellent new tariffs which might save you money. Can I tell you about them?'

Shelley's head had been thick all day from disturbed sleep the night before. Then her boss Steve had been on the phone to ask if she'd thought any more about applying for the management role in the new company. He'd only emailed it over yesterday and she'd barely had a chance to look at it. Why was he being so pushy about it?

Steve had only been with the company for about eighteen months. Until relatively recently, she hadn't seen that much of him around the office because, generally speaking, he was out and about drumming up new business. It must have been the imminent takeover that had seen him hanging around more often. When he first started appearing at her desk unannounced, it had been so out of the ordinary that she and Flora had wondered whether he was checking up on them. Then, with her usual fingernail grip on reality, Flora had teased that he might be plucking up the courage to ask Shelley out, which was clearly absurd. It had been a pleasure to tell Flora that she'd heard him talking to his girlfriend on the phone. Less so when Flora had arched an eyebrow and asked if she was disappointed. Was it any wonder she felt herself flush every time she spoke to him these days?

Steve's call about the management role wasn't the only reason she'd had a stressful day. Most of her colleagues – Flora included – were starting to look around at other job opportunities, and it made for a very unsettled atmosphere. Trying to keep herself focused on the job at hand was exhausting when all around her people were talking about CVs and recruitment companies and what they'd heard on the grapevine about the jobs going at the new company.

Now, on the phone to this sparky salesman, the little energy she had left seeped out of her and drained away. Gas and electric: that had been Greg's domain. Paperwork tasks had always been split down the middle: Greg knew all the dates for the car tax, house insurance and utilities. She did all the social paperwork – birthday cards, family weddings, gifts, etc. Now she was doing all of it. And there always seemed to be *more* to do, more she had forgotten. It had taken four weeks for her to get in the habit of putting the bins out on the right day. And now this man wanted to talk to her about electricity prices.

'I don't think so. I've just got in from work and—'

'It won't take long. I can see from our records that your husband registered on our website last year to be kept up to date with the latest offers. According to our records, your current tariff expires in four weeks' time. Is that right?'

Greg had asked them to call? For a moment she was bewildered and then she realised what the man had said: a year ago. 'I… I… don't know. My husband dealt with all that and…'

'Maybe it would be better if I spoke directly to your husband?'

Shelley's throat started to close up. When you share a home with someone, there are so many things you take for granted that the other person does. It's not that you're not capable of doing those jobs, just that you haven't been the one to do them for a long time. Or ever. Somehow, over time, jobs become yours or his. You always change the bedding; he always puts the bins out.

She held the phone in her left hand, her right hand clenched. 'No, he's not here.'

Justin didn't give up that easily. 'That's no problem. When's a good time to call to catch him in?'

Pushing, pushing. It was too much. Why wouldn't he listen to her? Why could he not just stop talking at her? *Shut up. Shut up. Shut up.* 'He's not here. He's not coming back. You can't talk to him. Goodbye.' She slammed the phone down. Hard. Then she picked up the receiver and slammed it down again.

Being abandoned and having to deal with the rejection and disappointment and loneliness was bad enough. Managing life alone was just about achievable if she wasn't expected to deal with job changes and room sort-outs and decisions about the bloody energy supplier. She opened a cupboard door then slammed it shut. Then did it again. And again. She roared. Loudly. Why the hell couldn't people just leave her alone?

As usual, the rage burned fierce for a few seconds and then died, throbbing pain left in its wake. Shelley slumped against the counter in the kitchen with her hands over her face. Her shoulders jumped as she coughed out tears. Gradually, her body calmed and the tears slowed. She pressed her fingertips into her eyes and squeezed the last of them away. Then she ran the cold tap and splashed water on her face, wiping it away with a square of kitchen roll. *Deep breath and on we go.*

She'd stopped at the Tesco Metro on the way home from the office to pick up some salad, but there was no way she was ready to eat now: emotion and digestion didn't mix well. She opened the fridge to throw the prepared salad inside. There was a bottle of wine there, looking at her. Had she put that in there last night? Maybe one glass wouldn't hurt. She grabbed it from the fridge and had her hand on the screw top when there was a knock at the door. *Who is that?*

'Hiya. I'm not too early, am I?' Lara stood with an armful of packets that looked like olives and houmous and pitta bread. 'I brought supplies.'

The brain fog, busy day and Justin from the electricity company had driven their arrangement from Shelley's mind. Matt was out until late tonight at some work function and Lara had suggested she come over for the evening so they could carry on sorting out the box room. Why had she agreed? She was too tired for this tonight. 'Of course not, come in. Tea?'

Lara followed her back to the kitchen and dropped the contents of her arms onto the counter. If she'd noticed Shelley's face was blotchy, she didn't mention it. 'Were you just about to have a glass of wine? Don't stop on my account. You don't have to be boring because I am.'

'No.' Shelley returned the wine to the fridge and pulled out the ready-made salad. She reached up into the top cupboard to get a salad bowl and some smaller bowls for Lara's antipasti. 'I bought it for the weekend.'

That was a stupid thing to say. Now she was going to have to make up something she was doing at the weekend. Sure enough, Lara asked, 'Are you doing anything nice?'

Dammit. What could she say? Lying got complicated if you didn't watch yourself. 'Nothing much, just meeting up with some work colleagues.'

Lara was transferring the contents of the clear plastic containers into the small bowls. They barely knew each other, yet here she was making herself at home in Shelley's kitchen. Why was she here anyway? Didn't she have real friends to hang around with when her husband was away?

Lara had clearly had the same thoughts about Shelley. 'Must be nice to have colleagues you want to hang out with. Do they live around here?'

Was this a tactful way of asking why Lara never saw anyone come or go from the house except Shelley, who was home alone most evenings and all weekend? 'Not really. Since I've been on my own, I've been having some time to myself.'

Lara nodded slowly as she tapped the bottom of a plastic pot to release a couple of reluctant olives. 'It can be difficult when a marriage comes to an end, unfortunately. People seem to feel like they have to pick a side. Did you say that you and your ex-husband have a lot of friends in common?'

Until last year, Shelley hadn't realised that all of their friends were mutual. If she was honest, they were all more Greg's friends than hers, so it wasn't surprising that they'd slipped away from her over the last few months. To them she was just Greg's wife. And now she wasn't anymore, they probably didn't know what to do with her. She thought of Dee. Then pushed the image away. 'Uh, yes, quite a few.'

If Lara knew how uncomfortable her questions were making Shelley, she didn't show it. 'Did you read the foreword to *Make Way for Joy*? She went through a really rough marriage break-up and the ideas for the book came from that.'

Shelley opened a cupboard so that the door would hide her face. She didn't want to admit that she had only dipped in and out of the book. She also didn't want her face to tell the truth that her lips weren't ready to. 'Did she? I skipped that part.'

There was a pause before Lara spoke again. 'Actually, she found out her husband had cheated on her. More than once.'

Lara's words hung in the air. Was she waiting for Shelley's reaction? Did she suspect something? Was she hoping that Shelley would take the opportunity to tell all? If she was, she was about to be disappointed. Now the food was all in bowls, Shelley could seize the opportunity to divert Lara's conversation. 'Shall we take all this through to the lounge?'

A large cardboard box was perched on the coffee table in front of the sofa, some of its contents already spilling out. Lara put the dips and pitta onto a side table and sat down. 'What's this? Have you got started without me?'

Shelley scooped some of the loose prints from the table and dropped them back where they'd come from. 'It's just a box of really old photos. School and baby photos mostly. Feel free to look. As long as you don't laugh at the dodgy haircuts.' At least this might distract Lara from the talk of mutual friendships and broken marriages.

'What's this one?' Lara opened an album of the photos Shelley had put together from her interrailing trip. It was covered in the country stickers they had picked up along the way. She'd wanted to collect souvenirs but space had been limited in her bright blue rucksack. Stickers had been the perfect solution, and she'd been pleased she had them when she'd had the brainwave to customise the photo album. This album was the main reason she'd brought the box down in the first place. Uncovering Dee's photo in the box of shoes had started her mind wandering. One of the reasons she'd had such a bad night's sleep.

'This looks like a blast. You're so cute in these. So young. How old are you here?'

'Eighteen.' They'd finished their A levels and taken off straight away, travelling around Europe for four weeks, home in time for exam results mid-August. It had been Dee's idea, of course. Once she'd conceived of the idea, she was full speed ahead on choosing destinations, finding youth hostels, checking train routes. Shelley had been pulled along in her back draft.

Lara looked surprised. Was it shock that Shelley could do something so exciting? 'You were brave to go away, just the two of you. Is this the same girl in those photo booth photos from the other day? Are you still in touch?'

Shelley had spent almost an hour flicking through these photos last night. But it still hurt to look at them. The one in Lara's hands had been taken at the Gare du Nord by a blond guy from Denmark they'd met on the train. They had their arms around each other's shoulders, backpacks looming behind them, wide expectant smiles. 'Yes. That was my best friend, Dee. And no. We're not in touch anymore.'

'That's a shame. Friendships slip sometimes, don't they?' Lara stared at the photo too, longer than was necessary. Was she thinking about a lost friendship of her own? Shelley knew so little about Lara – and vice versa – and yet here they were, with Shelley's past spread out in front of them. It was strange that this didn't feel weird. Lara *was* a little pushy, but somehow it wasn't unpleasant. Dee had been pushy too. Shelley shook her head. That wasn't a path she wanted to go down with Lara. At least, not yet.

Lara also seemed happy to change the subject. She picked up another picture. 'And what about this one? Who is this in the middle of you and Dee?'

Shelley took the photograph that Lara was holding up. It wasn't surprising that Lara didn't recognise him from the wedding photo. They were all pulling funny faces at the camera; the reason why escaped her now, but they looked so comfortable in each other's company. If only it had stayed like that. 'That's Greg. About a week after we got together.'

CHAPTER TEN

Shelley

Before

Two hours, four different outfits and three shades of lipstick later, Shelley was on her way. It hadn't helped that she couldn't ask Dee for help with choosing an outfit; Dee was still upset with her for choosing Greg over her current boyfriend's best mate.

Greg was six years older than Shelley, and at eighteen, that made a big difference. He worked in the City; she was only just finishing sixth form. To be honest, she didn't really understand what he did for a job. It was something to do with stocks and shares and he earned a lot of money if his car and the clothes he wore were anything to go by. She'd known him and his group of friends for a while, often chatting to them in one of the pubs on the high street, but couldn't believe her luck when he had asked her out: just the two of them.

Busy with young, stylish people drinking champagne and eating small plates of beautiful food, the restaurant Greg had booked near his office in the City was more than a little intimidating. Years later, he confessed he'd been trying to impress her. She never admitted she'd realised that all along. Due to train times, she was uncharacteristically early and was sitting at the table waiting, head down scrutinising the menu, trying to pretend that she did things like this all the time.

When he arrived, she watched the hostess lead him to their table. He had a slight swagger: Dee thought he was arrogant, but Shelley just saw confidence. Greg was comfortable in his own skin; he knew who he was. As he leaned in to kiss her cheek, she could smell his cologne and it made her stomach flip over. His smile made it flop back again. 'Hi. Glad you found the place okay. Do you like it?'

'It's great. And so were your directions. It was super easy.' Her insides were churning with nerves. She would have waited outside the restaurant but the rush hour pavements were more overwhelming than sitting alone at the table. The sight of him in his suit and tie, looking so handsome, wasn't helping. Why was he interested in someone like her? Surely, he could have anyone he wanted? Even the hostess had looked at him approvingly as she brought him over. Everyone liked Greg. Apart from Dee at the moment.

'Would you like another drink?' He motioned towards the glass of water she had ordered for herself while she waited. 'Maybe something stronger? Orange cordial? Or blackcurrant?'

She laughed and leaned forwards conspiratorially. 'I was too scared to order a grown-up drink in case they didn't believe I was eighteen.' The thought of being asked for ID in a place like this filled her with horror.

Ice broken, they had a lovely evening. Greg had been here with colleagues several times so he knew his way around the menu. Having stared at the many food choices for fifteen minutes before he arrived, she'd pretty much decided the chicken breast was the safest option, but he persuaded her to try the sea bass, which came with aubergines and tomato pesto and other ingredients she'd never tried. It didn't matter that the fish wasn't really to her taste – it was only because she wasn't used to eating this kind of food in these kinds of places. She could get used to it. And it wasn't only the food; he knew how to order their meals exactly the way he wanted, what wine to drink, how to get the waiter's attention without being rude. He was funny and considerate and worldly and sophisticated. Greg was at home here. She was quite possibly in love with him before the chocolate mousse even arrived.

All the way there, she'd worried about what they would talk about, running through potential topics in her head. But the conversation flowed easily: he chatted about his job and the flat he was in the process of buying; she told him about the universities she'd had offers from. Greg had been to university too, but he had been surprised by how many people he worked with who hadn't. He asked her what she planned to do with a degree once she had one; it was embarrassing to admit she hadn't thought that far ahead. The two hours they were there practically flew by. After paying the bill – he insisted, she was relieved – they left to get their train home.

On the way to the station, they passed a shoe shop, its small window artfully decorated with only five shoes displayed like works of art. Shelley pointed out a pair of red patent peep-toes with really high heels. 'Look at the height of those!'

Greg stopped walking, pulled her with him as he leaned towards the window for a closer look. 'Do you like them?'

She laughed and tugged at his hand; shoes like that were not for the likes of her. 'They're beautiful, but it would be impossible to walk in them.'

Greg shrugged. 'Lots of the women at work wear shoes like that every day. It must just take practice.'

Shelley could imagine those women. Tailored, beautiful professionals like the other women in the restaurant. Not clumsy, unconfident sixth-formers. She didn't like the comparison in her head and wasn't about to draw Greg's attention to her deficiencies.

'Maybe. Come on.' She pulled at his hand, which had held hers all the way from the restaurant.

Earlier, she'd taken the Underground from Waterloo to meet him, but they decided to skip the Tube ride this time and walk back to the station. Greg knew his way through all the back roads to get them there. His confident stride was a relief; she would have been lost within two streets of the restaurant. Not that they were rushing. They walked so slowly, in fact, that they almost missed the last train home. Well, it was probably also because they were holding hands and stopping every hundred metres to kiss. It wasn't until they got to Waterloo and looked at the departures board that they realised they had two minutes to get to their platform. Greg squeezed her hand and looked at her. 'Can you run? It's that or I book a hotel room.'

Excitement fizzed in her chest but was rapidly replaced by the cold fear of her mum's reaction if she called her to say she'd missed her train and was staying overnight with a man. 'Let's sprint!'

They were doing so well until she skidded on a spilt McDonald's coke and her left leg swept out at a tangent from her body. Thankfully, Greg still had hold of her hand and he pulled her upwards. The only thing that snapped was the thin ankle strap of one of her cheap shoes. There was no time for a post-mortem; she slipped them both off and held them aloft. 'Keep going!'

They made it to platform fifteen just as the whistle blew and they stood breathless inside the train doors. She doubled over at the hips, laughing, and he panted, holding onto the rail and placing a hand on her waist to stop her from toppling as the train pulled away. 'You were magnificent.'

She righted herself and looked at him. Pulling her close, he kissed her gently.

Their second date was only two days later and, when he picked her up from home, Greg presented her with a beautifully wrapped box. 'To make up for breaking your shoe.'

The red peep-toes weren't her kind of thing, but it was a very sweet gesture. Romantic even. 'I can't believe you bought them. Thank you.' There had been no price tags in the shop window, which probably meant they were expensive. Since her dad had left, there wasn't a great deal of money around at home; there was no way she could have bought herself a pair of shoes like that. Even if she'd wanted to.

Dee rolled her eyes when Shelley showed them to her. 'He's just being showy. When are you going to wear shoes like that? Do you even like them?' But that made Shelley even more determined. Even if it took her hours of walking up and down the hallway like Bambi, she was going to wear those red patent heels and be just like the glamorous women Greg worked with.

When he took her to dinner again two weeks later – their sixth date – she did.

'Wow. You look fantastic.' His face made the blisters worthwhile. But she couldn't help but wonder what would happen if she told him that high-heeled shoes weren't her kind of thing. That she really did want the chicken rather than the sea bass. Would he feel the same way about her then?

CHAPTER ELEVEN

Lara

Open boxes, piles of clothes, random objects of uncertain purpose: the trouble with having a clear-out was that it often looked a hundred times worse before it got better. On Tuesday night – after flicking through the photographs – Lara had shown Shelley how to follow the system from *Make Way for Joy*, plucking items from boxes and assembling them into rough piles to keep, sell or throw away. Judging by Shelley's overwhelmed expression as they walked into the room on Wednesday evening, she might need reminding of the process. Lara nudged her. 'It's organised chaos. Honestly.'

There was one pile at least that should be very easy to get rid of. 'We could bag up all your ex-husband's clothes tonight. To be honest, I don't really understand why he hasn't taken them. I mean, you might take it into your head to throw them all away? Or burn them?'

She'd meant the last part as a joke, but Shelley didn't smile. 'Not my style. Look, let's just move them to one side for now and I'll deal with them later.'

There was quite a big heap, but Shelley seemed intent on scooping it up all at once. She slid both arms underneath like a forklift. As she lifted, the pile must have obscured her view because she stumbled as if she'd been struck, a jumper falling from the pile.

Lara picked it up and followed her to the wardrobe with it, slid the door open. Shelley threw the clothes in so hard that a pair of jeans fell back out. She snatched them up and slammed them back in. A T-shirt dropped and she kicked it, grabbed the jumper from Lara, threw that on top and yanked the door across. As it slid closed, she caught her fingers and winced in pain. Twisting to face Lara, her eyes bright, she brushed her palms together and stuck out her chin. 'Done.'

Lara felt a stab of guilt. Was she pushing Shelley too fast? It could take a long time to get over the breakdown of a marriage and she still hadn't managed to find out what had happened between Shelley and her ex-husband. The aggression with which she'd moved the clothes showed she was clearly very angry with him. And in pain.

She put a hand on Shelley's arm. 'We don't have to do this tonight if you don't want. We can—'

Shelley pulled back her arm as if Lara had hit her. 'No. Let's get on with it. What's next?'

This was a new side she hadn't seen. Was Shelley about to burst into tears or shout at her? Frankly, it was nice to see her with a bit more fire in her belly. Although, Lara didn't want to make her upset. There must be something less personal in here that they could do today? 'What about that box next to you? It says CDs. Shall we start with that?'

Shelley nodded but still didn't meet Lara's eye. Clearly, she *had* pushed her too quickly. Dammit. She was supposed to be helping her not making it worse. They didn't speak as Shelley pulled over the box and opened the flaps. This one wasn't stuck down. Lara racked her brains for something funny to say to lighten the mood but came up with nothing. It would be so much easier if Shelley just told her what had gone on between her and Greg – then she would know what subjects to avoid. She reached inside the box and lifted out a small pile of CD cases.

Shelley placed a hand either side of the box. 'Shall I just tip the whole lot out? It'll probably be easier.'

The CD cases clattered from the box and Lara watched her, unable to bear this atmosphere between them. She had to say something. 'Look, I know it's difficult when you split up with someone. Especially if you are not the one who did the leaving. I'm sorry if I'm being tactless about throwing stuff out. I was just trying to make you laugh.'

Shelley pressed her middle fingers to the corners of her eyes, wiped away two large tears in one stroke. 'Honestly. I'm fine. It was just the wardrobe door; it caught my finger.'

That wasn't the pain she was in. Did she think Lara was stupid? 'I know. I know. But it's okay. To be upset, I mean. It's actually good to get it off your chest. I'm not trying to pry; I just want you to know that I am happy to listen if you ever want to offload.'

Shelley took a deep breath and looked Lara in the eye. She smiled. 'Thanks, honestly. But there's nothing to say. Let's just get on with this. How should we organise them?'

'Well, first you need to decide if you actually want to keep them. Matt and I don't own a single CD anymore.'

Shelley nodded. 'These are the only ones left in this house. Greg ripped all the ones that we had and put them onto our computer. Then he just used Spotify.' She motioned to the mini-Everest of CDs in front of them. 'These were my ones. He was pretty evangelical about becoming totally digital, and I had to save them from the cull.' She smiled and the mood in the room lifted a little.

Lara poked around in the pile. 'Wow. How many Madonna albums do you have? You're quite a fan.' Lara held up her hands, which were full of every album from *Like a Virgin* onwards.

Shelley smiled. 'Yes. I was a big fan back in the day.'

'Why don't you listen to them anymore?'

Shelley scratched her head. 'I don't really know. I suppose I just got out of the habit.'

'Right. We need a system. You have to decide whether owning each album brings you joy. Let's start with…' Lara held her hand over the scattered albums like the grabber at a fairground then plucked one and held it up. 'The Spice Girls!'

Shelley held out her hand for it. 'Oh my word. I'm surprised the laser didn't melt this one, I listened to it so many times. I got it for my birthday. My mum bought me a portable CD player and Dee bought me this album to go with it, and I played it over and over.' She stared at the cover for a few moments and then laughed. 'Crikey, we also used to dance along to it together in Dee's bedroom. I would be Baby Spice and Dee was always Ginger Spice. We used to make up routines, until Dee's dad would shout upstairs, "Stop that banging before you come through the bloody ceiling!"' She deepened her voice to mimic him and laughed again. Lara was really enjoying this new Shelley today. Perhaps she'd just needed time to warm up.

'Well, I can tell by the smile on your face that *that* one brings you joy. I was a big fan too. Let's listen to it now.' Lara pulled out her phone and with a few taps and swipes they were listening to the opening of 'Wannabe' at full volume. Shelley even joined in when Lara sang a couple of the lines, but then she blushed and shook her head.

Lara turned the volume down. 'So, what's it to be? Do you really, really want to keep that one?'

Shelley laughed. 'Yeah, I reckon I do. Plenty of good memories. But a lot of these other ones can go.'

Lara held up another case between her finger and thumb as if it was something unpleasant. 'Like this one? Hear'Say? What were you thinking?'

Shelley pulled a face. 'Actually, I think my dad sent me that one. I don't think he had a clue what to get me. My parents divorced when I was pretty young and I didn't see him much. I usually got a birthday gift about three months late if I got one at all. I have no idea why I kept it, though.'

Lara held it over the black plastic bag destined for the charity shop. 'Oxfam?'

Shelley gave her a thumbs up. 'Oxfam.'

Lara's phone rang. It was Matt. He'd been held up by a tanker spill on the M1 and was probably calling to update her. 'Sorry, need to quickly speak to him.'

'No worries, I'll pop to the toilet while you're talking.'

Lara swiped to connect the call. 'Hi, honey.'

'Hey, beautiful. Traffic has started moving again so I should be home in a couple of hours. Sorry you've been on your own again all evening.'

'Don't worry, I'm fine. Actually, I'm next door with Shelley.'

There was a pause. 'You said you were going to watch a film?'

'Yeah, well, I couldn't settle to it in the end. Thought I'd continue with my *mission*.' He had been teasing her about it again last night. Asking if she was going to start a tidying cult and recruit all the neighbours.

She could almost hear him frown at his handsfree speaker. 'You're not carrying boxes around, are you?'

Lara sighed. 'No. Just sorting through CDs. I think they only weigh a few grams, so I should be fine.'

He sighed at the other end. 'Lara. You don't need to be sarcastic. I just—'

'I know. I know. You're just looking out for me. But I'm not an idiot, Matt. And I'm going nuts in there on my own.'

'It's just another three months, Lar.'

He didn't need to tell her how long it was. She knew how long she had left in days. Shelley reappeared. Time to get Matt off the phone so that they could go back to laughing about dubious music choices. 'I need to go, Matt. I'm fine, okay? Drive safely and I'll see you later.'

'Hold on, before you go. I found a group you might like. My client recommended it – the one I get the tea from. It's not therapy, exactly, it's more—'

Not this again. 'Matt, please. Enough with the self-help groups. I need to go. I'll speak to you when you get home. Bye.'

She clicked off the phone and put it behind her.

Shelley tilted her head. 'Everything okay?'

If she only knew. 'Yeah, he was just checking in. Fourth time today. He was out early and woke me which makes him feel bad; he knows I can't get back to sleep once I'm awake. My head starts buzzing and I'm better off getting up.'

Shelley nodded. 'Thinking about the baby?'

Lara scrutinised one of the cases then put it back on the pile. 'Yes. Mostly. Or just random stuff.' How could she explain what it was like to wake up early with your mind at full throttle? Your heart racing as if you were late for something or you'd forgotten to do something vital?

'I suppose at least you can take a nap in the afternoon if you need one. Not having to go to work, I mean.'

Lara began piling up some of the cases. Not having anywhere to go made it worse but she didn't want to get into that. 'Yeah, that's what Matt says. He thinks I'm better off at home and that everything can be solved with a nice lie-down.'

Shelley looked as if she was about to say something and then changed her mind. She picked up a couple of love ballad compilations, pulled a face and chucked them into the Oxfam bag. 'He works long hours, doesn't he?'

'Yes, the nature of the job, unfortunately. He's a medical sales rep – drives halfway round the country most days. I've already told him he needs to make sure that he can't go more than twenty miles away when I get near my due date.'

'That explains why you don't mind helping me sort out all my old crap. It must get a bit boring for you some days. Do you miss your job?'

So much more than she could have anticipated. School, college, university, work: Lara had always had a sharp brain, enjoyed learning and analysing and having to work out solutions. Now the only decision she had to make was what to cook for dinner, and at the weekends, Matt would even do that. 'Yes, I really do. You don't have time for dark thoughts when you're rushed off your feet at work. I loved it too – the cases, the research, the people. I'm going crackers next door some days. Thank goodness for you and your junk, eh?'

Dammit. She shouldn't have said *dark thoughts*. Now Shelley was frowning at her and was going to ask her what she meant. After her trying to press Shelley about her ex-husband, she would only have herself to blame if Shelley started to ask questions about Lara's business. But she didn't. 'We aim to please!'

She'd dodged a bullet there. It was bad enough having Matt watching her like a hawk. When he got home tonight, he would slowly and tactfully bring up the subject of this group he'd found for her to attend. Why wouldn't he get it that this wasn't what she wanted? Sitting around in a circle listening to other people's misery would only make her feel worse. Or even more guilty that their problems were worse than hers. Sorting through Shelley's stuff was better therapy than that. 'What about your job? What's happening there?'

Shelley shrugged. 'The company is definitely being sold. I need to decide if I am going to apply for a job with the new owner.'

This was a safe subject. 'Don't you want to?'

Shelley sighed. 'To be honest, I don't want to think about it.'

Her face also made it obvious that she didn't want to talk about it. For a few moments, the only noise in the room was the clattering of plastic as Lara rummaged through the rest of the pile, wanting to get back to the lighter atmosphere before Matt had called. *Say something funny.* 'Do you seriously have every single copy of *Now That's What I Call Music!* that was ever released?'

Shelley laughed. 'I obviously shouldn't have been allowed loose in HMV. I'm just not generally a music person. I mean, I like listening to music but I've never been someone who goes to gigs or talks about the latest albums. Greg really knew his stuff. He played guitar a bit when he was at school and college. Listened to all the cool bands. Radiohead and Portishead and all the other heads probably. When he explained it all to me, I got into it too and then I stopped listening to the pop stuff.'

'Radiohead and Portishead? Crikey, that sounds a bit dreary. Did he wear black a lot too?' Lara pulled her fringe down over her left eye, emo-style.

Shelley laughed again; they were back on track. 'No. He was more of a designer label man. It was just the music he liked. He was the one who bought me my favourite album of all time.'

Lara was sorting the plethora of *Now That's What I Call Music!* albums into numerical order. 'Really? What was that?'

CHAPTER TWELVE

Shelley

Before

Music stores were like the third circle of hell. Men of various ages shuffling around, flicking at CD cases, plucking one from the rack and studying it before replacing it and continuing on and on and on. This one had a vague smell of greasy hair and dust. It was for serious music-lovers only. And their bored partners. And, God, she was bored.

To be fair, she only had herself to blame. Without once complaining, Greg had followed her around twenty shops looking for a gift for her mother, so she owed it to him to wait it out as he scoured the shelves for obscure releases by Tim Buckley and Leonard Cohen. But, seriously, how long did it take?

Ten almost unbearable minutes had given way to another ten in which the click-clacking of plastic cases made her want to scream for freedom. 'They need chairs for bored girlfriends in this place. With maybe some magazines to read.'

'Hmmm?' Greg looked up, his eyes blurred. He was lost somewhere in music land. 'Have you had enough?'

She felt bad then; he hadn't murmured when she'd read the contents of every single 'Mum' card in Clintons. 'No, it's fine. I'm joking.'

Another five minutes passed. Click-clack. Shuffle shuffle. 'I mean, if they had an area for girlfriends to sit, they might keep the boyfriends in here longer and then they might sell more.'

He laughed at her, knowing she wouldn't say something that sexist and really mean it. 'Why don't you look for something. I'll buy it for you. What music do you like?'

She hated this question. She knew she was supposed to say someone cool like The Cure or The Smiths but the truth was she liked pop music. How could she say that to Greg though? He would think her an idiot if she told him that her favourite album at the moment was *NSYNC's *Celebrity*. They'd been dating for a few months, but there was still the risk that he would realise she was actually dull and clueless. What could she say? 'Actually, I like lots of different stuff.'

Damn, he looked genuinely interested. His fingers didn't leave their place on the CDs, but he put his head to one side and gave her his full attention. 'Okay. Like who?'

Her mind went completely blank. She didn't want to look stupid, not when things had been going so well between them. Although they were only six years apart in age, that felt like a lot of experience she needed to catch up on. Best to play it safe. 'Actually, I have a lot of compilation albums.'

He shuddered. 'Compilation albums? They are for people with absolutely no taste in music. The type of thing your nan buys you for Christmas. You need to find a band you like, or a singer. Wait a minute, I know what you might like.' He moved up to the 'K' section and started to thumb through before plucking one out and waving it at her. 'Here you go!'

He passed her a CD featuring a cool-looking woman in a bright green hat. 'Who's this?'

'Alicia Keys. You must have heard her single? "Fallin'"? It's been played relentlessly. You'll love the album. It's brilliant. Why don't you come over to mine later? We can play the CD on my new stereo and you can hear how fantastic it is.'

She turned the CD case over and read the tracklist. Normally, she wouldn't pass up the opportunity to spend the evening with Greg but there was a small problem. 'I'm supposed to be seeing Dee later.'

Greg went back to flicking through the CD cases. 'I would say we can all do something together but I don't think she'd be keen on me hanging around. I think she's cross with me.'

Shelley felt uneasy. She'd begun to suspect the same thing. 'What makes you think that?'

Greg shrugged; he didn't look hugely bothered. 'Because I'm monopolising you. I think she feels left out.'

Shelley got that familiar fluttering feeling in her stomach. Confrontation made her uneasy. 'That's silly. She's my best friend. You're my boyfriend.' She still got a thrill saying that word. 'It's two different things.'

Greg picked up another CD: Edie Brickell. 'You might like this one too – it's an old one but she's got a great voice.' He passed it to her. 'I think I'm on Dee's *list*.'

Dee used to say people were 'on her list' if they were annoying her or had done something to upset her. Greg's mocking tone made Shelley regret telling him about it.

Shelley felt torn. It was horrible having to choose between the two of them. Dee was her best friend – they'd done everything together for the last seven years, including the trip around Europe. During that month they had become even closer, and Shelley wouldn't have got through her homesickness and fears about new places if she hadn't had Dee there to take her hand and pull her along. Sometimes literally.

Up until now, Dee had always been the one with the boyfriends. Outgoing, pretty and fun to be around, she was a magnet for boys. Shelley always ended up being the one chatting to Dee's boyfriend's creepy mate; there was always a creepy mate. Dee never left her out but it was uncomfortable being her accessory sometimes.

This time it was *her* turn. She was really falling for Greg and it seemed like he felt the same. After Dee had gotten over her initial annoyance, she had been all right about their relationship, but the more Shelley saw of Greg, the more irritated Dee got. Now she would sigh dramatically every time Shelley even mentioned his name. 'That's all you ever go on about these days,' she'd said last night. 'Greg this and Greg that. I'm bored of how great you think he is.'

Shelley was hurt. She hadn't said she was bored when all Dee had wanted to do was lie on her bed crying because Pete Murphy had a new girlfriend. Or when she'd had to trail around the fair with Lanky Lewis because Dee fancied his best friend Lucas. Wasn't it fair to expect that Dee might give her the same support?

She flipped over the Edie Brickell CD to read the tracklist: 'What I Am'. What was she? A good best friend or a good girlfriend? And why wasn't it possible to be both?

'I'll call Dee and see what she has planned for tonight. Maybe she'll want to rearrange.'

'It's up to you. Let me buy these two CDs for you anyway. If we don't get to listen to them tonight, you can take them home and we can listen to them together another time. Whatever you want. Or you can listen to them with Dee, give her a bit of a musical education instead of those boy bands she still listens to.'

Shelley laughed and sent up a silent prayer of thanks that she hadn't mentioned *NSYNC. She would call Dee and invite her over to Greg's flat to listen to these new albums. If the three of them spent some time hanging out together, it wouldn't be so weird. Or maybe she should encourage Dee and Greg to spend some time together without her there to play referee?

CHAPTER THIRTEEN

Lara

Some friendships are short, only lasting while you have circumstances in common. Maybe you were colleagues or neighbours or had kids of the same age. Other friendships last longer – you make a real connection, meet up just the two of you for the odd coffee or lunch until you slip out of the habit and, before you know it, you only ever chat via posts on social media. But there are some friends who are there for the long haul. Ups and downs, celebrations and commiserations, weddings, births, relationship breakdowns, house moves, career changes: whatever life throws up at you, the friend is there. Those friends are more precious than gold.

When Shelley had talked about Dee – recounting how they'd grown up together, been travelling together – Lara had got the impression of a real closeness. Shelley was an only child and she'd mentioned a couple of times how quiet it had been at home, just her and her mum. When she'd recalled a story about Dee and the things she'd said and done, her face had lit up at the memory. Never once had she explained why Dee wasn't in her life, and Lara hadn't felt as if she could ask.

Maybe there was no big story. People just drifted apart sometimes, didn't they? Life got busy. You made plans and had to cancel. Didn't get around to rearranging and then, before you knew it, six months had gone past and you hadn't seen each other. Like her and Natalie.

Six months. That's how long Natalie said it had been in her text this morning.

Hey, stranger. It's been six months! When can I see you? How's the new house?

Why had the message filled her with fear?

Matt had urged her to answer, make an arrangement. 'Ask her over tomorrow. A Friday Girls' Night; like the old days. It'll do you good.'

She'd just turned over in bed. She was getting fed up with him telling her what would do her good.

Now she stood in the kitchen with a cup of tea and stared at the message again. They'd met at work. With a similar sense of humour, it hadn't been long before she and Natalie had started to take their lunch hour together, then a glass of wine after work, then meeting up on a Friday or Saturday night – sometimes with the husbands too. When Natalie had left to have a baby, they'd stayed in touch, and Lara and Matt had been to hers and Chris's for a takeaway, taking gifts for their baby girl and making all the right noises about how cute she was.

Natalie had returned to work part-time a year later and they'd resumed their lunch dates. She wasn't one of those women who constantly shoved pictures of their child under your nose. She was great, she really was. But things had changed. And then she'd got pregnant again. This time around, Lara hadn't been to visit during her maternity leave.

Lara knew that the problem was with her, not Natalie. Natalie was her friend. She was fun and caring and supportive. It didn't matter that their circumstances were different. She should just pick up her phone right now and make an arrangement to see her. It wasn't as if she didn't have the time, was it?

But she couldn't do it. Just as she couldn't text Louise or Kerry or Theresa or any of the other friends she'd avoided for the last six months or longer. She could make all the excuses she wanted about being busy or focusing on the pregnancy or feeling tired, but that wasn't the reason. They had been her friends over one of the worst periods of her life. They knew everything that had happened and would want to support her and reassure her and encourage her to talk about how she was feeling. She couldn't face that. Not yet. Not until she knew how this was all going to work out.

Ignoring the message would just be rude, though. She typed a response with her thumb:

All good but everything in boxes! Will be in touch when life isn't so crazy!

Then she put the phone face down on the kitchen counter and pushed it away.

Maybe Natalie was as bored as she was. Stuck indoors with a baby and a toddler must be pretty tough. When she'd come back to work the first time, she'd joked several times that it was easier to be at work than at home with a baby: 'It feels so good to *think!*'

Watching Shelley leave for work this morning, Lara had felt a twinge of envy. Shelley might be at home alone most evenings but at least her days were busy.

Why *was* Shelley at home so much? If she and her ex-husband had lived in that house for years, surely she would have some local friends. Though she wasn't spying out the window at all times of the day, Lara had never seen anyone visiting. Other than Greg and Dee, the only people Shelley had ever mentioned were two work colleagues – Flora and Steve – and her mother, who lived an hour away. Shelley wasn't the most outgoing of people, but she must have *some* friends?

The more she thought about Shelley, the more Lara realised how much she was beginning to enjoy Shelley's company, looking forward to their sorting-out sessions next door. When Lara had been at school, she'd always been the quiet, studious one, but when she'd got to university, she had reinvented herself as a confident party girl. Friends from home would not have recognised her. That was the advantage of meeting new people: you got to be whoever you wanted to be. Meeting Shelley was a bit like that. Shelley didn't know anything about the last few years of Lara's life. She'd presented herself to Shelley as someone confident and calm, with a clear joy-focused ethos for life. The upside to this was Lara was beginning to actually feel more like that person again.

She picked her phone back up from the worktop. Shelley was the closest thing she had to a friend right now, and even if that friendship was based on circumstance rather than choice, they needed to do something together other than sit in her box room. She thumbed another text:

Hi. Just had a thought. I'm going to the gym later. Do you fancy coming after work?

The reply pinged back immediately:

When you say 'gym', do you mean 'bar'?

Lara smiled. The more she got to know Shelley, the more she seemed to loosen up. She tapped away again:

If only. Pregnant, remember? It's the one round the corner. Are you a member? If not, I can get you a free pass. I'll buy you a posh coffee after? Going around 6ish.

No reply pinged back. Had she misread the situation? Did Shelley only see her as a neighbour? Was she sitting at work trying to think up a plausible excuse for why she couldn't go to the gym with her? Lara screwed up her eyes until tiny lights appeared. What had she been thinking?

Her phone pinged:

Sorry, can't make that tonight.

Oh no. She *had* been trying to think of an excuse. This was so embarrassing. How could she go next door again now that she knew Shelley didn't want—

Her phone pinged again:

Sorry, hit send too soon. Can't make tonight because I'm staying late at work to help my colleague Flora with her CV. I can make it tomorrow night?

Relief flooded through Lara.

Tomorrow night will be great. I'll sort out a pass for you.

It was ridiculous that she'd felt so anxious about inviting her neighbour to come to the gym. What had happened to her that something so small could send her into a spin? She needed to get a grip of herself.

Another ping:

Okay. But I'm not signing up to anything. Last time I did that, I ended up paying £35 a month to sit at home feeling guilty.

Lara laughed. This would be nice. Shelley could be her friend. Shelley, who had no children and who didn't know about her past and everything else. It was better that way.

CHAPTER FOURTEEN

Shelley

After a relationship ends badly, the first moments after waking can be the worst. Somehow your brain plays tricks on you in the night and lulls you back to a previous time when you had a husband lying next to you. So, when you wake up and stretch and your palm hits the cold side of the bed, there is a physical jolt which brings you back to reality. There's only you.

Shelley peeled her head off the pillow. She'd woken up so often last night, it had barely been worth coming upstairs. This couldn't go on. But she didn't want to go back to the doctor for sleeping pills. He'd been so keen on her coming off them, and she didn't have the energy to argue her case. She should be sleeping better by now – was it the room clearance making her feel worse?

Dragging herself out of bed and into the shower, she stood with her face turned up to the water, letting it push the dreams from her mind. They were more painful than the nightmares because she was relieved to wake up from a nightmare. With a dream, she just wished she could go back.

Much as she didn't fancy going to work this Friday morning, she was grateful for it. Those first couple of months after Greg went, life had been erratic, and she'd floated from hour to hour like a kite that'd had its strings cut. The routine of her job had given her something to cling to when it had all been too much.

This Friday she even had plans after work and, though it was only a session at Lara's gym, it felt good. It would also give her something to tell Flora when she nagged her about doing something in the evening. She smiled and shut off the shower. Time to go to work.

She must have been late if Flora was at her desk already. As she slipped into her seat, Shelley glanced across the sales floor to check that no one had noticed her absence. She needn't have worried: half of them were on job websites applying for new positions elsewhere. Would that be her soon too?

Flora threw a globe-shaped stress toy at her. 'What time do you call this? Steve just called. He's due in any minute – you'd better look busy.'

That was the last thing Shelley needed. 'I bet he's going to ask me about the job again. What can I say?'

Life for Flora was always pretty black and white. 'You should do it. If he thinks it's a good idea, he'll put a word in for you. What's the problem?'

The problem was that just thinking about it made her feel exhausted and overwhelmed. Work had been her safe place for the last twelve months and now everything was changing here too. Maybe this was where the dreams were coming from? Greg was on her mind because he was the person she would have spoken to about this. He would have helped her work out the pros and cons. Made a list of all the worries she had about it and worked through them. Helped her to work out what her journey to work would be and how long it would take. But Greg wasn't here. Greg was gone. She shook her head and pulled her palms down her face. 'I don't know, Flora. It's not something I would have thought about if it wasn't for this place going. I've been fine just ticking along.'

Flora sighed like a mother talking to a recalcitrant child. 'That's the problem: you've been ticking along for years. It's about time you got a promotion.' Flora squinted her eyes. 'And you're going to need some new clothes. Those ones don't even fit anymore.'

Shelley looked down at her fitted blouse, which flapped about over a skirt with a waistband that gaped when she sat down. To think of all the years she had tried and failed to lose the extra stone she'd gained since getting married.

When she looked up again, Steve was standing there. 'Morning!'

She almost jumped. Why was she always so nervous around him lately? 'Morning. Sorry, I didn't know you were coming in. Was I supposed to prepare anything for a meeting?'

Steve unbuttoned his jacket and slipped his omnipresent mobile into his inside pocket. The patterned silk lining called to mind Greg's old suits and she wrenched her mind away from them. Steve shook his head. 'No need to prepare anything. I'm only popping in to make sure that everyone has seen the job information. I'll set myself up in the conference room for this morning in case anyone wants to have an informal chat about the opportunities.'

Had she imagined it or had he emphasised the word 'anyone' and directed it at her? She could feel Flora's eyes burning into the back of her head too. 'Uh, okay. Do you want me to send an email round?'

'Don't worry, I'll get myself set up in there and then I'll come out and see who's around. I need to make some calls first anyway.'

As soon as he was out of earshot, Flora nudged her. 'You definitely need to speak to him about the job. He clearly wants you to do it.'

She could see Steve through the glass windows of the conference room, striding up and down as he spoke into his mobile. He was laughing and running his hands through his short blond hair. She'd wait until he finished and then go in; might as well get it over with.

Fifteen minutes later, he opened the door of the conference room and she took this as a sign that he was open for conversation. She knocked on the frame of the door and he smiled as he looked up from his laptop. 'Shelley. Great. Let's talk about that job. I'm hoping that's what you're here to talk about?'

The warm way he looked at her was clearly designed to put her at her ease but it had the opposite effect; her stomach fizzed with nerves. 'Uh... Yes... I wanted to ask if—'

She was cut off by his phone buzzing along the desk. Steve closed his eyes and opened them again. 'I'm so sorry, Shelley, but I have to get this. I've been waiting for this call. I'll take it out in the main office.'

He pushed his chair back as he stood up and slid his finger across the screen to accept the call. She couldn't help but hear him before he strode across to the other side of the office. 'Hi, Dana? I'm so pleased you called. I'm so sorry about this morning...'

Dana? Another one?

As she drove to the gym, Shelley ran over the conversation with Steve in her mind. After finishing his phone call, he'd been very persuasive about her applying for the team manager role, listing personal qualities that she didn't know she possessed. His enthusiasm made her suspicious, like there was something he wasn't telling her. It was stupid, but the conversation she'd overheard with another woman hadn't helped. She hadn't pegged him for the kind of man who would date more than one woman at a time. It was none of her business, of course, but it didn't sit right with her. Could she trust him?

She pulled into a car park full of shiny new four-by-fours. Her little Fiat looked out of place and she couldn't help feeling the same. The side walls of the gym were made of glass and she tried to get a sneaky look as she walked towards the entrance. Though she'd managed to dig out some old leggings and a vest, they weren't in the league of the bright Lycra of the glamorous women facing outwards, thundering away on exercise bikes.

Lara, on the other hand, looked as if she fit right in. 'Hi. You made it! Do you realise this is the first time we've seen each other in the real world?'

It *was* odd to see her away from one of their homes. Did this mean they were proper friends now rather than just neighbours? 'Are you sure you wouldn't rather cut out the getting sweaty bit and go straight to the posh coffee in the café?'

Lara shook her head. Her long ponytail swayed to reinforce it. 'No. I've organised a trial session now; you just need to fill out a Health and Safety form and we're in.'

'Okay.' Shelley took the health questionnaire from the receptionist to record her medical history. There was a whole section on the heart, but no tick box for 'broken'.

The instructor who showed them around the lethal-looking equipment looked about fifteen, and he spent ten minutes explaining to Shelley how to use the running machine, seeming to take pleasure in emphasising how easy it was to have an accident. It didn't matter that she interrupted him three times to tell him she'd used one several times before.

Lara stood to one side and pulled funny faces at her when he was speaking, which definitely took the edge off his patronising explanations. Once he'd left Shelley alone – still hovering in the vicinity, ready to swoop if she lost control of her legs on the conveyor belt – Lara put her hand to her chin and frowned mockingly. 'Do you think you got all that or shall I ask him to run through it one more time?'

Shelley laughed. 'I think I'm okay. What about you? Are you going on anything? Can you?'

Lara shrugged. 'I'd love to. A session on the cross trainer would blow some cobwebs away, but I've promised Matt I won't. I'm going to have a swim if you're okay here on your own for a bit? We can meet in the café in an hour?'

Shelley would rather be on her own – getting red and sweaty was not a spectator sport – but she was surprised by how quickly Lara acquiesced to what Matt told her to do. She was so upfront and confident. Why did she give in to everything he said? It was uncomfortably familiar. 'I'll be fine. Enjoy your swim.'

Lara reached into the small rucksack she had on her shoulder and brought out an iPod and a pair of headphones. 'I brought you this to help keep you going for longer. I know you like pop, but what kind of music do you like to run to?'

Anything that doesn't remind me of Greg. 'I don't know. Something upbeat?'

Lara thumbed through her selection. 'I've got a workout playlist on here that's perfect for running. Here you go.' She passed the iPod over and Shelley tucked it into a hidden pocket on the front of her leggings, inserting headphones into her ears. Lara gave her a little wave goodbye – and a salute for the youthful instructor, who was still watching from a distance – and left for the pool.

Two minutes of progressively faster walking and Shelley was ready to pick this up into a jog. It must have been at least two years since she'd been on a running machine, but she managed to find a rhythm to Beyoncé's 'Halo': the first track on Lara's iPod. As her breath quickened, her lungs worked harder to take in oxygen and expanded within her chest. Halfway along the earphones cord was a volume switch, and she turned it up and picked up the pace until the jog became a run. With music pounding in her ears, and her feet doing the same on the treadmill, she couldn't think about anything else. The thoughts buzzing around her head couldn't move: they were paralysed by the music. There was no room inside her ribs for anything but her burning lungs. This felt good. Really good. Her chest was screaming, her legs wobbled as they quickly tired, but the anger, the resentment, the gaping loneliness – it was as if she was crushing them beneath her feet.

It wasn't long before her lack of fitness caught up with her and she had to slow it down again, then stop and get off the machine. She bent over to catch her breath. And that was when she realised that she'd been crying.

In the café, Lara treated her to the posh coffee she'd promised. 'How was your run?'

Shelley's lungs felt ragged and her calves were going to be screaming tomorrow, but she felt better than she had in a long, long time. 'I'll be honest – I was a bit confused why you invited me to the gym, but I'm so glad you did. It was amazing. I'm definitely going to go for a run more often.'

Lara tapped her water bottle on the side of Shelley's cup. 'I knew it would make you feel good. It's the best thing ever for blocking out the world and getting the mess out of your head. I really miss it.'

She looked at Shelley and, just for a moment, Shelley saw something in her eyes which was deep and dark. Lara understood. There was pain in her eyes too. But why?

Then, in a blink, it was gone again. Lara grinned. 'I might even allow myself a hot chocolate to celebrate.'

CHAPTER FIFTEEN

Shelley

'It's all about the photographs. We need to catch the colours in it somehow.'

Shelley's legs ached on Saturday morning but today – Sunday – she'd managed a slow jog around the park. Ten minutes after emerging from the shower, a text pinged, suggesting Shelley come next door with the unwanted jewellery they'd uncovered; Lara had big plans for it apparently.

Now Lara took the dark grey throw from the back of the sofa and laid it over a cushion, placing the pendant and silver chain across it. The milky sheen of the large opal had never suited Shelley, and she'd only worn it once to a work dinner of Greg's. Lara seemed to think it was lovely though. 'There you go. Something like that.'

Shelley wasn't convinced. 'And you really think someone is going to want to buy that?'

Lara looked at her as if she was crazy. 'Yes. You've got some really nice pieces.'

Objectively, Shelley could see that they were well made and attractive, but like the shoes, they had never been the kind of jewellery that she would have chosen for herself. 'Greg used to buy me a piece of jewellery every time we went on holiday. It was a tradition, I suppose. To be fair, he was very generous.' It wasn't just jewellery. He would see something in a shop window or online and just buy it for her. It felt ungrateful to say she didn't want something so she would wear it once and then hide it away in the wardrobe. She didn't have to do that anymore.

Lara closed her right eye as she peered at the necklace with her left. 'I'm actually wondering if you should get some of these valued before you put them up. You want to make sure you get a good deal.'

Lara held her phone towards the cushion and took three photographs of the pendant from different angles. She had the air of a crime scene photographer: precise and accurate. After a quick check, she held the screen out to Shelley. 'See. Looks good, doesn't it?'

It looked like an old necklace on a cushion but Shelley didn't want to dent her enthusiasm. 'So, do you do this a lot? Sell stuff on eBay?'

'Yes, and we used to buy a ton of things on there. Before *Make Way for Joy*, obviously. Don't you?'

Shelley shook her head. 'Greg had a weird thing about second-hand things. He used to like everything to be brand new.' He hadn't even wanted the household things that Shelley's mum had tried to give them when they'd first moved in together. Dee used to say he liked to show off how much money he had by buying flashy things, and there was a small part of Shelley who had suspected that might be true. Not that she would ever have admitted it to Dee.

'Then you've really been missing out. It's full of bargains. Go and make another cup of tea and I'll show you.' Lara held her phone nearer to the cushion and took a close-up of the silver chain.

By the time Shelley got back from the kitchen with the drinks, Lara had opened up her laptop on the dining table and was scrolling through eBay. She patted the chair next to her. 'Look: you just type in what you're looking for. Say, necklaces, and it brings up everything that is for sale.'

Shelley peered at the screen. There was a variety of different-length chains with various pendants hanging from them. It was a shock to see how cheap some were. Although she wasn't keen on hers, Greg had paid quite a lot for it. 'That one's less than a quid! There's no point selling it for that; I'd rather give it to the charity shop.'

Lara rolled her eyes. 'Hold your horses, cowboy. That's only the starting price. People place bids and it goes up and up until the end of the auction.'

From memory, it had cost about three hundred times that. 'It wants to go up a lot from ninety-nine pence.'

This was beginning to feel uncomfortable. Was she really going to sell the jewellery that Greg had bought her? It wasn't as if she was ever going to wear it again. She hadn't liked it when he'd bought it, let alone now. But still. It felt... like closing a door.

'Hang on.' Shelley leaned towards the screen again. Something bright had caught her eye. 'Scroll back a bit.'

Lara did as asked. 'What have you seen?'

Shelley pointed. 'I like that necklace. The one with the buttons.'

She pointed at a necklace made from several strands of lime green and hot pink buttons of various sizes. Lara's eyebrows nearly hit her fringe. 'This one?'

What was so wrong with it? 'Yes. Why? Isn't it any good?'

Lara dropped her eyebrows, started to backtrack on her surprise. 'It's not that. I just haven't seen you wear anything like that. Your normal taste seems more... conservative.'

Now she understood. 'Boring, you mean?'

'No. Not boring.' Lara flailed around for the right word. 'Classy.'

That was a euphemism for dull if she'd ever heard one. Was that how Lara saw her? Staid and uninteresting, like the opal pendant laid out on the cushion? There was more to her than that; Lara just hadn't seen it yet. 'I like that button necklace a lot. How much is it?'

Lara clicked the mouse to enlarge the window on the screen. 'Well, shopper, you're in luck. It's a *Buy It Now*, so you don't have to bid. You can just order it.'

Shelley leaned in again. Would she wear it? Did it go with anything she had? Maybe it was best to leave it for now. She was supposed to be getting rid of stuff, not buying more. But then she looked at Lara's face. Classy? Or boring? What did it matter if it didn't match anything she had? She could always buy new clothes. Ones that *she* had chosen. 'Yes. I do want to order it.'

Lara grinned. 'Great. Let's do it. Shall we set you up an account? I'll need your credit card details. We can start listing the pieces you want to sell.'

Shelley's purse was in her bag, hanging on a peg in Lara's hall. As she left to retrieve it, her stomach felt decidedly unsettled. Could she really bring herself to sell her jewellery? She'd had some of those necklaces and bracelets for a long time. What did the book say? *Do you need it? Does it bring you joy?* She definitely didn't need them. And joy? Looking at them right now was more painful than anything else. She pushed down the uncertainty and grabbed her bag from the peg. This was a good idea. It was.

When she got back, Lara was staring at the laptop screen. Hers wasn't a happy face. Shelley placed a hand on her shoulder. 'Are you okay? Did something go wrong?'

Lara peeled her eyes away from the screen and shook her head as if to make them work again. 'No. It's fine. There are just some ancient messages on my account and I stupidly clicked on them.'

Who sent messages on eBay? It wasn't social media. 'Is it something mean? Is someone trolling you?'

'On eBay?' Lara smiled although the humour didn't reach her eyes. 'You really are a novice, aren't you? No, it's an old message from a seller asking me to leave a review for something I bought ages ago.' She turned her laptop so that Shelley could see the screen. 'A pram.'

It was plum-coloured with thick wheels and a cherry logo on the side. The date on the message was from two years ago. Why would Lara and Matt be buying a pram all that time ago? 'Looks great. I didn't know you had a pram already.'

'We don't. This was a while ago.' Lara took a deep breath. 'A different pregnancy. One that didn't make it.'

Deep down in Shelley's gut, a scraping sensation almost made her catch her breath. For a moment she couldn't speak. *Push it down. Focus on Lara.* 'I'm so sorry. That must have been terribly hard for you.'

Lara flushed. 'Yeah. It was.' She looked back at the screen. 'We were stupid to buy the pram so early. Everyone tells you not to, but you never think it'll be you, right?'

You never think it'll be you. So incredibly true. 'Well, I suppose you were excited. It's easy to get carried away when you're excited.'

Shelley thought it would be best not to delve too deeply into this, but Lara clearly wanted to share it. 'We hadn't even had the first scan. We were shopping at the retail park, getting some part for Matt's computer, and there was a Mothercare. We only popped in to look but I saw the pram and we were messing about. Matt took a picture of me pushing it as a joke – said he was going to make it into a meme when we announced the pregnancy.'

Shelley could see the two of them in her head; she'd imagined the exact same scenario many times herself. Buying a pram was a big moment. 'And you ended up going home with it?'

Lara shook her head. 'Not exactly. Matt was browsing on eBay – he had a borderline addiction – and saw the previous year's model on offer for a stupid price so he said we might as well get it. He doesn't believe in all the old superstitions. Well, neither did I really, but…'

Did she know Lara well enough to put her arms around her? It felt heartless to just sit there. Best to stay still though; even touching Lara's hand might start one or the both of them crying, and that wouldn't help anyone. 'I'm so sorry, Lara. But look how well you're doing this time. How far along are you now?'

'Twenty-nine weeks and one day.' Lara put a hand on her stomach and smiled. 'Roughly.'

'There you go. I know… I mean, I've *heard* it's incredibly common to miscarry the first time. It's just because no one talks about it and you don't know until it happens to you.' She needed to stop speaking. Had she said too much?

Lara's smile froze and she turned back to the computer screen, where she clicked out of her messages and back to the homepage. 'Yes. I know. Anyway, let's get you set up. Have you got your credit card?'

Clearly, she was done talking about it. 'Here you go.' Shelley slid her credit card over and Lara tapped in her account details.

Lara was back in business mode. 'While I fill this out, why don't you start sorting through the box? Work out which bits and pieces you want to list first.'

The box was on the coffee table, staring at her accusingly. This was as good a time as any to sort it all out. It needed doing. And what was the point of hanging on to it if she was never going to wear it? *It's just stuff.*

Shelley perched on the edge of the sofa. Spread out in front of her like a pirate's treasure were rings and bracelets and earrings; large gems in different colours and sizes; thick bands of white gold and platinum. Everything showy and sparkly and not her style at all. Why hadn't she told him? Why had she pretended that she loved it? Dee's voice rang in her ear: *If you don't tell him, I will.*

Picking a small, white box at random, she found a ring: the first he'd ever bought her. A large, square sapphire in a white gold setting that had caught Greg's eye in a window. He'd taken her to see it, so excited by his find that she'd had no way of telling him that she hated it. And that's how it had started.

CHAPTER SIXTEEN

Shelley

Before

'It's your birthstone. Sapphire. For September.' He glanced at the shop assistant and she nodded confirmation. A co-conspirator.

It was their first trip away together. Greg had booked a hotel in Southwold and they'd had a wonderful weekend on the beach, sitting in front of the beach huts, drinking coffee in a dark café that you had to go down some steps to get to. Shelley had never been on holiday as a child – there hadn't been the spare money once her dad left – and Greg had pulled out all the stops to make sure she enjoyed it. She was a little in awe of how easily he organised everything from booking the hotel to finding the ideal restaurant for dinner. She'd never felt so grown up and sophisticated with anyone else. Greg made everything perfect.

Last night in bed he had announced that he wanted her to have a memento of the trip and suggested they go shopping the next morning. Naively, she had assumed he'd meant a fridge magnet or postcard.

She stared at the ring lying innocently in front of her on a dark purple velvet-lined display tray. It wasn't the blue stone she didn't like – although the size of it practically shouted 'bling' – it was the setting. The white gold band was thick and chunky and modern. Would she even be able to lift her hand with that on her finger? If that wasn't enough, there were small diamonds set into the shoulders of the setting, which caught the light and drew her eye: *Look at me! Look at me!*

Greg seemed blissfully unaware of her reluctance to try it on. 'I spotted it in the window this morning when I came out to get the paper. When I asked what the stone was – and found out that sapphires are the birthstone for September – I knew it would be perfect for you.'

He'd sneaked out of the hotel room early that morning with a plan to surprise her with a newspaper and coffee when she woke up. It had been very sweet of him. No one had bought her a pristine copy of *The Times* before. He'd sat on the end of the bed in his long, checked shorts and white T-shirt looking like a young boy in his excitement to show her what he'd found. It would be churlish not to at least try it on. She held out her right hand and he slipped it onto the ring finger. With any luck, it would be too small.

The fates were against her: the ring might have been made to measure. Greg's smile got even wider. 'See, I knew it would be perfect. Look. Stay here with it. I'm just going to go down the road and get some cash out. There's a discount for cash.' He paused and dipped his head until he was looking Shelley in the eye. 'You do like it, don't you?'

This was her chance. With the red shoes, he'd already bought them. This time she could say no, it wasn't for her. Thanks, but no thanks. Channel her inner Dee – polite but assertive.

But Greg looked so hopeful, so excited. It would spoil the end of their perfect weekend if she said she didn't like it. It would be like kicking a puppy. She had one last try at avoidance. 'Of course I like it. You're so clever to have found it. It's perfect. But really, it's too much. You've already paid for this whole weekend. I can't let you buy this too. Really.'

Greg was already at the door before she finished speaking. The bell tinkled as he pushed it open. 'Just give me five minutes. Don't take it off.'

She turned back to look at her right hand, which was still splayed in front of her, the offending article on her ring finger. The large sapphire mocked her. Why did it have to fit so perfectly?

As the door clicked shut, the elderly shop assistant spoke for the first time. 'You don't like it, do you?'

Shelley looked up. The assistant stood a little back from the counter, hands linked in front. Her grey hair was cut well and she wore a navy suit. Her smile was kind. Trustworthy. Even though Greg was halfway to the ATM, Shelley lowered her voice. 'Is it that obvious?'

The assistant laughed. 'I've worked here a long time, my dear. When people are being treated to a ring, they usually look more enthusiastic about it.'

Shelley's face grew warm. This woman must think she was awful. 'Sorry. I know I sound ungrateful, and the ring is lovely, it's just…'

'Just not your thing? Don't apologise. It's a very personal choice.' She nodded at the other ring on Shelley's hand. On her little finger was a thin yellow gold band with tiny golden flowers dotted all the way around. She'd bought it in a German market when she'd been travelling with Dee. 'I can see your taste is more for the vintage.'

To be honest, she didn't have enough jewellery to actually *have* a taste. But it definitely wasn't this huge blingy shouty thing that Greg had picked out. Dee had helped her to choose the gold ring with the flowers as she'd dithered back and forth between it and one with a spiral shape. *This one is more you*, Dee had decided.

She felt guilty again. 'They don't really go together, do they? Maybe I should take off the yellow gold one? See if the sapphire looks better on its own?' She twisted it off, leaving an imprint in her finger where it had been. The improvement was marginal.

The assistant could clearly read Shelley's face. 'You should just tell him. Believe me. Otherwise he will think that this is the kind of jewellery you like and you'll be getting it every birthday for the rest of your life.'

She raised a warning eyebrow at Shelley as the tinkling door heralded Greg's reappearance. He slipped the cash across the counter at the assistant, who paused before she took the money, looking to Shelley for her reaction.

Shelley took a deep breath and turned to Greg. 'Thank you. It's beautiful.'

The smile on his face confirmed she'd made the right decision. It was just a ring after all. It wouldn't hurt her to wear it now and again if it made him happy.

While the assistant processed the payment, Shelley wandered to the other side of the shop, where there was a tray of antique gold bangles; they were much more her style. Greg came up behind and looked over her shoulder. 'That's the kind of old tat that Dee likes, isn't it? Shall we buy her one? Might help to get me back in her good books after taking you away from her this weekend. Mind you, if I buy it, it's sure to be wrong.'

And she would tell you, Shelley thought. *Because she's not scared to say what she wants. And she makes sure she gets it.*

CHAPTER SEVENTEEN

Lara

Matt had tried to creep out quietly this morning but his alarm had woken Lara and she hadn't been able to go back to sleep.

'Sorry,' he'd whispered. 'Early one this morning.'

Trying to pretend that she wasn't actually awake, she'd kept her eyes closed, still upset from their conversation last night.

He'd got back late. Again. It was the nature of a field sales job, which meant lots of time on the road. One traffic jam on the M40 followed by a broken down car on the M25 could mean at least a two-hour delay. He would call her from the handsfree in the car: *Sorry. Are you okay?* It wasn't his fault. But after another day spent at home alone, she'd been desperate for company.

Still, it had been stupid to start a conversation about the birth on a Monday night when he was tired and hungry and still had a raft of emails to clear.

She'd been picking at the bowl of salad in the middle of the table. 'What will you do nearer the birth? About meeting customers at such a distance, I mean.'

He'd looked up from his carbonara with heavy lids. 'Sorry? I was miles away. Distance? No, I'll try and sort my schedule so that I am no more than an hour's drive from home once we get to… near to… the actual thing.'

Thing. It. Why couldn't he say it? Irritation had scratched at her. 'Even an hour is quite a long way. I mean, an hour could be as far as the M4 junction, and if you got stuck at the top of the M25, which is more than possible…'

She'd tailed off when he'd sighed deeply. 'I know, Lara. I know. But what can I do? It's my job. I'm trying to work my backside off at the moment so that I can take two weeks' paternity leave but it's not that kind of job. You know that. And if I can make my target this quarter, the bonus will really help make up the shortfall.'

Lara had bristled. The shortfall caused by their new circumstances – only one wage coming into the house. 'It was your idea that I give up work.'

Matt's head had drooped, his voice monotone. 'I know that, Lara. Are you trying to pick a fight with me? I'm not complaining. I'm just tired.'

He was always tired at the moment. The move had reinvigorated them for a while, given them something else to think about. But now the unpacking was done – and with far fewer possessions that hadn't taken long – they had slid back into this… stasis.

Time to change the subject. 'I've seen an advert for a local antenatal group. It's on a Monday evening. Shall I book us onto it?'

Matt had shaken his head, moving pasta around his plate. 'Mondays are tricky for me, love. Why don't you ask a friend to go with you? Maybe Shelley?'

Irritation had grown to annoyance. He was happy to suggest groups for *her* to attend. 'This is something we should do together. Mother and father. It's what everyone does, Matt. All normal expectant couples go to antenatal classes.'

Matt had laid both his palms on the table. He wasn't a man who got angry. He wasn't a man who showed much intensity of emotion at all. It was part of what attracted her to him: he was the yin to her yang. But right then, he'd seemed to be fighting to stay calm. 'Lara. I've done everything you wanted. We are doing this because you want to do it. But you need to stop pushing me to do more.'

This isn't fair. 'But it has worked out. Hasn't it? It was the right thing to do?'

He'd finally looked up at her, his eyes unreadable. 'Has it? How can you know that?' He'd crumpled a little. 'I'm sorry. I'm really tired. I think I need to go to bed.'

Now, she waited in bed for a while for the baby to move, wiggling her hips a little, tapping and rubbing her stomach. 'Come on, little one. Time to play ball.'

The way Matt had spoken last night had made her out to be one of those women who had pushed their husband into having a baby, and that just wasn't true. He had wanted a baby as much as she had – more, if anything, in the beginning. She had been the one trying to work out when it would be the best time for her career-wise. He had just been eager to get started. 'Come on, babe, let's start popping them out!' had been his actual words.

Rolling onto her side, she pushed gently into the area where her waist had been. 'Come on, bubba. Mummy needs you this morning.'

A twinge turned into a flutter and Lara let out a breath she hadn't even realised she'd been holding. If only Matt could feel this, he would understand.

Being up that early meant even more hours to fill. A walk would be a good idea. Fresh air, physical exertion – all positive things for mental health. It was good to explore the neighbourhood a little more; the whole area was beginning to feel more familiar. Here was the school with the tabletop sale banner. Might as well take a picture of the details now. Last time she hadn't noticed that half the proceeds were going to Tommy's. Even more reason to persuade Shelley into it.

Phone back in her pocket, she continued to walk. These streets were less familiar, but she'd always had a pretty good sense of direction, and the map on her mobile would see her home anyway. As the sun moved across the sky, it melted the clouds and it became warm enough to take off her jacket. Gradually, she felt lighter, freer, happier. The endorphins were doing their job and she did feel a whole lot better. Until she got to the park.

It was the bench which had enticed her. It was early enough that no one was there yet, so she was safe from other people's cute children. The swings were still and the climbing frame was empty. She tried to imagine herself, and Matt, holding onto a pudgy toddler as they climbed the steps to the slide. It was almost there and then... no. It still didn't feel real.

Maybe that was why it was so difficult for Matt. She was finding it difficult to imagine a real-life baby and he was inside her. All she could do was keep trying to make Matt a part of this. Try to get him to feel positive about fatherhood again. She clicked a picture of the swings and sent it to him.

Not long now.

Fifteen minutes later and her mood had changed. A heavily pregnant woman with a toddler wheeled a buggy into the park. Sitting down next to Lara with a bump, she let out a long sigh then smiled. 'We're about the same size. How long have you got left?'

Though this mother was only being friendly, it was the kind of conversation Lara avoided like the plague. She'd learned to her cost not to compare herself to other women. 'About three months.'

The woman rubbed her belly. 'Me too. My ankles are starting to swell already. How are you feeling?'

'I'm okay.' Conversations like this didn't used to make her so tense. When she'd found out she was pregnant the first time, she'd confided in Natalie and loved it when Natalie had checked in with her every day, sending emails about the size of her baby at week seven, eight, nine. Natalie had still been on maternity leave with her first daughter then and had joked that she would try and get pregnant again so they could be off work together and rip up the mother and baby clubs.

The toddler started to squawk and strain at her buggy straps. The woman sighed again and unbuckled her. 'Try and relax as much as you can for the next few weeks. You won't be allowed to rest again for a very long time.' She hauled herself off the bench and followed her daughter to the swings.

Advice. Lara had had so much of it in the last couple of years that she wanted to scream. *Relax. Exercise. Be calm. Stay busy. Eat this. Drink that. Avoid medication. Take an aspirin.* Everyone knew someone who'd had a miscarriage and had some wisdom to impart.

And then there were women like this. Women with happy, healthy children who complained about being tired and having no time to themselves. Lara knew she was being unfair – this woman and others like her did look completely knackered – but having no time was infinitely preferable to having way too much.

Matt was probably right about the antenatal classes. The pair of them were too damaged to sit with optimistic couples on their first try. Any mention of what they'd been through would be bad form, like they were cursed. No. She was much better off with Shelley. Shelley was safe. Pushing herself off the bench with her hands, she slipped away from the park before she met anyone else.

At 5.45 p.m., Shelley pulled up outside her house as usual. Lara had been itching to see her all afternoon but forced herself to wait and allow her fifteen minutes to get in and make herself a drink before she knocked on the door.

Shelley opened the door with a mug in her hand, looking surprised. They weren't quite at the popping-over-unannounced stage.

'Only me. Don't worry, I'm not coming to make you sort more stuff out. I'm too knackered today to think about that.' She did feel tired: the early morning, the unpleasantness with Matt last night, even the long walk had taken their toll. 'I just needed a bit of company. Do you mind?'

Shelley held the door open. 'Of course not; it's nice to see you. Come in. Have you had a busy day, then?'

After scurrying home from the park, she had stayed safely indoors for the rest of the day. 'No. Unless you count scrolling through Netflix to put some new box sets on my planner busy. I'm going to die of boredom before this baby comes.' That was tactless. Shelley had been at work all day. 'How was your day? Any more news?'

Shelley led the way through to the kitchen. 'It was fine. Flora was debating whether she wants to retrain as an air steward or become a holiday rep. She's decided that a desk job is not for her anymore.' She smiled and then sighed. 'I'm really going to miss her. She's completely bonkers but she's been a good mate, you know? Tea?'

'Yes, please. I'll have a proper one for once. Do you think you'll stay in touch with her when you move to the new office?'

'*If* I move to the new office.' Shelley reached into a cupboard for another grey mug. Everything in this kitchen was coordinated. It was beautiful. 'I'd like to see her again but I doubt it. We don't see each other outside of work now, so it's unlikely we'll manage it when we're no longer colleagues. You know what it's like.'

Lara did know exactly what it was like. She remembered Natalie's text message. *Hey, stranger.*

Taking the mug of tea, she followed Shelley through to the lounge, sinking into the huge sofa. She could close her eyes and sleep here, no problem. This house was starting to feel more like home than her own. 'I love this sofa so much. I'm so glad your ex-husband didn't take it. Actually, one of the reasons I've descended on you is because I walked past that primary school again and the tabletop sale is this weekend. I took a picture of the banner across the school gates with all the info. There's so much in that pile of stuff to get rid of, and eBaying it all will take forever. This way, you can make a bit of money from the decent stuff. There's sure to be a ton of Surrey yummy mummies splashing the cash.'

Shelley sat in the armchair opposite. 'I'm not sure.'

Tiredness made Lara more irritable than normal with Shelley's reticence. Yes, she was pushing Shelley out of her comfort zone, but some people needed that, didn't they? And Lara would bet Shelley's ex-husband wasn't sitting at home every weekend like she did. It was only a tabletop sale, not an all-night rave. 'Oh, please. I need to have something to do that isn't too strenuous. Come on, it'll be fun.'

Shelley picked up her mug and sipped. 'Maybe I could give you a few things to sell if you want to do it? I'm not sure it's for me.'

Oh, for goodness' sake. 'I don't want to go on my own. I thought it would be something fun for us to do together. Plus, it's in aid of Tommy's – a charity that raises funds for research into stillbirth, premature birth and miscarriage.' It was a low strike, pulling the charity card, but she'd been thinking about the sale all afternoon, had even looked on Pinterest for ideas to set out Shelley's shoes to maximum advantage. Occupying her mind with anything non-baby was a good idea.

The emotional blackmail must have worked as Shelley nodded. 'Okay. I'm being silly. Yes, let's do it.'

CHAPTER EIGHTEEN

Shelley

Saturday morning was bright and sunny, which was a good thing because the tabletop sale was on the school field. Matt had made Lara some kind of construction with wire to display the shoes on, and she was putting this together as Shelley wrestled the table up, having already refused Lara's help. 'Thanks for letting me borrow your pasting table.'

'No problem. Matt pretended to be awfully disappointed that he couldn't make a start on wallpapering the nursery, but the installation of his Sky box yesterday took the edge off his disappointment somewhat.' Lara rubbed at her eyes; her smile looked painted on. Was this too much for her?

Shelley hadn't seen Matt this morning but she wondered how he felt about his pregnant wife playing at being a market trader for the morning, given that he hadn't wanted her to help Shelley with sorting out the box room. She didn't want to upset him. 'Doesn't he mind that you're out doing this with me?'

Lara shook her head. 'I've had the fourteen warnings about not lifting, moving or pulling anything. To be honest, it'll do us both good to do our own thing for a few hours.'

It wasn't Shelley's business to comment on someone else's relationship. Now she knew about the miscarriage, she could understand Matt's protectiveness, but it still seemed way over the top. For Lara's sake, she hoped it would calm down once the baby was here.

She was attempting to lay the objects out on the table nicely, but there was so much stuff jostling for space that she couldn't see half of it. 'How are people going to find something that they want?'

'Don't you worry. People love a rummage.' Lara nodded back at the entrance. 'Here they come.'

Advancing towards them was a small regiment of people holding carrier bags. It was like a walking race. Before Shelley knew it, a wiry old lady with fingers covered in rings was brandishing a cat ornament under her nose. 'How much for this, love?'

A price? How had she not thought about that beforehand? 'Oh, er, a pound?'

The old lady nodded and put the cat back. Was that too much? 'Or, uhm, fifty pence?'

The old lady smiled at her sympathetically, nodded and walked away. Should she have said thirty pence? Had she failed already? Was the woman an expert haggler or could she smell Shelley's desperation over the aroma of the van that had started frying bacon and sausages at the end of their row?

Lara was laughing beside her. 'You're going to be giving the stuff away at this rate. Hold your nerve, Shelley, hold your nerve.'

Shelley laughed as well. 'Sorry, I've never really sold things before. I'm overthinking it, aren't I?'

Lara scrunched up her nose. 'A bit. You tell them what you want for it; if they don't like it, they walk away. Worst-case scenario, we take the stuff you don't sell to the charity shop on our way home. Nothing lost. It's fun. Honestly.'

Despite expecting it to be the polar opposite of fun to be hawking her worldly goods in a school field on a Saturday morning, Shelley had to admit that Lara was right. It had actually felt quite a relief to offload some of this stuff. Especially some of the awful ornaments that Greg's mother had insisted on buying them, which had only ever seen the light of day when she was due to visit. By 10.30 a.m., she'd sold about a quarter of what was on the table. 'This is better than I thought it would be. Thanks for persuading me into this.'

Lara looked a lot brighter too. 'See, I told you. It's like the book says. These things can weigh you down, keep you rooted to a time you no longer want to inhabit. It is not the fault of the objects themselves; you can send them on their way to make someone else happy.'

Sometimes she quoted from the book as if it were a religious text. As if to prove her point, a small voice interrupted their conversation. 'Excuse me, please. How much is this bag?'

A young girl of around seven, her two front teeth missing, was holding out a sequined clutch bag, hopefully. The sweetness of her voice and her high pigtails almost unravelled Shelley. 'How much have you got?'

The girl opened her palm to show a sweaty pound coin. 'This.'

Shelley smiled and held her hand out for the money. 'Well, that is exactly what it costs.'

The girl beamed, clutched the bag tighter and ran back to her mother, who was stood watching her, a tiny baby strapped to her chest.

Lara nudged Shelley gently. 'See how happy you made her?'

Shelley watched as the girl's mother leaned down and kissed the top of her daughter's head. How did that feel? To be a mother? It was something she hadn't thought about in quite a while.

Now Lara was watching too, but her face was darker somehow. Before Shelley had a chance to ask if she was okay, a man started to pull the clubs out of Greg's golf bag and examine them.

It felt so odd watching someone handling those clubs. They'd been Greg's pride and joy at one time. He'd stopped playing golf regularly when he'd changed his job and his new colleagues weren't into it, but it still felt disloyal.

She'd tried to explain that to Lara this morning. 'It feels wrong to be... getting rid of them without...'

Lara had shaken her head. 'Do you mean without checking with him first? Look, if he wanted them, he should have come and got them. What are you? A storage facility?'

And she was right. He obviously didn't need them. She didn't want them. But still. Watching this man scrutinising the head of each club was just... wrong somehow.

'Oi, love. How much for the clubs?'

A combination of the 'oi', the fact he couldn't be bothered to take his other hand out of his pocket and that she hated being called *love* by complete strangers made Shelley less than polite. 'Two hundred quid.'

He nearly swallowed his own tongue. 'For second-hand clubs? You won't get that, love. What about fifty?'

She knew for a fact that Greg had paid a lot more than two hundred pounds for those clubs. The bag alone had cost that much. And she didn't like this man's tone. 'They're a top brand. It's two hundred or nothing.'

He made a mocking sound and looked at her as if she were stupid. 'Maybe, but they're second-hand. These are titanium clubs; looks like they've not been used in a while, judging by the dust. And I'm assuming you *ladies* don't want to be carrying these back home again. Especially her.' He nodded at Lara's stomach.

God, she hated men like this. Mansplaining, patronising idiot. Her face grew warm and she gritted her teeth. 'Well, *this* lady wants two hundred pounds for those clubs, and if you're not going to pay that, can you move along so that someone else can take a look?'

When he walked away, shaking his head, Lara put a hand on her arm. 'Are you okay? I thought you were going to hit him.'

Shelley's anger ebbed as she looked at the concern in Lara's face, unable to explain – even to herself – why he'd made her so angry. 'I'm fine. Just don't like men like that. I'm going to get a coffee from the stall at the end. Do you want anything?'

There was a short queue at the refreshments table, and Shelley was still thinking about the ignorant golf club man, which was why she didn't notice Steve until he was standing right in front of her. 'Hi, Shelley. Fancy seeing you here.'

Dressed in jeans and a polo shirt –his face unshaven, hair tousled – Steve looked very different from the confident salesman she knew from the office. Either that, or the surprise of seeing him here, made her stomach flutter and it took her a moment to reply. She swallowed. *Speak you idiot.* 'I could say the same. You don't strike me as the tabletop sale type.'

He laughed and waved a cup of insipid-looking tea. 'I'm just here for the hot beverages.' He stood to the side to let someone pass. 'No, I live near here and just needed to get out of the house for a bit. Saw the sign and thought I'd take a look.'

She hadn't realised they lived close to each other. In fact, she didn't know much about him at all. Like why he would be stuck in the house. Before she could speak again, an attractive woman in full make-up clapped him on the shoulder. 'Steve! What are you doing here?'

He flushed and shuffled from foot to foot. 'Hi, Abbie. I'm just having a walk round.' He glanced at Shelley. Was he not going to introduce her?

The attractive woman had a faint accent, but Shelley couldn't place it. 'Perfect! I've seen something I think your mother would love. Come and see.'

Steve didn't put up any resistance when she took hold of his arm and pulled him away. He put up his hand by way of goodbye. Was she his girlfriend? And did she know about the others? The fluttering in her stomach turned to something bitter: maybe he wasn't such a nice guy after all.

When she got back to her table with a cup of instant coffee in a polystyrene cup, Shelley found Lara staring at a slim, blond woman pushing a pram slowly past their table: close enough that she could look at their wares, far enough away that they wouldn't start speaking to her. Over the course of the morning, Shelley had learned to recognise the technique. Every so often, the woman would glance in at her baby, readjust the blanket, wave away a fly, move a toy. Her husband caught up with her and kissed her cheek, leaning in to check the baby himself. It was touching and sweet. And oh so painful.

Shelley turned to Lara. 'That'll be you in a few months. You and Matt.'

Lara closed her eyes for a moment. When she opened them, they were wet. 'Oh God, I hope so.'

Why was she crying? That had obviously not been the right thing to say. 'Hey, don't get upset. It will all be fine. The doctors are happy with you, aren't they? There's no reason that it won't all be okay, right?'

But Lara didn't answer. Her lips were trembling. Shelley's stomach fell; she recognised that look. 'Lara? What is it? Are you okay?'

Lara shook her head and started to rearrange some of the costume jewellery they had displayed on the end of the table. 'I'm fine. Ignore me, it's nothing.'

But Shelley couldn't ignore the fact she looked so upset. She turned her body to shield Lara from the people walking past; dwindling numbers now the sale was coming to an end. 'You're not fine. Talk to me. What is it? Did I say something wrong?'

A necklace dropped from Lara's fingers because they were suddenly shaking so hard. 'Sorry.' She knelt slowly to the ground to pick it up.

Shelley knelt too, putting her hand on Lara's. They were behind the table now; no one could see them. 'Lara, what is it?'

Lara looked up at her, her eyes two dark pools. 'I haven't been honest with you. Well, not completely.' She paused. 'I've lost more than one baby, Shelley. And there's no guarantee I won't lose this one too.'

CHAPTER NINETEEN

Lara

Lara sat in the car waiting for Shelley, who'd insisted that she could pack up on her own. Other people were returning to their cars with cardboard boxes full of remnants from the lives they'd lived. She'd cleared out everything that reminded her of the last two years of her life. She didn't want to look back. Only forwards. *Make way for joy.*

So why had she told Shelley? One of the reasons she enjoyed her company so much was because Shelley didn't treat her like a fragile object or look at her with sympathy. And now she'd blown it by telling her about the miscarriages. It was that woman who'd done it. The perfect family of three that Lara so desperately wanted for herself.

It was so easy for some people. They decided to get pregnant. They tried for a couple of months. They got pregnant. Nine months later they had a baby. Simple.

But it hadn't been; not for her.

It wasn't as if she'd always been desperate to have a baby. Two months before their wedding they'd actually thought she might be pregnant, and she'd been relieved to find it was a false alarm because it had been too soon. Looking back, she wondered now if that had been another very early miscarriage. Her naive relief back then made her feel sick now. What a fool.

Shelley was walking towards the car with the last box. Once they were on their own, Shelley would expect Lara to tell her what had happened to her pregnancies, wouldn't she? How much should she tell her? All of it? Or just enough to explain why she lived like a virtual recluse?

The car jolted slightly as Shelley slammed the boot, then she opened the driver's side door and slipped in. 'All done. I can drop it off at the charity shop next week.'

Lara nodded. They had planned to go to the charity shop straight from here, but she didn't feel up to it now and Shelley had obviously realised that. 'I'm sorry for getting all upset back there.'

Shelley shook her head. 'Don't be silly. I'm sorry if I was insensitive, pointing out that baby. I didn't realise…'

Now Lara shook her head. 'Don't apologise. You didn't know because I didn't tell you. Matt's just texted me to say he's popped out for lunch with a mate. Let's get back to mine and I'll explain.'

Back in her own lounge with a cup of herbal tea in her hands, Lara felt a little stronger though less willing to let Shelley in on the whole sorry story. But she couldn't say nothing. Not when Shelley looked so concerned.

'So? Are the doctors keeping a close eye on you?'

That was one way to put it. She'd had so many blood tests and urine tests and scans that she was beginning to feel like a laboratory test subject. 'They are now. After the first miscarriage, my doctor just told us to try again. Like you say, miscarriages are relatively common for a first pregnancy. After the second, they said the same.'

She could talk about it now as if it was a process they'd been through, but it hadn't been like that at the time. The first miscarriage had been a complete and utter shock. She hadn't even known anyone who'd had a miscarriage. Or rather, she hadn't known that anyone had. Since that day, she'd had friends and family members tell her that they had also miscarried the first time. Maybe she wouldn't have been as utterly shocked that first time if she'd known it was a real possibility.

Shelley looked grey. She seemed really affected by Lara's words. 'How long before they gave you some help?'

'It was after the third one. That's the stage at which they begin to investigate what's going on. Obviously, that's enough suffering for one person to have to go through.' She smiled, trying to lighten the conversation. Talking about it was hard. Too hard.

But Shelley wasn't smiling. 'I'm so sorry you've had to go through that so many times. It's truly awful. No wonder you gave up work when you got pregnant this time.'

Lara sipped at her tea. How much should she say? 'Actually... I misled you. I gave up work more than a year before this pregnancy. I was having so many tests it got impossible to fit them in around work. They were great about it, but the clients weren't too happy that they had to keep dealing with someone else. In the end, it was easier to give up. That's when we decided to move somewhere smaller, so that Matt could cover the mortgage on his wage.'

Shelley flushed. 'That makes sense. Also explains why Matt is so protective over you. Over the baby.'

It wasn't just the baby that Matt was worried about. But Lara wasn't going to get into that today. From Shelley's red face, she'd clearly had Matt down as a controlling husband. Poor Matt – if he'd been in control, they wouldn't be having this baby at all. A wave of exhaustion washed over her and she closed her eyes.

Shelley put her cup down on the table. 'You're shattered. I should go.' She stood and put up a hand as Lara shifted in her seat. 'I can see myself out. I know we planned for another sort-out tomorrow, but see how you feel. There's no rush.'

*

After Shelley had gone, Lara felt wrung out. Strong emotions had a habit of doing that. Still, it felt as if the morning had ended well. Shelley had seemed to understand. Really understand. More than she would have expected from someone who'd never mentioned children or wanting a child. It was surprising that the subject hadn't come up between them, considering Lara's pregnancy. But her reaction today suggested that she wasn't indifferent on the subject. Was that something to do with her separation from Greg?

She let her head fall back on the sofa. She was too tired to think about that right now, but she might be able to broach the subject another time. Opening up to Shelley about the miscarriages had made her feel closer to her. Maybe it wasn't such a bad thing that it had come out today. Maybe she should have gone further. Maybe she should have told her everything.

CHAPTER TWENTY

Shelley

Sunday had not been a good day – the usual boredom had been worsened by concern for Lara, who was out all day visiting family – so Shelley was both pleased and relieved to get a text from her at work on Monday. Matt had to work late again, so Shelley suggested Lara come over for dinner. It was funny: since they'd met, she'd assumed she was the broken one who Lara was trying to fix, but maybe Lara needed her just as much?

Thankfully, Lara looked a lot brighter than she had on Saturday. Her family day must have done her good. Renewed energy made her keen to get sorting out as soon as they finished dinner. 'We might as well get as much done as we can, then we can take it all to the charity shop next Saturday in one go.'

She had a good point. Shelley didn't want to prolong the bin bag obstacle course in her hallway. 'We could start on my clothes? There's a wardrobe of stuff I never wear.'

Lara grinned; she really did look better. 'Go get the book.'

Standing in the box room again, they appraised the pile of clothes Shelley had pulled from the wardrobe and the chest of drawers. Formal and summer dresses, linen trousers, blouses, T-shirts, jeans and skirts: she was amazed by how much there was. Had she really worn all of these?

Lara had the book open to the 'clothes' chapter and was reading aloud. 'You need to take each item, one at a time, and hold it close to you. How does it make you feel? What would you say to it?'

Shelley stopped mid-fold with a red striped T-shirt. 'Talk to a T-shirt? Are you serious? About what?'

Lara lowered the book and pointed at her. 'Aha! I knew you hadn't read more than the first couple of chapters. Busted!'

Shelley laughed. 'I skim-read it.'

Lara shook her head in mock disgust. 'You've really let me down. And, more importantly, you've let Joy down.'

It was so good to hear Lara joking again. Shelley threw the half-folded T-shirt at her. 'Come on. What am I chatting to my trousers about?'

Lara reopened the book. 'You need to decide whether to keep them or to pass them on. Speaking aloud your reasons for owning the item will help you to understand whether it should stay in your wardrobe or whether it is time to let it go.'

Was this a joke? Shelley picked up an old blouse she hadn't worn in years. 'Hey, blouse. How are things?'

Lara waved a finger at her. 'We need to do this properly.'

This was craziness, but Shelley was enjoying this process for the first time. These were *her* belongings; they had nothing to do with Greg. She brushed her open palm down past her eyes. 'Serious face.'

Lara nodded her approval. 'Good. Start with that dress. The psychedelic one with the collar. The one with the label that says: "What the hell were you thinking?"'

Shelley giggled and picked up the one Lara was pointing at. 'This one?'

'Yes, that one. And I really hope it is the only one you have that could fit that description. Now, say out loud why you bought it and whether it is something that you will wear again or whether it gives you joy for other reasons.'

Lara had an eyebrow raised and Shelley still couldn't work out if she was serious about this or not. She had to give it a go, though. Holding the dress at arm's length, she addressed it like an old friend. 'Hi, overly bright dress. I really liked you when I saw you in that boutique in Camden. But I think we both knew it was never going to work. You were always far too cool for me.'

She looked at Lara, who was nodding her approval. 'And so?'

'And so, I'm going to have to let you go.' She dropped the dress onto the floor.

'Nope, you're not done. You need to thank it first.'

Surely, this was a joke. 'Are you serious?'

Lara pointed to the floor, where the dress was a heap of luminosity. 'Yes, you need to thank it for being part of your life.'

Shelley scooped it back up. 'Thank you for making me feel like I was cool. Even if only for a short while.' This time she folded it up before dropping it onto the floor.

Lara clapped her hands together. 'Well done. Now the next one.'

Shelley picked up a white Gucci T-shirt. It had cost her a lot of money at the time, so she hadn't had the heart to throw it away, even though she couldn't wear it anymore due to a small brown stain. 'Hey, T-shirt. We had some good times. But that chocolate ice cream – it was the end of us. There's no going back.'

Lara's shoulders moved up and down as she laughed. 'And thank you for…'

'Thank you for growing with me that fortnight in Cornwall when I put on a stone. You had my back. And front. And the flabby bit around my middle.'

Lara tilted her head, struggling to keep a serious face. 'Cream teas?'

Shelley nodded gravely. 'And Cornish cider.'

Lara reached out and put her hand on the front of the T-shirt. 'Good work, Gucci. Good work.'

The more items they got through, the sillier – and funnier – it got. The absolute climax was the discovery of a pair of gold lamé hot pants.

Lara uncovered them with horror and then lay down on the bed with one hand over her face and the other holding the pants aloft. 'My eyes! My eyes!'

'What the hell are those?' Shelley snatched them from Lara's hand, then started to laugh. 'Oh my God, they were Dee's! She wore them to a fancy-dress party we had here one New Year's Eve. She was Kylie Minogue.' Dee had got very drunk that night and ended up staying over. She must have left them.

Lara was still groaning on the bed. 'I will never be able to unsee them!'

Shelley threw them at her and laughed. She hadn't had so much fun in a long time. She felt a rush of warmth towards this woman who had been a complete stranger a few weeks ago.

Before long, there was a sizeable pile of discarded clothes on the floor. Lara pulled out a roll of black bags that she'd brought with her and they shifted them inside. 'It's best to do it straight away. If you keep looking at them too long, you start getting sentimental.'

With every item that went into the bag, Shelley felt lighter. There was something liberating about clearing this stuff out. It wasn't just the wardrobe that would have more space: she felt freer too.

Lara started to hand her items from the other side of the bed: dresses, trousers, camisole tops. Some of them she hadn't worn in years. Why had she kept them?

Lara was passing a white denim jacket when she paused. 'I think there's something in the pocket of this one.'

Shelley took it from her, felt inside the right-hand pocket. There was something sharp and rough to the touch. She pulled out a key attached to a key ring made up of four, glittery capital letters: HOME.

Lara leaned forward. 'That's pretty.'

Shelley swallowed hard as she looked at it. Then again. 'Thanks. It's a key to my old flat.' The first home of her own she had ever had. The flat she had moved into with Greg when she was barely nineteen.

CHAPTER TWENTY-ONE

Shelley

Before

Dee's bedroom had been Shelley's second home for most of her teenage years. Now they were nineteen, the boy band posters had been replaced by art prints and collages of postcards. Disney princesses had lost out to colour-coordinated scatter cushions on the bed. And it was clean. Mainly because Dee hadn't been there in the last three months.

Shelley had got home from Warwick on Friday afternoon, leaving directly after her final lecture on medieval history. Dee had stayed on in Manchester for the weekend and had just got home.

'Did you bring home every single item of clothing you own? When you suggested I help you unpack, I didn't know I should bring rubber gloves.' Shelley's face was almost as screwed up as the ball of vest tops she had excavated from the bottom of one of Dee's numerous bags.

Dee sat back on her haunches and surveyed the piles. 'Pretty much. I've not been to the launderette for the last few weeks. And some of us haven't been coming home every weekend with our stuff.' She raised a judgmental eyebrow.

Shelley dropped the clump of clothing into the washing basket they'd dragged to the end of the bed. 'I don't come home every weekend.'

Dee started pulling books out of her suitcase and replacing them on her bookcase. Art students had a surprising number of textbooks. 'Most weekends, then.'

'What about the weekend I came to visit you?' Dee had begged her to come so she'd spent a stupid amount on train fare during reading week. It had been lovely to see Dee but her university experience was so different from Shelley's. Wherever they'd gone on campus, Dee had found someone she knew to say hello to or hug or share a joke with. They'd eaten out, been to a club in town, hung out at some random people's halls. It was a far cry from Shelley's experience.

Dee turned and waved a crisp copy of *History of Art: A Student's Handbook*, which looked as if it had never been opened. 'That wasn't a weekend. It was one night. And you left before Sunday lunchtime.'

Remembering how annoyed Dee had been about that, Shelley decided to change the subject. She picked up a copy of John Berger's *Ways of Seeing* and a couple of the other weightier tomes and passed them to Dee. 'Anyway. We're home now. Have you got any plans yet?'

Dee pulled a face. 'Mum wants us to have some *girl time* together, as she puts it. It probably involves us getting our nails done or something. I'm hoping to avoid a full-on spa day. Unless you come with us? That would make it a lot more bearable. Do you fancy it?'

Shelley didn't have the money for a day at a spa but she couldn't remind Dee of that without her offering to pay. Plus, the idea of spending a whole afternoon with Dee's mother looking down her nose wasn't appealing. 'I don't think I can. I need to spend some time with my own mum and I know Greg has some plans too.'

She picked up another carrier bag and started poking around in it as a way to avoid Dee's eyes.

She couldn't avoid her mouth though. 'What plans? I haven't seen you in weeks. You've seen him loads. Didn't he come up and see you last week too?'

Greg had come and spent the weekend with her and it had been lovely. He'd taken her for lunch at a restaurant in town that she hadn't even known existed. Then he'd insisted on taking her to the supermarket and buying her a week's shopping. They'd spent the following morning in her tiny student bedroom together and had managed to completely avoid the other students on her landing. It was as if they were the only two people there. Which was when he'd given her the key.

'The thing is…' How was she going to tell Dee about this in a way which wouldn't provoke a wave of condemnation? 'The thing is, there's something I need to tell you. Greg has given me a key to his flat, and today I was going to get some stuff together that I can keep there. You know, just my toothbrush, spare PJs, that sort of thing.'

She tried so hard to make it sound casual but she couldn't suppress the smile that came over her face. He'd been so sweet about it all. Just said that he wanted her to feel that she could come over whenever she wanted. Weekends, holidays from uni, anytime. Her mum had met someone, and she knew that he stayed over when Shelley was away at college. He wasn't there when Shelley came home but she didn't want to get in the way of her mum having her own life. It would be good to have somewhere else to stay.

Dee wasn't smiling, though. She was staring. 'You're moving in with him?'

Shelley shook her head. 'Not exactly. I'm living in Warwick, remember?'

'Exactly. You're living in Warwick. So why is he giving you a key to his place? It's not like you live around the corner and you're going to be popping over. Is it?'

This last question didn't sound rhetorical. 'What are you asking? Am I dropping out of university?'

'Are you?'

'No!' That wasn't what she was saying. She'd committed to going and she'd see it through. Even if she was hating it. And she was. Dee was still looking at her so she repeated herself. 'No.'

'You can't blame me for asking. It's not as if you are giving it a proper chance. And I know what Greg's like.'

Shelley felt defensive. On both her account and Greg's. 'What's that supposed to mean?'

'You don't talk about anyone from college, and when I ring you in the evening, you're always back in your room. I know you're finding it difficult to talk to people, but if you don't make an effort to go out, how are you going to make friends and start enjoying yourself?'

She was regretting telling Dee so much in her emails. 'I'm there to get a degree, Dee. And I just haven't connected with anyone there.'

'But you're not going to connect with anyone if you keep running back home to your boyfriend every five minutes. You need to give it a proper chance. Without being tied to home.'

These arguments were getting too common. 'So, you think I should break up with him just so that I can sleep around at university and get the full experience?'

'I didn't say that. I'm just saying you're not giving it a proper go. You would enjoy it. You've spent the last two years planning to be at uni, and now you can't wait to get away and come home.'

Actually, it was Dee who had spent the last two years planning it all, but Shelley didn't say that. 'I can do both.'

But she was beginning to wonder if she wanted to. Being at the flat with Greg these last two nights had been lovely. He had cooked for her; she had helped him to pick out some new curtains from the Next catalogue. Just hanging out together felt right. At university she never felt at home, never felt entirely comfortable. It wasn't as if she was even enjoying her studies. Most of the preliminary modules were about ancient history and it wasn't really her thing. Was it possible that she had made a terrible mistake in going to university in the first place?

Dee moved closer to her and took her hand. 'I don't want to argue with you about this, but I am just worried that you are going to make a decision that you'll regret.'

How could she make her understand? They were different. 'Do you like your degree course?'

Dee looked confused. 'Yeah, it's okay. Some modules are better than others. Why? Don't you like yours?'

'I've been wondering if I should think about changing to something else. Maybe history isn't for me.'

Dee nodded. 'Well, if that's how you feel, you should. Have you been to speak to anyone? You've only done one term – surely you can still swap and catch up?'

She hadn't been to see anyone yet because switching to another degree subject wasn't what she'd been thinking about. 'Not yet. But I have seen a course in London that looks good.'

Dee's face changed. 'In London?'

She'd started now so she might as well get it all out. 'Travel and hospitality. It's not a degree course but it looks really good.'

Dee was staring at her. 'Travel and hospitality. In London. Let me guess: so you can commute from Greg's flat?'

That had crossed Shelley's mind, but that wasn't the reason she'd picked it. It wasn't. 'I'm going to save a lot of money if I move back home and go to college from here.'

'But you're going to miss out on so much. It's not the course – I don't care what degree you do – but you're not going to have the same experience if you live at home. That's not what university is about.'

Shelley had known this was going to be Dee's reaction. That was why she hadn't said anything in her emails when she'd started to research degrees in London. She'd wanted to talk to Dee face to face. 'It's different for you. You're outgoing. You meet people. I'm not like you. And I'm miserable where I am.'

The look of disappointment on Dee's face was worse than the look on Shelley's mother's. Her mum had just said that Shelley should do what she thought best. That she just wanted her to be happy.

The difference was, Dee thought she knew better what made Shelley happy. 'It was Greg's idea, wasn't it?'

She'd known that was coming. 'No, it wasn't. It was mine.'

But Dee wasn't listening. She stood up. 'Wait till I speak to him. He is so out of order encouraging you to drop out so that you can go and play house with him in his new flat.'

Now Shelley was annoyed. 'Don't you dare speak to him. It's got nothing to do with him or the flat. This is about what I want. If you are my friend, you'll understand.'

Dee sank back onto the bed. 'I don't want you to make a decision you're going to regret. I'm worried about you.'

Shelley put an arm around her. 'You don't need to worry about me. I feel good about this new course. It feels more like me. And when I get a job in the travel industry, think of all the cheap holiday deals I'll be able to get for us.'

Dee looked at her. 'Are you sure you won't be going on all your holidays with Greg from now on?'

'Of course not. You're my best friend. I'll always have time for you.' She took the key out of her pocket with its sparkly HOME key ring that Greg had bought for her. 'Want to come over and see the flat? There are two bedrooms, so you'll be able to come and stay when you're home from uni.'

CHAPTER TWENTY-TWO

Shelley

Shelley didn't actually know what mothballs smelled like but she would have guessed it was similar to this room. Stale clothes and old toys and a whiff of neglect. They'd picked the Oxfam shop on the high street because it was the shortest distance from the car park – she couldn't expect Lara to help with the heavy black sacks.

Since the clothes sort-out on Monday, they had barely seen each other, and Shelley had been surprised by how much she'd missed her new neighbour. It was strange how quickly she got used to having someone in her life. And how slowly she got used to having someone missing from it.

The rest of the week at work had been particularly trying. Everyone was feeling twitchy about the takeover and was starting to snipe at each other. Flora had never so much as raised her voice at Shelley, but on Wednesday she'd lost her patience with her about the team manager job. 'Have you at least filled in the application form for your job? The deadline is soon.'

Even though she still wasn't sure whether she wanted the job, she *had* filled in the application form the night before, more for something to do than anything else. 'Just to clarify, it's not *my* job. But, actually, yes, I have done it and I was going to ask you to look at it.'

Flora had focused on the part of the sentence she was interested in. 'Great! Good girl. Email it over to me and I'll pimp it up. I know you'll have undersold what you've done. Your CV should make you blush when you read it, otherwise you haven't promoted yourself enough.'

Shelley had rolled her eyes. Maybe asking Flora to read it wasn't the best idea. At least the CV had put her in a better mood, or a gossipy one at least. 'You know you said you saw Steve with his girlfriend at the tabletop sale last weekend?'

That wasn't quite what she'd said. 'I don't know whether she was his girlfriend.'

Details like this weren't getting in the way of Flora's story. 'Yes, well, I was speaking to Adele in accounts and she said his girlfriend is called Svetlana. She heard him on the phone to her and remembered because it's such an exotic-sounding name.'

Shelley knew it was absolutely none of her business what Steve did in his spare time, but she wasn't enjoying the gossip as much as Flora clearly was. Maybe he was on Tinder or one of those other apps. For some reason, it was an unpleasant thought. Was she jealous? Of what? *Get a grip.*

Now Lara was holding the Oxfam shop door open so that Shelley could stumble through with two big black bags of leftovers from the tabletop sale. A dark-haired woman in a bottle green cardigan smiled at them from behind the counter. 'Donations to the back, please. Give Sandra a shout if there's no one there.'

Navigating her way around clothing rails, Shelley left Lara behind looking at paperbacks and made her way to the back of the small shop. Rows of plastic toys were perched on a series of shelves on the back wall, and she avoided those and made her way towards a doorway.

The aforementioned Sandra was in the storeroom sifting through a pile of women's clothes. She looked up when Shelley appeared and held her hands out for the bags.

'What have we here?' She peered inside. 'Oh, these look nice, thank you.' She turned and placed them on the floor beside the rest of the clothes. 'If you've got a minute, can I take your details for Gift Aid? It makes such a difference.'

Lara appeared behind her. 'Good idea. We're going to be regulars over the next few weeks – there's a lot more where that came from.'

Sandra suddenly looked very excited. 'You're pregnant! Perfect timing. I am just sorting through a huge pile of maternity clothes which would look lovely on you. Do you want a rummage?'

Lara flushed. 'Oh, no. I don't need anything. Thanks. Actually, I'm feeling really hot. I'll wait for you outside, Shelley?'

Shelley recognised that look. Lara wasn't hot; she was uncomfortable. 'Okay. I'll be as quick as I can. Maybe we can go and get a cold drink?'

The café was quiet. Most people were out enjoying the early summer sunshine. With a cold glass of juice to sip, Lara looked much better. Shelley raised an enquiring eyebrow. 'Your love of eBay doesn't stretch to buying second-hand clothes, then?'

Lara shook her head. 'It's not that. It's just that I'm still managing with my existing clothes. The joys of Lycra.' She paused. 'Actually, that's not true. I've just not wanted to shop for that stuff, to be honest.'

'Because you're trying to save money?'

'Partly. And because I don't want to jinx anything.' She turned her glass of juice around on the table.

Shelley thought of the pram from eBay. 'Well, it's understandable that you've been cautious this time. After everything you've been through.'

The kitchen door squeaked open behind Lara and she looked over her shoulder. 'These look like our sandwiches coming over now.'

The woman who had come from the kitchen with their ham baguettes was wearing a cap over her hair, which may have been why Shelley didn't recognise her at first. But she recognised Shelley. 'Hello, Shel! I didn't realise that was you!'

Shelley panicked. She knew what was coming next. 'I didn't know you worked in here, Cindy.'

'Yes, I've been here about a year. Now the twins have started secondary school, I've got more time on my hands.'

Shelley could see that she was just about to put her head to one side and the sympathy was about to flow. She needed to head her off. 'Lara, this is Cindy. We were at sixth form together. Seems like forever ago now.' She smiled at Cindy. If she could just keep her voice upbeat, maybe Cindy would go back to the kitchen and they could avoid any awkwardness.

But that was impossible. She smiled at Lara and then her head was almost immediately back on her shoulder. 'I was so shocked to hear about Greg. I remember you guys getting married, such a lovely day. How are you doing?'

This was going badly. 'I'm okay, yes. Just catching up with my friend here.'

Shelley was being so obvious it was almost rude, but it was clearly too subtle for Cindy. 'Ah. You poor thing. I've seen Dee out and about but I haven't spoken to her. Terrible business. Terrible.'

Shelley felt sick. How was she going to stop her from spilling the whole thing in front of Lara?

Thank God, she was saved by the kitchen door opening and another hat poking out into the café. 'Cindy! Can you give me a hand?'

'I'll be right there!' Cindy turned back to Shelley. 'Anyway, you take care and I'll hopefully see you in here another day.' She patted Shelley on the shoulder and left.

Shelley turned back to Lara. She needed to get the conversation away from anything to do with Greg or Dee. 'So, the joy book.

How did you get hold of it in the first place? You don't seem the sort of person to have gone looking for a book like that.'

Lara was scrutinising her with what Shelley assumed was her professional legal face, but she was too polite to ask questions. She picked up her knife and cut the baguette into four pieces. 'It was chance, really. I was taking stuff to the charity shop and…' She sighed deeply. 'I told you that we'd bought the pram too early the first time? Well, we'd bought other stuff too. Clothes, a blanket, even a tiny little lamb toy with a yellow ribbon around its neck.' Her voice cracked and she coughed.

'Oh, Lara, I'm so sorry. That must have been so hard.'

Lara nodded. She pressed at the baguette in front of her, flattening it to make it easier to eat. 'After the… last time, I said that I couldn't do it again. It was over. I didn't want to try for another baby. Matt stayed quiet. He's always wanted kids. He's one of five boys and family means a loud, crazy home to him. But he stayed quiet. Said he would do whatever I wanted. And what I wanted to do was clear out every single thing we'd bought.'

Shelley's own mother had tutted about women who bought things before the baby was born. 'It's bad luck,' she would say with a shake of her head. It might be an old wives' tale – like not opening an umbrella indoors – but she could see the sense in it for occasions like this.

Lara sniffed loudly, waited a few moments, then looked up again. 'Anyway, when I was at the charity shop, I got chatting to the woman who worked there and she told me that they'd had an influx of donations after this book was released. *Make Way for Joy*. Had I read it? She went on about it so much, I ended up ordering a copy off Amazon so that I could get away. And that's how it all started. I bought the book and gave it a go.'

Shelley had taken a bite of her sandwich, so all she could say was, 'Mmm.'

Lara kept going. 'It was good at the beginning because it gave me a focus, something to do. The more I threw away, the better I felt. Not just the baby stuff – most of that went the first week – but other things as well. Clothes I'd said I'd slim back into. Lacy bras I'd never wear because they made me itch. Literary classics I thought I should read but didn't actually want to. Rigby and Peller went the same way as Jekyll and Hyde: if it wasn't in use and it didn't bring me joy…' She made a throwing motion with her hand. 'Out of the door it went.'

Shelley could see now why Lara had been so keen for her to do the same. And she was right, it had been cathartic. She did feel like she could breathe a little easier. But Lara's honesty was making her uncomfortable. If she was sharing, did this mean that Shelley should be honest too? They'd felt closer since their conversation after the tabletop sale and she'd felt increasingly guilty that she'd let Lara open herself up without returning the favour.

A little of the colour had returned to Lara's face as she spoke. 'Matt and I started to laugh again. The weekend we tore a Hawaiian shirt he refused to give away was a high point. We had a sleeve each and were tugging it between us, which ended up in us wrestling on the bed. We laughed so much. That's when I knew: I was ready to try again. Matt and I sat down and talked about it, and that's when we made the decision to sell the house and pay for a private consultation.'

'Wow. And everything went well from that point on?'

Shelley regretted her question when she saw the cloud that came over Lara's face. 'I'll save the rest of the story for when we're not out in public.' She picked up a piece of her baguette. 'I think you're right about the maternity clothes, though. When we've finished here, shall we go back and I'll try some on? Maybe we can look for an interview outfit for you, too.'

Seemed that she wasn't the only one adept at changing the subject.

*

Back at the charity shop, both of them were in a lighter mood. Lara tried on outfits and then sent Shelley out into the shop to find hats or scarves to set them off. 'Wait till Matt sees me in some of these. He's going to bust a gut.'

She was standing in front of a mirror and looking at herself, pulling faces as she repositioned a large-brimmed straw hat. From nowhere, Shelley got the old feeling. The flash of jealousy she used to get all the time when she saw a pregnant woman. She thought that one would have been put to bed but here it was, rearing its ugly head. She swallowed. 'You look beautiful.'

Lara turned and pretended to stick her fingers down her throat. 'Please don't give me that "all pregnant women are beautiful" tosh. I am well aware that I look like a hippo. Come on, why don't you try something on? I saw a dress over there which would look great on you. The red one.' She took the hat off and pulled the curtain to the changing room closed.

A red dress? Shelley hadn't bought a new dress in months, much less one in a colour that invited people to notice her. But she did as she was told and thumbed through the hangers on the nearest rail. 'I'm not sure that I need anything new – or nearly new. There's probably something in the wardrobe that would do.'

Lara stuck her head out of the curtain. 'But is there anything in your wardrobe that sparks *joy*?' She raised an eyebrow and then her head disappeared again.

Shelley couldn't help but smile.

Lara made it out of the changing cubicle and stood beside her, lowered her voice. 'Tell me if I'm speaking out of turn, Shelley, but it might be time for you to get back out there. You may not feel like it now, but at some point you will want to meet someone new. You don't have to be single forever.'

Lara's enthusiasm for life was infectious. But there was no way she was ready to get out in the world again. Just the thought of getting dressed up to go out made her feel a little queasy. Shelley opened her mouth to reply but was interrupted by a beep as someone opened the front door.

A young woman came in, glanced around and approached the counter. 'Excuse me. I don't suppose you have any wedding dresses?'

'Just a minute, love, I'll ask.' Bottle green cardigan lady held cupped hands to her mouth. 'Sandra!'

Sandra appeared in the doorway with a giant rabbit in one hand and a pile of CDs in the other. 'Did you call me?'

'Yes. Do we have any wedding dresses?'

'No. We had a couple in last month but they got snapped up immediately. Always do. Is it for you?'

The young woman nodded.

'I can take your name and give you a call if anything comes in. When's the wedding?'

The girl blushed. 'Not until next year but I'm trying to get organised – we're on a pretty strict budget. Yes, please, I'll give you my mobile number.'

As Sandra bustled back to the stockroom to get a pen, Shelley realised that Lara was looking at her intently. Was she suggesting that Shelley bring her wedding dress in? She shook her head at her. It was still too soon to face that.

CHAPTER TWENTY-THREE

Shelley

Before

When they had been planning their wedding, Shelley had had three non-negotiables: a white dress, proper speeches and a first dance to 'Crazy for You'.

It would have been nice to have lots more guests, a proper wedding breakfast and a bit more razzmatazz, but it was Greg's wedding too – she reminded herself frequently – and if he wanted something quieter and more intimate, so be it. His mother had helped her to find a venue and caterers, and Shelley's mum had seemed happy to take a back seat – Greg's parents had much more experience in organising social events. They had also pushed for something more formal but Greg had been firm with them: small and intimate. Her new mother-in-law's efforts hopefully meant that she had accepted Shelley as good enough for her son. Even if her face had still to show evidence of that.

Dee had also been a great help, which was a relief. She hadn't seemed too keen on the idea of them getting married, but once she'd got her head round it, she'd been a wonder. Coming with Shelley to look at wedding dresses, choosing flower arrangements for the church, looking at – and tasting – options for wedding cakes, finding a hog roast for the evening.

Greg was right: what was the point of paying out lots of money for a three-course meal when no one wanted to be stuck at a table with people they didn't know making small talk? It was better to have a buffet where guests could mingle as they wished, eat and then get on with enjoying themselves. The quicker the food was over, the quicker the dancing could start. *And the quicker it would be over.* That was the subtext. It was normal for most grooms to want to get the wedding over, wasn't it? As he'd said, it was the marriage that was important, not the day. He was only doing this for her.

Dee had helped her get dressed this morning. Her mum had been there too, but the buttons up the back of her dress were too fiddly for her mum's fingers. When she'd turned around to face them, they had both cried at the sight of her in bridal finery. Just the reaction she'd been hoping for.

'You do look beautiful, Shelley. Like a proper grown-up woman.'

Shelley had laughed; she knew what Dee meant. While Dee had spent the last year travelling and musing about what to do next, Shelley had gone straight into working at a local travel agency after finishing her travel and hospitality course. It was only a first step: she was hoping to get a job working in corporate travel – it sounded so sophisticated. They had joked that Shelley was booking holidays while Dee was on a permanent one. Shelley didn't mind; with Dee away, there wasn't the difficulty of splitting her time between her and Greg.

Now her mum had left for the church and Dee was downstairs with the other bridesmaids, waiting for the bridal car. Back in her childhood bedroom, which was now a guest bedroom coordinated within an inch of its life, she stood in front of the mirror, turning this way and that, looking at her dress. Dee had paid for someone to do her hair and make-up as a wedding gift. It was one of the only times in her life she'd felt truly beautiful. This was her day.

'All ready, love?' Her dad poked his head in the doorway, clearly uncomfortable in the house he'd not lived in for the best part of two decades.

She beckoned him in. 'Nearly there, just noticed a stray hair I need to tame.' She caught it with a kirby grip and patted it into place. 'Done.'

'Well, you look beautiful.' He took a handkerchief out of his pocket and dabbed it under his eyes. 'Really beautiful.'

She turned and smiled. 'Thanks, Dad. You look very handsome in your suit.'

He smoothed his hair down. It was greying and receding. 'Aye, well. I'm just glad you and Greg didn't go in for all that top hat malarkey. I would have felt a right picture in one of those.' Someone else who was pleased that the wedding was simple. It clearly was a man thing.

'You look great.'

He sat down on the bed, watching her as she turned her body this way and that in front of the full-length mirror. 'Listen, love. I know I haven't been the best of dads.'

She looked at his reflection in the mirror. He looked genuinely sorry. 'Not now, Dad. You're going to make my make-up run.' She smiled, trying to lighten the moment.

But he was intent on getting his point across. 'Please, let me just say this. After me and your mother split up, I know I wasn't very good at staying in touch. I should have made more effort, come to see you, but life gets busy. You know how it is.'

You were too busy with your new girlfriend. That's what Shelley wanted to say, but her wedding morning wasn't the time to get into this. 'Dad, honestly. It's fine. Me and mum were all right.'

He seemed to get the message. 'Yes. Your mother is a good woman. Better than me, eh?'

Shelley didn't want to talk about it now, or even think about it. That part of her life was over. She was marrying Greg and starting something new. She held out her hands. 'Will I do?'

Her father smiled. 'You look perfect.' He held out his arm for her to slip her hand through. 'Shall we?'

The wedding ceremony had been full of moments she would treasure. Greg's face as she joined him at the front of the church, the laughter when she'd struggled to get his ring onto his finger, the feel of his hand between her shoulder blades as they had their first kiss as man and wife.

Then it was all over – the bells had rung, confetti had been thrown and they'd arrived at the hall for their reception. Greg had gripped her hand tightly the whole time. 'It's okay, I'm not going anywhere,' she'd whispered.

He'd kissed her cheek and smiled at her. 'Make sure you don't.'

People had warned her that her wedding day would go by quickly, but she hadn't realised how quickly. Even with a smaller gathering, there always seemed to be someone else they needed to talk to, or a photograph to pose for. And then there had been the cutting of the cake, the speeches, the first dance. Greg had held her close as Madonna sang 'Crazy for You' – as promised – and he hadn't rolled his eyes once at her choice of song. In fact, his eyes had looked deeply into hers as if no one else existed. It had been magical.

After that, she'd danced with her father at the insistence of Greg's mother – apparently it was tradition – which had been rather wooden and awkward. But Greg had danced with Dee at the same time, and it had made her smile to see them getting along so well. Laughing and joking, then twirling each other round. She'd hoped someone was taking photographs – she could use them to prove to them later how much they loved each other really. She'd barely spoken to Dee all day; who knew you got so little time with your chief bridesmaid?

Later in the evening, she finally caught up with her, chatting with some of their old school friends at the bar. 'Thank God, there you are.' She lowered her voice. 'Can you help me pee?'

Shut in the cubicle together, they giggled as Shelley hoisted up yards of satin and kind of threw it forwards for Dee to catch. 'Okay, I am sitting… now!'

This wasn't the first time they had been in a toilet cubicle together, but possibly the first time when Shelley was sober. People had been buying her drinks all afternoon but she had no idea where they kept disappearing to. She would swear she hadn't had more than a few sips of Prosecco.

Dee, though, definitely looked like she'd been making nice with a good few glasses. 'Have you enjoyed your day? Has everything gone as you wanted?'

Maybe not exactly what she'd originally wanted but it had gone as planned. 'Yes. All good. Except I've barely seen my best friend and chief bridesmaid.'

Dee hiccupped, put her hand to her mouth, dropped some of the dress and stooped to gather it up again. 'That's because your new husband hasn't let go of you all day.'

Was she going to be funny again? Best to just laugh it off. 'Well, I am quite a catch, you know.'

Dee nodded. 'You are. He's a lucky man. I hope he realises that.'

If only she could make Dee see that he did realise that. The way she spoke sometimes, you would think Greg had abducted Shelley, not that they had just fallen in love. She understood that it was difficult for Dee, but it was time to move this on. 'Right. Mission Wee accomplished. I'll stand, you drop my dress.'

Once they had navigated their way out of the cubicle, Shelley washed her hands as Dee reapplied her lipstick in the mirror. 'The colour of your dress really suits you. That plum satin looks lovely on your skin.'

Dee turned with her hands on her hips. 'Of course it does. That's why I chose it.' She gave a little wiggle.

Shelley laughed. She loved her so much. Dee had been such a big part of her life for so long. It had been hard when they'd gone to separate universities, even harder when Shelley had moved in with Greg. But that was life – things had to change, didn't they? A sob rose unbidden in her throat. 'Thanks for all your help with everything. I'm not sure I could have got everything organised without you.'

'Hey, you, don't get all teary on me.' Dee put her arms out and they squeezed each other tightly. 'I loved helping. I love you, you soppy woman.'

Shelley sniffed as they let each other go. Grabbing some tissues from the box on the vanity unit – Greg's mother had thought of everything – she dabbed under her eyes to make sure her mascara didn't run. 'Look, nothing is going to change, you know. Between us, I mean.'

Dee took the tissue from her and took over the dabbing. 'I know that. I just… well, I just want you to be happy.'

That nearly started Shelley off again. Maybe she had drunk more than she realised. 'I am happy. Very happy. We both are.'

Dee stopped dabbing and looked her in the eye. 'I just…'

The toilet door opened and strains of 'Dancing Queen' followed Auntie Beryl inside. Shelley grabbed Dee's hand. 'Come on. They're playing our song.'

CHAPTER TWENTY-FOUR

Lara

'Art is subjective. What is beautiful to one person can be quite ordinary to another. When deciding whether to keep a picture, sculpture or work of art, you must always come back to the same decision. Ask yourself: does this bring me joy?'

Lara stopped reading, lowered *Make Way for Joy* and looked at Shelley. For the last ten minutes, she had been tugging three frames from the side of the wardrobe, where they seemed to have been wedged, refusing any help that Lara offered. It was probably for the best; Lara had zero strength today. Around month four, when the sickness had stopped, she had felt really well. Surely she couldn't yet be past the 'blooming' period that everyone talked about?

Now most of the boxes had been emptied and any unwanted contents dropped off to the charity shop yesterday, this room was coming back to itself: it actually looked like somewhere you could invite a guest to stay. Though there was still work to do, it was a far cry from the junkyard it had been the first time Lara had seen it, when it had been so full that a frame had fallen out and hit her on the head. These last few weeks had gone quickly; it wasn't just the room that had changed. Who could have predicted that her quiet, buttoned-down neighbour would become the person she most wanted to spend time with?

They had almost missed the paintings altogether; they were hidden so far back. At least, Lara had missed them. She had her suspicions that Shelley had been trying to ignore them. Finally, with a grunt, Shelley managed to pull them free. 'This is the sum total of our art collection, I think.'

After all the work they'd already done, the floor space was pretty much clear, so Shelley had laid the first two frames flat so they could appraise them. Stark and modern, framed in chrome, bold, bright paint strokes filled the white background and challenged any onlookers. There was something powerful about them, very masculine. 'These are striking.'

Shelley folded her arms. 'I hate them. Greg had them in his old office and they came back here when he moved to another company. They never matched the décor anywhere in the house, so they've just been stuck up here. Like hostages.'

Hostages? That was an odd comparison. Not for the first time, Lara wondered if there was a reason that Shelley still had so many of Greg's belongings. Was she hoping to use them somehow? Was there something she wanted from him? Did she still want *him*?

Lara gave that idea some serious consideration. It was odd that Shelley hadn't told her why Greg had left. Apart from his name, some photographs and a few random memories, Lara knew very little about him. Up until now, it had not felt like something she should question, but now they were closer, perhaps she could ask? Shelley had admitted how much better she felt after offloading her old clothes. How much happier might she feel offloading about their split? It wasn't as if she was the one who had anything to be ashamed of, was it? Or did she not want Lara to think badly of Greg, in case he came back? Where was he? And who with?

Shelley was still holding the third frame, leaning it against her legs so that Lara couldn't see the picture. Lara pointed at it. 'Are you going to lay that one down, too?'

Tilting it backwards so that she could look at it, Shelley narrowed her eyes. After a few moments, she took a deep breath and placed it between the other two. 'There you go.'

Completely different in style from Greg's two corporate pictures, this was a portrait. Quite traditional. Two young girls of around eleven or twelve, one of whom – even with much darker hair – was undoubtedly Shelley. Lara could guess who the other one was. 'Is that you and Dee?'

'Yes.' Shelley stared at the painting for a few moments. 'This was my Christmas present two years ago. Dee painted it from a photograph of us when we were first friends.' She swallowed. Bit her lip.

The girls in the photograph were smiling, possibly laughing. Almost mirror images of each other in their hairstyle and clothes. At that age, all girls want to look just like their friends; Lara could remember her own parents complaining how she and her friends all looked the same. Individuality came later, like self-confidence.

From the few things Shelley had told her, Lara knew that she and Dee had been very close friends. Something pretty major must have happened to split them apart. If this gift was from two years ago, that had to have been pretty recent. Cogs started to turn in Lara's brain; suspicions got stronger, but she would need to tread carefully. 'It's a great painting. Is she a professional artist?'

Shelley looked up, her face proud. 'A graphic designer. Incredibly talented. She's worked on some pretty big campaigns. She doesn't paint very often these days. At least, she didn't. This was a special project. It took her weeks.'

Lara didn't know much about painting, but there looked to be a lot of love in this portrait. The girls in the painting were laughing, happy, close. What had happened twenty years later to split them apart? Although Dee's name seemed to come up a lot in conversation, Shelley had skirted around the subject of why they were no longer friends so many times. Surely they were close enough now for Lara to ask… 'Why don't you see her anymore?'

Shelley took a deep breath, still staring at the painting on the floor. 'We… fell out. Something happened and… we just lost touch.'

Greg and Dee had both disappeared from Shelley's life at the same time. Her husband and her best friend. It didn't take a detective to work out what that something was. No wonder she'd been living the life of a hermit when Lara had first moved in. And that would explain why she'd cut herself off from most of her friends too; she was embarrassed to see them. Poor Shelley. 'You don't have to answer this if you don't want to. But does Dee have something to do with Greg leaving?'

Shelley looked up from the painting and frowned. 'What do you mean?'

Lara had asked the big question; now she had to follow through. Surely Shelley knew what she was getting at? *Just say it.* 'I mean… did Greg leave you for Dee? Are they together? Is that why he left?'

It would explain why Shelley was so hurt. Why she couldn't bear to talk about Greg even a year later. Why she no longer had Dee in her life. The double betrayal of her best friend and her husband. Lara's heart ached for her. It was awful.

But Shelley looked completely confused. Either she was a great actress or Lara had got it very wrong. 'Leave me for *Dee*? No. No, of course not.'

Lara's face grew hot. Had she pushed her too fast again? She was wrong to have asked. Yes, they had become closer, but this was a big thing for Shelley to tell her; she should have waited until Shelley was ready to open up herself. 'I'm sorry, I shouldn't…'

She tailed off when she realised Shelley was shaking her head. 'Greg didn't leave me for *Dee*. I'm not sure you… why you…' She took a deep breath. 'Dee is Greg's sister.'

CHAPTER TWENTY-FIVE

Shelley

Before

'I am so happy for you.'

It was true. Shelley *was* happy for Dee. So why had her first emotion been one of disappointment? Or was that... envy?

Dee was sat on the bed, legs crossed, looking a lot younger than her thirty-one years. 'It's insane, right? The idea of me becoming a mother? Totally crazy?'

It did feel a little bit crazy, but mainly because Dee was telling Shelley her news back in her old childhood bedroom.

The whole family had been summoned to Greg and Dee's parents' house for their dad's birthday. Their mother had cooked her famous lemon chicken and they were having a short respite before dessert. Their dad had taken Dee's new husband Jamie for a tour of his garage, and Greg was helping to load the dishwasher. When Shelley had gone upstairs to use the bathroom, Dee had followed, pounced on her when she came out and dragged her in here.

Despite her protestations of insanity, Shelley could feel her friend's excitement. She pulled her close and hugged her. 'You'll be a brilliant mum.' She kept her held there long enough to blink her eyes hard. Any tears had to look like happiness, not jealousy.

When she released her, Dee grabbed her hands. 'You need to get pregnant too! We could do this together!'

Her words fell like a stone inside Shelley. 'We're not having children.'

'What?' Dee's eyes widened. 'Not ever?'

Shelley shook her head. 'Greg doesn't want children. We talked about it before we got married. I agreed.'

'But that was years ago! Have you talked about it recently? Things change.'

They hadn't talked about it recently, but Greg never hid his feelings. At dinner with his friend Max last weekend, he and his wife had taken turns to leave the table every ten minutes and deal with a toddler who refused to stay in bed. When both parents had joined forces the seventh time, Greg had poured Shelley another glass of wine and said, 'Thank God we haven't got kids.'

'It's fine. You don't need to have children to have a full life, you know?' Shelley had been repeating this to herself like a mantra every time she saw a pram going past or a baby in a high chair at the café.

Dee narrowed her eyes. 'But that's Greg's opinion. What do *you* want?'

Shelley knew how hard it was to hide her feelings from someone who knew her so well, but Greg was her husband and she wasn't about to paint him as the bad guy. 'I made a decision, Dee. I wanted Greg more than I wanted a baby.'

'But what about *now*? I don't think Greg knows what he wants. If you were pregnant, I know he'd be happy. It's just the thought of it. He can only see the negatives. Once I have this baby, he'll see how easy it is and he'll change his mind.'

Shelley shook her head again. 'I don't think so. Anyway, this is not about us. It's about you. I'm so happy for you.'

Maybe it was the first-trimester hormones but Dee became quite insistent. 'Let me talk to him. I'm his sister. I'm sure I can persuade him into it.'

What made her think she had more sway than Shelley? 'No, Dee. This is between me and Greg.'

'But he's being an idiot and someone needs to tell him.'

Greg's voice rang up the staircase. 'Shelley! Dee! Are you coming down anytime soon? Mum wants to do the dessert!'

Shelley got up from the bed. 'Come on, preggers. Let's go.'

But Dee reached out and held onto her wrist. 'Hold on. I want to finish our conversation. Do you want a baby? Because this is not something you can decide based on what Greg wants, just like everything else.'

It was the 'everything else' that started it. 'What do you mean?'

Dee sighed deeply. 'Like all the other things you've changed so you like the same things as Greg.' She stopped, shook her head. 'Oh, it doesn't matter. Let's just go downstairs and eat baked bloody Alaska.'

But now it was Shelley who wanted to finish this conversation; Dee's words had stung. 'What other things?'

Dee shrugged as if Shelley wasn't giving her a choice. 'Like Greg going on about your "new favourite wine" at dinner like the two of you are one person.'

Why was she so upset about the wine? 'Well, that's ridiculous. Greg's boss recommended a wine to him so he bought a bottle and we both liked it. You're completely overreacting.'

Now Dee looked irritated. 'It's not just that.' She glanced around the room as if for inspiration, and her eyes rested on the pop posters still on the wall. 'You only ever listen to the music he likes, for example. We used to love Westlife, didn't we? When did you last listen to them?'

Now she really *was* being ridiculous. 'When was the last time *you* listened to them? It's called growing up, Dee.'

Dee wasn't giving up. 'Bad example. But you used to love pop music – we both did. Now you only listen to Greg's stuff.

The Cure. The Smiths. Stuff we used to laugh at because it was so depressing.'

There was a burning in Shelley's stomach. Was there an element of truth to Dee's words? She didn't mind The Smiths these days. It had taken a bit of getting used to, but she quite liked it now. 'People change, Dee.'

Dee looked at her intently. 'You read the books he recommends; go to restaurants that he chooses. Hell, you don't even want to cut your hair because he likes it long.'

Shelley put a hand to her head. 'I don't think—'

Dee sensed she was hitting home and interrupted her. 'How many times have you looked at pictures in magazines of women with cropped hair and said how good you think they look? But you won't change yours, will you? It's still halfway down your back like it was when you were eighteen. Why is that?'

Where was all this coming from? The burning was quite intense now. 'Those styles wouldn't suit me anyway. I don't have that kind of face. It's not because Greg tells me how to have my hair.' Of course, he hadn't. But he did tell her often how beautiful it was. How long hair was just more feminine.

Dee was just getting warmed up. 'And holidays. When we went interrailing, you made a long list of places you wanted to visit before you were thirty. How many of those have you been to?'

'That's not fair. You know how Greg feels about flying.'

'Yes. But there are trains, or cruises.'

'I get seasick, Dee. You know that too.'

'Or, and this is *really* controversial, you could go on your own or with me or another friend. Not that you have a huge number of those around these days.'

Shelley's throat was tight. 'Is this a complete character assassination? What have I done to upset you, Dee? Why are you attacking me like this?'

Dee crumpled. 'I'm not attacking you. I'm worried about you. I miss you. I never see you anymore. And you have… lost yourself.'

'I don't know what you are talking about. I'm absolutely fine.'

Dee looked her in the eye. 'Are you? Because I don't recognise you anymore. I don't know where my best friend is. I never see you. We never do the things together which we enjoyed. All I see is—'

Greg's voice called up the stairs again. 'Shelley! Dee! Mum's about to get the baked Alaska out of the oven, and if you're not at the table, she's going to go spare!'

The baked Alaska had been the usual triumph, but Shelley hadn't made eye contact with Dee for the rest of dinner.

When Shelley and Greg got in bed that night, he asked her about it and she told him what had been said.

'Wow. I wonder where that all came from.' He looked thoughtful. She loved the way he looked in bed: T-shirt, boxers and messy hair. 'It's not true, is it? I mean, what she's saying. It's utterly ridiculous, right?'

The burning sensation was back. 'Utterly ridiculous.'

'Good, because if I thought that I had done anything to make you give things up, I would feel… terrible. I mean, I love you the way you are, I really do.'

'I know.' She reached over to kiss him. But was the way she was her actual self? And if not, what was?

As he encircled her in his arms, she pushed Dee out of her mind. Right now, she wanted to lose herself in Greg and not think about the questions that Dee had put in her head. She closed her eyes as his hands stroked her back and— 'Hold on.'

Greg pulled his head back to look at her. 'What is it?'

'I've run out of the pill. I've been meaning to take my repeat prescription in and just haven't had time. I haven't taken it for the last two days.' Although they had a good sex life, she and Greg weren't an *every single night* couple. It hadn't been a huge priority.

Greg moaned. She could feel a pressure on her leg which suggested he was as keen to make love as she was.

They had always been sensible about birth control. Right from the first time they had slept together and they had used condoms. They had never been the type to throw caution to the wind. Weeks later, she would wonder to herself if she would have made her next statement if it hadn't been for the conversation she'd had with Dee. 'I'm sure it'll be fine. No one gets pregnant that easily, do they?'

But it turned out, some people did.

CHAPTER TWENTY-SIX

Lara

Lara hadn't needed to look in the mirror as she left the house this morning to see how washed-out she looked: Shelley's concerned face as she opened the door would have done it for her. Shelley stood back to let her in. 'Are you okay? Why don't we leave it today?'

It was like a hangover: her limbs were heavy, she felt tired in her bones. The mirror in Shelley's hallway showed puffy eyes and a pasty complexion. She tried to smile but she wasn't convincing anyone. 'I'm fine. Just didn't sleep well last night, that's all. It's getting to the stage where I can't move once I'm in bed. I normally sleep on my back, and that's out, so I have to wrap myself around a long maternity pillow to support my bump. Then I can't move. Then I need the toilet. Blah blah blah. Anyway, that's boring. We were going to start under the bed today. Let's get cracking.'

Getting cracking in Shelley's bedroom was the lifeline keeping her going this morning. Both she and Matt had realised the significance of today's date, as much as they tried not to. It was probably why her night in bed had been so restless. Even Matt had been tossing and turning, and he usually slept like a log. Breakfast this morning had been a subdued affair and he had asked her how she felt so many times that she'd wanted to scream. Today she was twenty-nine weeks plus one day pregnant, and it didn't need to be circled on the calendar for them to know what that meant.

It had been an absolute stroke of luck that Shelley had decided to take a random Monday off work today. Apparently, she had loads of holiday allowance left and they were pushing her to take some of it. However, she was definitely less keen than Lara to get started with the stuff under her bed. 'Shall I make us a cup of tea so you can have a sit-down first?'

Lara rubbed her stomach while she walked into the lounge; she felt so uncomfortable this morning too. 'That sounds like a stalling tactic to me. I'll have a glass of water. Then we need to get started.'

She sank into the sofa, closed her eyes and leaned back while Shelley got her water. It would take very little to just fall asleep right now. 'You're in the third trimester,' Matt had said this morning. 'You'll start feeling better soon, love.' She hadn't asked whether he meant physically or mentally. The first time she'd been pregnant, she'd subscribed to an email that gave her daily alerts about her baby's progress – *Your baby is the size of your fingernail* – but she hadn't done it this time. When she'd logged into her personal email account a week after the first miscarriage, it had been excruciating to see what her lost child might have been doing in its twelfth week.

Shelley brought her a glass of water and she sipped it slowly as Shelley watched her like a worried parent. 'I'm not sure we should do this today. You look beat.'

Lara shook her head. 'I need to do something. I'm going crackers next door and Matt keeps calling every hour to check in on me. I feel like a child. A very bored child.'

Shelley tilted her head to one side. 'Why don't you just turn your phone off and try and get some sleep?'

Lara gave a hollow laugh. 'Last time I did that, he left work and came home to check on me. No, it's easier to take the call and assure him that I've had a sit-down and eaten something.' She raised her water glass. 'Maybe we could text him a picture of me drinking this? Although not from your phone. I told him I was going to stay home and sleep today.'

Shelley folded her arms. 'Well, if Matt doesn't know you're here, I'm not really comfortable with getting you to work on my sorting out. Maybe he's right. Maybe you need to rest today.'

There was more to this than concern; Shelley was doing everything she could to stop Lara getting to the bedroom. What was she hiding up there? 'Don't you start mollycoddling me. What happened to *everything is going to be fine this time*?' Lara put her glass down on the coaster and shuffled forwards on the sofa, pressing her arms into the seat to push herself to standing. 'I'll have the rest of that later or it'll be Niagara Falls every half hour. Come on, let's make room for some more joy.'

Behind her, she heard Shelley take a deep breath before following her up the stairs.

The floor of the room was remarkably empty now. The carpet was almost new: they must have barely used this room before Greg had walked out. The two of them had done well in the last few sessions. All that was left to sort out were the smaller boxes under the bed. Shelley brought in some cushions from her bedroom and laid them against the wall on top of the mattress. 'You sit there. I'll pull the stuff out.'

The first couple of boxes were just full of papers, so Shelley pulled them out and then pushed them against the wall under the window. Then she seemed to be under the bed for a while, half her body shielded from view and her bottom sticking up in the air.

'Are you okay under there? You're not stuck, are you?'

Her voice was muffled. 'No. There's nothing left under here now.' Then there was a loud ringing sound against the metal bed frame which revealed the lie of her words.

'What was that?' Lara leaned forwards, trying to peep under the bed. *Oof.* That wasn't a good idea. Her head swam a little and she righted herself.

Shelley's voice was so uncharacteristically light, anyone could have detected that she was lying. 'Nothing, I've got everything out. I must have banged my arm on the leg of the bed.'

Banged her arm? That excuse might have worked if she had a robotic hand or something. It definitely wasn't going to fool a lawyer. Lara shook her head. 'Are you telling fibs? There's another box, isn't there?' She moved one of the cushions and leaned back so that she could peer down the gap between the mattress and the wall. 'I can see it. It's a pretty box. Why don't you want to look at that?'

Shelley backed out from under the bed and sat back on her heels. She was flushed, but was that a reflection of her mood or the exertion of pulling boxes from under the bed? She bit her lip. 'Not yet. I'm not ready.'

Shelley looked every inch the guilty suspect: not making eye contact, diverting attention away by opening a box of old bills and starting to sort through them. Lara opened her mouth to speak but was interrupted as her phone rang. Matt. Again.

She knew this day was as hard for him as it was for her. Worse probably. Because her only worry was the baby, whereas he was worried about Lara too. But it was difficult not to get irritated by having the same conversation on repeat. She picked up his call, mouthing, *Matt. Sorry*, at Shelley, who looked positively relieved at the interruption.

'Hi, Matt.'

'Hi. Are you feeling any better?'

'Yes, much,' she lied. 'I'm just next door with Shelley, and before you ask, no I'm not lifting anything. I'm just sitting on the bed chatting to her.'

Matt sounded suspicious. 'As long as you are. I know it's difficult Lara, but—'

'I really need to go, Matt. Shelley has just brought me in a drink.' She held up her crossed fingers at Shelley; it was only a white lie. And listening to Matt made her more anxious than she felt already. 'I promise to be good and I'll see you tonight. I love you.'

Matt sighed in defeat. 'I love you too, Lara. I really do.'

She clicked to end the call and sighed. She should be nicer to him. He'd been through a lot too.

Shelley reached over and squeezed her hand. 'It must have been so tough for you both. I understand now why he wants to check on you.' She seemed to hesitate before adding, 'You must feel a bit more confident now though? You're through the danger zone?'

Lara was so tired. She'd kept the details to herself because she wanted a normal friendship, someone who didn't know every little detail from her gynaecological past, someone who would see this pregnancy as something positive and possible: the way Lara wanted to see it. The way she wanted Matt to see it. But she hadn't expected to get so close to Shelley. It was time to tell the truth. 'When I told you about the miscarriages that time in the café, I didn't exactly finish the story. There was something more I was holding back.'

'Oh?' Shelley sat up straight, expectant. Hopefully she wouldn't be upset that Lara hadn't been ready to tell her everything.

Lara picked up a cushion and laid it on her lap, stroking the soft fabric, staring at it to avoid looking directly at Shelley. 'It was true that it took three miscarriages before anything was done. After the third one, the doctor referred me to a specialist unit for recurrent miscarriage. Matt and I both had blood tests for chromosomal abnormalities, and I had hormonal tests to check for polycystic ovaries. They checked my uterus shape, the strength of my cervix. Nothing explained why I couldn't hold onto my babies.'

Lara felt her chin wobble. It didn't matter how many times she talked about this; it did not get easier. Shelley reached out to her but Lara waved her away, put a hand to her mouth to steady her lips and then continued. 'Matt kept saying he thought it was stress, and the doctors agreed it might be a factor. My job was pretty full on and – like I said – it was difficult to keep leaving work to go for the appointments at the clinic. So, I gave up my job.'

When she glanced up at Shelley, she saw her face had paled. But she nodded supportively. 'I see.'

'It made sense. I could get to all the appointments, and if we got pregnant again, I'd be able to rest.' Lara wrapped her arms around herself. She felt cold. 'But being at home on my own all day brought its own problems.'

Days and days at home where the clock seemed to go backwards. When the whole day was a trial to be got through, fighting her mind not to wander into painful territory.

'Waiting for test results and appointments was excruciating. Almost physically painful at times. I know everyone says, "No news is good news," but it doesn't feel like that when you are waiting to know your fate. I've never been an anxious person. One of the reasons I was so good at my job was because I was able to be rational and dispassionate. But those few months, I couldn't stop my mind from spiralling towards the worst possible scenario. We would never have a baby. I had some incurable disease. Matt was going to leave me. It just went on and on and on. Round and round my brain like a catastrophe carousel.'

She smiled weakly, and this time Shelley reached out and squeezed her hand. 'Oh, Lara.'

Lara held up her other hand. 'It gets worse. I had two more miscarriages. The last one was late. Really late. I was twenty-nine weeks pregnant. Twenty nine weeks and one day.'

CHAPTER TWENTY-SEVEN

Lara

Shelley's hand covered her mouth; her eyes widened in shock. She didn't speak.

It was easier for Lara to speak if she didn't look at her. 'I was out at the supermarket when the contractions started. Well, it was just a backache to begin with and a feeling that something wasn't quite right. I can't really explain it, but I knew. I knew it was happening again.

'I left the basket where it was and called a cab, then called Matt to tell him to meet me at the hospital. He stayed on the phone to me while he ran to the station for a train. "We're twenty-nine weeks," he kept saying. "We're twenty-nine weeks. Babies survive at twenty-nine weeks." He repeated it over and over, being positive. He tried so hard.' Her voice cracked and she had to stop speaking.

Shelley held Lara's hands, her own face streaked with tears. 'Oh, Lara. I am so sorry. So, so sorry.'

Lara regained control of her voice. She needed to get this all out. To tell it all. No more secrets. 'By the time I got to the hospital, I was having contractions. They came on suddenly, sharply. Somewhere between the cab and the entrance to A&E, my waters broke.'

Her memory of those minutes was hazy. People came from everywhere, she was sitting in a wheelchair, she was on a bed with her feet in stirrups, there were people, strange people, talking to her about trying to slow things down or stop things? She really couldn't remember. She just remembered being in a sea of people and yet being so terribly, terribly alone. 'Matt got to the hospital as quickly as he possibly could but he couldn't get there in time. He didn't see our son born.'

Their son. A boy. 'He was so tiny, Shelley. So tiny and yet so perfect. They wrapped him up and I held him. Just me and him. A mother and her son. I wanted him so much. I don't even know how long it was until Matt got there. He came in and put his arms around us both. And we cried. Because he was gone already.'

It may as well have been yesterday; the pain was still so raw. Lara's shoulders jumped as the sobs wracked her body. She had tried so hard to be strong, to be positive, to stop thinking about the past and focus on the future. But she was tired, so tired. And scared. No, terrified. Absolutely terrified that it might happen again.

Shelley didn't speak, just waited for Lara to be ready to talk again. 'After we buried Aaron, our little boy, everything got so dark and I couldn't see my way out. I'd wanted a baby from the beginning, but it became almost an obsession to get pregnant. At the same time, I was terrified of getting pregnant because I couldn't see myself surviving another miscarriage. I actually felt like my heart was breaking.' One tear ran down Lara's cheek and dripped onto her stomach before she could catch it with her palm.

Shelley was crying openly too. Lara took a very deep breath and stared at the wall over Shelley's shoulder; maintaining eye contact was too hard. 'There was one particular afternoon. It was all too much. I was sore from an exploratory investigation, I was tired from being up in the night. I'd turned on the TV to drown out the mess that was in my head and there was that show *One Born Every Minute* on the TV. A teenager giving birth. She was seventeen. She hadn't even wanted to get pregnant. It had been an accident. An accident! And there I was... there I was...'

A sob from Lara's chest sounded loud in that small room. Shelley got up on her knees and put her arms around her new friend, held her close as they both cried. Lara's stomach between them the only difference.

Lara sniffed when they parted. 'Well, I flipped out. Smashed up the TV. Threw stuff around the living room. Then just sat in the middle of the mess and howled. When Matt got home, he was beside himself. He didn't know what to do.'

'He must have been so scared for you.'

'He was.' Lara nodded. 'I was so angry and I couldn't stay home and just wait to find out what was going on. It was killing me. Everything took so long. We talked about it that night. Matt wanted to stop trying for a baby, wanted to stop putting ourselves through it all. But I couldn't even think about giving up. I had this huge hole in my life, and if I couldn't fill it, it was going to swallow me whole. I wanted to pay privately to speed things up, and Matt said he'd do anything that would make me happy. That's the other reason we had to sell our house and downsize – we used every penny of our savings, plus a loan, to pay the medical bills.'

Shelley spoke quietly and gently. 'And you found out what was causing the miscarriages?'

Lara nodded. 'I have something called antiphospholipid syndrome – or, in layman's terms, sticky blood syndrome. Basically, my blood makes clots which prevent the placenta from working properly. I have to take blood thinners to prevent the clots, which would deprive the baby of oxygen and nutrients. Plus a load of other medication.'

Shelley nodded slowly as if trying to get her head around the information she was being given. She pressed her right palm to her heart as she continued to hold onto Lara's hand with her left. 'I can't even begin to understand how hard this has been for you.

Every day must be so frightening, living on hope that these blood thinners are doing their job. You are so brave.'

Lara looked down at her stomach and paused for a while, ran her free hand slowly across her bump. When she looked up, there were fresh tears in her eyes and her voice was thin. 'I'm not brave, Shelley. I'm terrified. I am twenty-nine weeks plus one day pregnant *today*. The exact same stage I was at when I lost Aaron. I know that Matt wants me to take it easy, but sitting next door on my own, staring at those walls. I just can't do it. It's driving me crazy. I need to stay busy.'

'I wish you'd told me. I would have supported you more. Looked after you.'

'You've helped me more than you can ever know. Sorting out this room with you, tidying, organising, talking through your memories, it's all given me something to focus on that's outside of me. Helping you has saved me.' Until she spoke those words, even Lara hadn't realised how true this was. It was amazing how close the two of them had got in this short space of time. She'd distanced herself from the friends she'd known longest and yet here was this woman next door who she barely knew and who had somehow – unknowingly – kept her afloat.

She wasn't prepared for Shelley's reaction though. Shelley put both hands to her face and breathed in deeply a few times. Then a sob escaped from between her fingers.

Lara reached out for her wrist. 'Shelley? What is it? What did I say wrong?'

Without answering, Shelley took her hands away from her face. She took another deep breath and reached under the bed, feeling around for a few moments and then pulling out the object that she had been so intent on hiding from Lara.

It was a wooden box, white with yellow and green flowers. Shelley ran a finger over the embossed lettering – *Memories* – pressed her lips tightly together and opened it.

There wasn't a great deal inside. A pregnancy test. A photograph of a smiling Shelley. And a tiny delicate baby blanket. Shelley pulled it out of the box and held it up to Lara. 'I wasn't honest with you either.'

CHAPTER TWENTY-EIGHT

Shelley

Before

Shelley had taken the pregnancy test with Dee. Mainly because she really didn't think she was pregnant but also because – if she was – she would need time to plan how to break it to Greg. When they had first decided to get married, he had told her that he didn't want kids. At the time, she hadn't really been too troubled about it, not even knowing if she would ever want children anyway.

When had it started? This gradual need that had built in her to have a child of her own? Maybe it was when Greg's friends had asked him to be a godfather to their son. Baby Seb was a tiny, screwed-up creature who had held a tiny fist around Shelley's finger and made tears leak from her eyes. Watching Greg hold him and smile down at him had shifted something deep within. She wanted a child.

Then Dee had got pregnant and the desire had turned up a notch. She'd tried a few times to broach the subject with Greg but it always got changed somehow. He'd make jokes about the people they knew who had children. How they were all skint and tired and never had time to themselves. How could she complain when he had always said that he didn't want to have children? He hadn't changed; she had.

They were at an age when all their friends seemed to be having children, and the desire had grown as she watched them with their babies and toddlers until it became a deep need within her. A physical need. It became difficult to see Dee and her husband getting excited about becoming parents without experiencing a tearing desire for her own child.

But she'd had to accept that Greg had not changed his mind. He did not want a child of his own. He did not want her child. They would never have a baby.

And then she had missed a period.

Her biggest fear when she had told him about the pregnancy was that he would suggest they didn't go through with it. But she needn't have worried. He had been shocked, of course, but his first question had been to ask her how she felt about it. When she had admitted – albeit tentatively – that she was happy, he had hugged her. 'Okay, then,' he'd said. 'Let's do this.'

Today was their twelve-week scan. Maybe Greg would be more enthusiastic once he saw the baby on the monitor? Her stomach flip-flopped at the thought of it. With no change to her stomach shape and a complete lack of morning sickness, she sometimes felt like she had made the pregnancy up. Seeing a baby on the screen was going to be surreal.

They'd got to the appointment really early and had sat in the waiting room with several other women. Some looked like Shelley – you'd barely know they were pregnant; others were much further along and were leaning back in the waiting-room chairs under the weight of their huge stomachs. Shelley couldn't wait to look like that. She had already stuck a pillow up her top several times to see what she might look like by month six or seven. It was silly, she knew.

She squeezed Greg's hand; he hated hospitals and had looked white all day. 'Okay?'

He smiled at her, lifted his arm and laid it across the back of her shoulders. 'Yes, fine. You?'

She couldn't hold back the smile that spread across her face. 'Yeah, all good.'

It would have been better if Greg wanted this child as much as she did, of course it would. But she'd been on lots of parenting forums online, and many of the women had said that their partners hadn't seemed enthusiastic until the baby arrived. It was different for men, she supposed. The baby wasn't a part of their body. When he or she arrived and there was a tiny little baby who looked just like Greg, how would he be able to stop himself from loving it? Her stomach fluttered at the thought of him holding their baby. Dee had reassured her several times – amidst squeals of excitement about them being new mums together – that it was all going to work out fine.

The gel they spread on her stomach was really cold. Lying on the bed with her trousers open and a blue paper towel tucked into the top of her knickers, she felt exposed and vulnerable. For the first time, she felt nervous. Would everything be okay with the baby? She reached for Greg's hand and squeezed it again. He was watching the sonographer.

'Okay then, let's have a look.' The sonographer turned the screen away from them and placed the scanner onto Shelley's stomach. 'Is this your first pregnancy?'

'Yes. First one.' From the look on Greg's face, it might be the only one. An observer would think she was being scanned for something horrible, not a new life.

'Okay. I'm just going to check over the baby and take some measurements. Bear with me for a few minutes.'

While the sonographer worked, the only noise was the click of her mouse. It was so quiet that Shelley could almost hear the pounding of her heart. What if there was no baby? She'd taken four pregnancy tests at home and they'd all been positive, but this was the moment she would get confirmation. The silence became unbearable. 'Is everything okay?'

'I just want to ask someone else to come in for a moment. Bear with me.' The sonographer flashed a brief smile and left.

Now Shelley's heart was in her ears. What was going on? She looked at Greg. If possible, he was even whiter than he'd been in the waiting room. 'Do you think this is normal?'

He put his other hand over the one he was holding and stroked it. 'It might just be a problem with the machine. Or maybe she's training, or—'

He was interrupted by the door opening. The original sonographer was accompanied by a younger woman in a different uniform. Was she a doctor?

'Good morning, Mrs Thomas. I'm Dr Lane. I just want to have a look at your scan if that's okay?'

Shelley nodded dumbly. Her mouth wouldn't open. Why was there a doctor here?

Dr Lane sat down on the stool beside her bed and squeezed more of the gel onto her stomach – *Sorry, this might be cold* – then stared intently at the screen, which was still turned away from Shelley's view. The sonographer stood behind her, looking over her shoulder. The scanner was pressed firmly onto her stomach and moved across. The doctor clicked off the monitor and turned to face her. 'I'm very sorry but I have some bad news. Would you like to sit up?'

The rest of what she said was a blur. *No growth… About ten weeks… Will need to perform a procedure…* Wind rushed in Shelley's ears and she grew hotter and hotter. The baby was dead. *Very common in the first trimester… doesn't indicate that you won't have other successful pregnancies… Take your time…* How had this happened? What had she done? *Just one of those things… It really is very common…* She felt sick. Was there a bowl? *I need to go now, but please take your time…*

The doctor left and the sonographer followed. 'I'll give you a few minutes alone.'

Greg slid his arms around her and held her tight. 'I'm sorry, love. I'm so sorry.'

He rubbed her back and kissed the top of her head, but she didn't move. He was probably expecting her to cry but nothing came. Her heart felt as if it was freezing, calcifying within her. She wanted to close her eyes and not wake up.

How could everything have changed so quickly? She pulled herself away from Greg's chest and looked at him. For a fleeting second, before he arranged his face into sympathy, he looked completely relieved.

Numb, she picked up her coat from the chair and followed him back to reception, where they made an appointment for her to come back the next day. A procedure that would clear away any trace that she had ever been pregnant. Wiping it away as if it had never existed.

It was 3 a.m. when she finally cried. Curled up in a ball on the bed in the spare room. Deep, thundering sobs that overtook her body.

Two weeks later, Greg told her he had booked himself in for a vasectomy. There would be no second baby.

CHAPTER TWENTY-NINE

Shelley

The miscarriage had happened over a year – and yet a whole lifetime – ago. As she recounted the events of that day, it was like telling herself the story too. Slowly unwrapping the memory like an unexploded device, waiting for the emotions to strike. How could she put into words how she had felt that day? And the days that followed. Disbelief? Fear? Pain? Anger?

Anger.

Even now, her jaw stiffened as she explained what had happened. 'Greg didn't want to take the risk that I would fall pregnant again. It had been an accident the first time but it was obviously not meant to be, and, according to him, we should go back to our original plan. He just wanted a relationship to be about two people. He didn't want a family. Never had. That's why it's so hard now…'

Lara looked as if she might be sick. 'Oh, Shelley. Would he not even discuss it? Did he not support you? I know how awful it is to lose a baby. Truly awful.'

It had been awful. It had. She'd thought it was the worst possible thing that could happen. She'd been wrong.

The blanket in her hands was so tiny. She rubbed at it with her thumb. 'I have no idea why I kept these things. It was stupid to buy them in the first place.' Her voice sounded so bitter. She attempted a weak smile at Lara, whose face was wet with fresh tears.

'No, it wasn't stupid. No more stupid than me buying a pram or a baby bath or any of those other things I bought the first time. You were excited. That's natural. You *should* be excited about having a baby. That's how it's supposed to be.'

A lump rose in Shelley's throat and she struggled to swallow it down. Greg hadn't been excited. Not at any point. She'd just fooled herself into thinking it would work out. 'But why did I keep them afterwards? I should have done exactly what you did and got rid of everything. Taken it to the charity shop or given it to someone else. Not just shoved it in here with the rest of the junk.'

When Shelley glanced up, Lara's eyes were full of pity. The same eyes she had seen over and over in the last year: she hadn't wanted to see them from her. She wanted Lara to be her friend because they enjoyed each other's company, not because she felt sorry for her.

Lara reached forwards and put a hand over Shelley's. Another familiar reaction. 'I can't believe that he wouldn't even discuss the possibility of another baby. Did you want to try again? Did he know that?'

God, this was hard. She shouldn't have started this; it was too painful, too difficult. How was she going to get this all out? *Breathe. Breathe.* 'Yes, he knew. When I found out that he had booked the vasectomy, I tried to persuade him out of it. It was so final. No chance for a change of heart.' She refolded the blanket and put it back into the box. 'But he knew *he* wouldn't have a change of heart.'

He had been very straight with her, very gentle. He was worried that it might happen again. He was convinced that the miscarriage had happened because of a heart defect – it didn't matter how many times she told him that miscarriages were common with a first pregnancy. He'd had a heart murmur as a baby, he'd told her for the first time. Nothing serious. An 'innocent murmur', the doctor had described it to his parents. But he had got it into his head that the baby might have had the same thing and they shouldn't risk passing it on.

'That's just an excuse!' she'd screamed at him; the first time in their marriage she had ever raised her voice. They weren't a couple who argued. Because, she now realised, she had never challenged him before; never pushed back; never demanded, asked, wanted anything. He had been the one with the ideas, the plans, the vision for their life together and she had just… gone along with it.

Lara rubbed at her forehead. 'But he knew that you wanted children? And still wouldn't discuss it? That's terrible, Shelley. So selfish.'

Shelley shook her head; it wasn't as simple as that. 'The way he saw it, he'd been honest from the beginning. Before we even got serious, he'd spoken about the fact he didn't want children. It was a deal-breaker for him. That's what he said. I made the choice. I chose him. I wanted him more than I wanted children. I was wrong to expect that he would change his mind because we'd had an accidental pregnancy.'

She'd rowed with Dee too. It had been irrational and unkind, but when Dee had even *suggested* speaking to Greg on her behalf, she'd practically roared at her, blamed her for putting the idea of a pregnancy into her head. It hadn't helped that Dee's stomach had been swelling with her own child. Shelley hadn't even wanted to look at her.

Lara blinked as if she was trying to process what Shelley was saying. 'I'm sorry, but… I can't… I mean, did you just give in? I understand that Greg didn't want children, but surely he could see how you might have changed your mind? I'm not saying that having children is the be all and end all for everyone, but…' She motioned to the box. 'It looks to me like you really wanted to be a mum.'

Shelley's hands trembled and she tightened them into fists, her heart beating right out of her chest. 'Maybe I had changed my mind. But he hadn't. I could rage all I wanted but he wasn't going to back down. Being a parent was a huge thing, he said. You couldn't just do it because someone else wanted you to. It wouldn't be fair on anyone.'

Lara opened her mouth. Closed it again. Shook her head. Shelley knew how she felt. Greg's explanations had been sound. No one should be forced into being a parent. But it hadn't stopped her trying to persuade him... until she realised that he really wasn't going to budge. He had been honest and clear and consistent in what he wanted. What else could she have done but accept it?

'I told myself that once everyone around us was through the baby stage, all our friends, it would be okay. I loved my husband. We had a good life. We enjoyed each other's company, had meals out and great holidays, and, like Greg said, we couldn't have had all that if we'd had kids. But now... now he's gone I don't have that either.'

Lara's face reddened. 'What an absolute bastard. I'm sorry, Shelley. I know he was your husband and I am trying not to be judgmental. But to make you sacrifice that and then to just abandon you anyway—'

'He didn't *make* me,' Shelley interrupted. Despite her anger with Greg, it wasn't fair to blame him for this, and she didn't want to give Lara the wrong impression of him. 'It was *my* choice.'

Lara's eyes glinted. 'Yes, but you made that choice thinking he would be there forever. That you were choosing a marriage over a baby. And then he *left* you. I'm sorry. I know you loved him, but I just can't believe anyone could be that cruel.'

Shelley swallowed. There was no getting away with it any longer. It was time to tell Lara the truth. She deserved the truth. 'You don't understand.'

Lara reached out and took her hand. 'I do understand. I do. Because I wanted a child so badly it almost killed me. I understand that longing. And he put you through that and then left you and I know that you are a good person but… Oh, don't cry… I'm sorry. I'm sorry.'

Tears threatened to choke her but Shelley had to explain. 'No. You *don't* understand. You can't understand because I haven't… because… because Greg didn't leave me like you think. He died, Lara. My husband died.'

CHAPTER THIRTY

Shelley

Before

Since the miscarriage, something had shifted between them. Anger and disbelief were unwanted guests in their house that they couldn't get rid of.

In the days after the scan, Shelley saw babies everywhere. On billboards and magazine covers, and in real life. It was as if she was conjuring them up from the depths of her mind, willing them into being.

It was absolute torture.

Once it was all over, Greg had been so kind, he really had. Telling her to stay in bed and rest after the D&C procedure which had left her sore and tender. It wasn't the pain that stayed with her; it was the emptiness.

How could she broach the subject with him? Surely most normal women would be in a period of mourning after something so terrible. Instead, she felt as if something had awoken in her. Something she couldn't ignore.

Initially, he had been gentle. 'You've been through a lot, Shel. And your hormones will probably be all over the place. It's not the time to be making big decisions.'

Maybe that was true. But this feeling was strong. She wanted a baby. She wanted to try again.

When he realised that she wasn't going to let it go, he had taken it more seriously. 'But I don't want a child. You know that. We talked about it before we got married. You were okay with that.'

He was right. He had made that clear to her at the beginning. He had done nothing wrong. But she hadn't known then. Hadn't known that she would want this someday. And want it so badly. For a week, she shouted and argued and cried and then… then she gave in. As he probably knew she would.

This morning, on the surface, all had been fine. He'd brought her tea in bed and kissed her goodbye as usual. She'd gone to work and was sifting through her paperwork when she felt Flora's hand on her arm.

'This call is for you. It's Greg's boss.'

That was strange. 'Put it through to my phone.'

The conversation with Greg's boss was brief. He'd collapsed at work. They'd called an ambulance and he was on his way to the hospital. Could she go straight there?

The shock must have been apparent on her face because Flora insisted on asking someone from the finance team to drive her to the hospital. When he dropped her off outside A&E, she stood in the busy reception area for a few moments, lost, unsure where to go. What should she do? Who could she ask? A receptionist smiled at her. 'Can I help?'

Once she'd stammered Greg's name, the receptionist looked him up on the computer then led Shelley to a small room, assuring her that someone would come and speak to her shortly. Greg was in resuscitation – she wasn't allowed in. They asked her if she wanted to call anyone to wait with her. She'd called her mum but the phone had gone to answer machine. Greg's parents were away visiting friends and she couldn't get hold of them either. It would have to be Dee.

Since Dee's pregnancy announcement, things had been weird between them. Greg had called Dee to tell her about Shelley's miscarriage, and Dee had wanted to come over, but Shelley had asked Greg to put her off. She hadn't wanted to see her. Luckily, right after it had happened, Dee and her husband had been about to fly out to Spain for two weeks: a last-minute holiday before she got too big to fly. They'd been back a few days now, but Shelley had managed to avoid her so far. There was no avoiding calling her now though. She found Dee's name on her mobile and pressed it with a shaky finger. Voicemail.

'Would you like a cup of tea?' A large woman with dark hair and some kind of uniform – Nurse? Orderly? Volunteer? – stood in front of her, her hands on her hips. Her face kind.

Shelley's throat was so tight, she wouldn't have been able to drink anything. 'No, thank you. I really need to see my husband. He was brought in by ambulance. Collapsed at work. I was told someone would come for me, take me to see him. Greg Thomas. Do you know if he is still in resuscitation? Do you know if he's okay?'

The woman looked at her. Just looked at her for a few moments. Saying nothing. 'I don't know, I'm afraid. I'm sure someone will be here shortly. I'll get you a cup of tea in the meantime and leave it on the table. You don't have to drink it but it'll be there if you change your mind.'

She bustled away and Shelley heard the clang of a metal trolley, followed by the scrape of a spoon in a china cup and the clatter of cutlery.

The woman reappeared. 'Here you go, love. I brought you a couple of biscuits too. Chocolate. Is there anyone you can call so you're not waiting here on your own?'

Why were they all obsessed with her calling someone? She didn't need anyone to wait with her. And why couldn't she see

Greg? Still, she tried Greg's parents again. And Dee. Still no
answer. This time she left a message.

A knock on the door and a doctor came in, followed by a nurse.
'Mrs Thomas? I'm Dr Winters.' He shook her hand. 'Is there
anyone on their way to be with you?' When she shook her head,
he glanced at the nurse and sat down. 'Your husband had a severe
heart attack at work. The ambulance crew worked hard to keep
him alive on the way here and there is a team trying to repair
the damage right now. We will keep you informed, but I have to
warn you, it's not looking very good. I really think you need to
have someone here with you. Can we call them for you?'

She shook her head again. 'I've left messages.'

The doctor nodded and left, promising to keep her updated.

Who knew how long she sat there watching the tea go cold?
It might have been five minutes or five hours. It was warm in
the room, really warm. But when she pressed her fingers to her
mouth they were ice-cold. What was taking so long?

Then it happened. She had been sitting still, hands back in her
lap, staring at the poster on the opposite door which explained
all the safeguarding measures that had been put in place in the
A&E department. It was the twelfth time she'd read it; anything
not to think.

How could she describe the feeling? It started with a warmth
on her chest and then she felt arms go around her back and a
pressure as if she was being held in an embrace. Three, four, five
seconds. Then it slipped away.

There was a knock on the door and the receptionist entered.
'Mrs Thomas? Your husband's sister has arrived. Is it okay to
show her in?'

Although she knew Dee was pregnant, it was still a shock seeing
a visible bump. The last time she'd seen her, Dee had begun to

thicken about the middle, but now there was no mistaking that there was a baby in there.

'Where is he? Why aren't they letting us go in?' Dee swept in with her usual energy and noise. 'Have they told you anything? Are you okay?' The legs of the plastic chair scraped along the floor as she moved it to sit closer to Shelley. She tried to take one of her hands but Shelley kept them clasped in her lap. Dee's questions hammered onto her head.

'Heart attack. They're working on him.'

'Oh my God. I came as soon as I got your voicemail. I'm sorry I missed your calls. I'd turned it onto silent mode for a midwife appointment and forgot to turn the ringer back on.'

Dee's face was stretched and white. It had been the right thing to call her, of course it had, but it was harder to have her here than be alone. She always wanted to be in charge of everything.

Shelley had wondered before now if Greg blamed Dee for Shelley's change of mind about becoming a mother. He had certainly not been in any rush to speak to her after she got back from her holiday.

Dee stood and started to pace the small room, her hands on her burgeoning stomach. 'What have they told you? Do you know exactly what they're doing?'

Shelley's hands gripped each other more tightly. Dee needed to stop talking. Why was she pacing like that? Why was she taking up so much space in the room? *Just focus on the poster. Don't look at her.*

She was in that position when the doctor and nurse knocked and entered again. The doctor looked relieved to see Dee. 'Oh, good. You have someone here now.'

Dee held out her hand to shake his. 'I'm Greg's sister. What's going on? Is he okay? Can we see him?'

Still with the questions. Shelley ignored her and looked at the doctor. 'I want to see my husband.'

The doctor motioned for Dee to sit down. He and the nurse took the two remaining chairs. He looked tired. They both did. 'Mrs Thomas, as I explained earlier, your husband had a severe heart attack this morning. We did all we could to repair the damage, but then he suffered a cardiac arrest. There was nothing we could do.'

She continued to stare at the doctor. What else was there? Where was Greg now? What did this mean?

Dee leaned forwards. 'So, what do we do now? Does he have to go on a register for a transplant? Is he on life support? What kind of condition is he in?'

Each question she asked burrowed into Shelley's skull. Ignoring Dee, she focused on the tired doctor. 'I need to see him.'

The doctor nodded. 'We will take you to see him in a moment. We're just moving him to the high-dependency unit, where you can stay as long as you like.' He glanced at Dee and then back to her. 'At the moment, he has machines keeping him breathing. We will send him for a scan shortly to confirm, but there appears to be no brain activity. I'm so sorry but he's not going to come back from this.'

Dee was up on her feet again. 'What do you mean? Why have you stopped? What have you done? There must be something else you can try!'

Shelley gripped the sides of the chair with her hands. She couldn't take these questions anymore. A scream tore from somewhere at the bottom of her stomach. 'He's dead! He's dead, Dee! Stop asking these fucking questions. Shut up! Shut up! Shut up!'

She went on, screaming and shouting at Dee. No idea what she was saying. They sedated her. An injection which felt as if someone had squeezed her head so tight that she couldn't escape. She was aware of everything going on around her. People speaking. Signing forms. More cups of tea arriving. But she couldn't feel it. Couldn't quite understand.

*

Once the scan was completed, they took her to Greg's bedside, but it wasn't him lying in the bed. It was a man who looked like him, but he was pale and grey and empty. So empty. She had told Dee to wait outside; she wanted to see him alone first without her noise and her tears and her interference.

A nurse spoke to her very quietly. 'It looks as if he is breathing, but that is the machine breathing for him. As the doctor explained, your husband is now classed as clinically brain-dead.'

She sat down on the chair they had placed beside the bed for her. Slipping her arm under his, she bent her head and laid her cheek across the back of his hand. Her voice was barely a whisper. 'Don't leave me, Greg. Please don't go.'

CHAPTER THIRTY-ONE

Shelley

Lara had her hand to her mouth. 'Oh, Shelley. Why didn't you tell me all this? You said he left you.'

A wave of tiredness swept over Shelley. She pressed her fingers into her temples. 'It was just easier. And in a way, he did. That's how it felt.'

Since Greg's death, everyone had treated her as if she were an invalid. Talking to her in hushed tones. Offering platitudes about life. Either that or they crossed the road to avoid speaking to her altogether. Lara hadn't known anything about Greg that first time and she had wanted to just be Shelley. Not Shelley the Widow.

Of course, she felt guilty. Lara had been so good to her these last few weeks. Especially recently, when she'd been so open about her own pain and grief. All this time Shelley had been hiding this huge secret. She owed Lara an explanation.

'Greg's death was a shock. The murmur he'd had as a child turned out not to be as insignificant as they'd believed. He was here one day and then he wasn't.'

She paused for a moment. Even basic details were painful to remember. It was impossible to say these words aloud without feeling each one of them. Lara didn't interrupt her; her face showed she knew how difficult this must be. *Just keep going.*

'Anyway. For a little while after he died there were people around all the time. All. The. Time. My mum stayed for a week. His work colleagues all came to see me. Even people we barely knew came to pay their respects. It was kind but also too much at once. Overwhelming. I couldn't understand what I was supposed to do. How I was supposed to act. People were in my house but I wasn't the host, I was… well, in the beginning I was somewhere else entirely most of the time. I'd been given sedatives by the hospital and then my doctor prescribed antidepressants and everything was blurry at the edges for a while. Still, there was so much emotion around me and it was stifling; I just wanted everyone to go away. To leave me alone.'

Lara nodded slowly. 'People don't know what to do for the best, do they? Or even what they should say.'

Shelley interlaced her fingers on her lap to stop them trembling. 'What *can* they say? When an old person dies, you can at least talk about the long and happy life they had. But a thirty-eight-year-old man? What can you say about his death?'

Lara put a hand to her own chest. 'Oh, Shelley. I'm so sorry.'

Shelley needed to keep talking, get the whole thing out before the tears overwhelmed her and she couldn't speak. 'I overheard someone at the funeral say, "At least they don't have children." Can you believe that? Why would you say that? I mean, I'm sure they meant it would be difficult for children to lose their father. But what about me? How am I supposed to get through this on my own?'

She paused again, her chest felt so tight, but she wanted to get it all out. 'I read some forums online. For widows, I mean. Lots of them said the same thing: "It's the kids who are getting me through." I get it. When you have children, they are your reason to keep going. You have to keep going. You have to be there for them and that gets you through. But when you don't… What's going to pull me through, Lara? From the age of eighteen, whenever something bad has happened, whenever I am upset, whenever I have a decision to make, it's Greg that I turn to. But he's not here. He's not here.'

Shelley's voice got louder and louder, the rage lying dormant in the pit of her belly caught fire and words she hadn't even said to herself came tumbling out of her mouth. 'I did everything his way – the food he liked, the clothes he liked, the holidays, the jewellery – everything. Dee told me I was doing it and I said she was crazy, but it was absolutely true. I never minded, I didn't even notice it, but I let him have his way on everything. And then the one thing I wanted, the one thing, was a baby and he wouldn't even think about it. It wasn't up for discussion and I was so angry, so very angry.' Her whole body was trembling but she hadn't finished. 'I know I said I'd accepted it but I hadn't, not properly. And I don't think I'd realised that until he'd gone and I didn't have the chance to ever ask him about it again. It was too late. Too late.'

The force of her final words made her bend over and her shoulders shook as her whole body gave in to the sobs as they came. This was why she didn't let them out; once she started, she couldn't stop. She felt Lara's arm across her shoulders, Lara's face resting on the top of her head.

Once she could breathe freely again, Shelley sat up and brushed the tears from her cheeks with the palms of her hands. She attempted a smile. 'This is why I don't like telling people.'

Lara had tears running down her own cheeks. 'I understand that one. I really do. And I feel terrible that I didn't work it out. When did it happen?'

Shelley sat back with a sigh. 'A year ago. I was telling the truth about that. After the first couple of months or so, my doctor started encouraging me to come off the antidepressants. It wasn't a long-term solution, he said. I went back to work towards the end of the third month. Everyone told me not to. Said it was too soon. I needed time to heal. But I knew that I wasn't going to heal. How could I? Everything about me was so entwined in everything that was him. If I was going to have to learn to live without him, I might as well get on with it and start this new life on my own.' She wiped at her eyes. 'Actually, work was my respite. Flora, especially. When I was at work, I was busy and useful and I could pretend that nothing had changed.'

Lara turned her face upwards. 'Which is why this company takeover has been so difficult.'

Shelley nodded. 'Exactly. And why I haven't been able to make a decision about applying for a new job in the new company. That office has been my safe place. It was here in my own home that I found it difficult to be. A few months before you moved in, I took everything from the house that reminded me of Greg and I put it into this room. I couldn't look at any of it anymore. It hurt too much. I knew I needed to get rid of it but I couldn't do that yet either. It was easier to lock it away for now, deal with it when I was stronger.'

Lara screwed up her face. 'And then I blundered in and tried to make you get rid of all your precious memories. I can't believe how awful—'

Shelley shook her head. 'Stop. Please. It was a relief to be with someone who didn't know I was a widow. Who didn't treat me with kid gloves or whisper at me or apologise when they said something that they thought might upset me. It's been nice to be normal with someone again.'

Lara covered her face with her hands. 'I can't believe I even tried to persuade you to pass on your wedding dress to that girl at the charity shop.' Her face was red when she took her hands away again.

Shelley reached out and took her hand. 'Honestly, please don't apologise. You have been a lifeline these last few weeks. Without you, I would have been sitting on that sofa downstairs, staring at the TV and trying to summon up the energy to put a frozen lasagne in the microwave. You've been good for me. Really good for me.'

Her voice cracked as she spoke. The truth of her words bounced back at her. It *had* been wonderful to spend time with someone who saw her as a single entity, and not just the remaining half of a broken whole. It was a relief to tell Lara the truth, but it was like tearing a mask from her face, leaving herself raw and exposed. Would this change things between them? Would Lara become a fountain of sympathy? Because she really didn't need – or want – that right now. She just wanted a friend.

She needn't have worried. Lara took a tissue from the box, blew her nose loudly and wiped the tears from her eyes. 'Okay. No more sympathy for either of us. We are mates now and we are going to get through your stuff and my stuff together. My new house, your new job and anything else life decides to throw at us. And after I have had this baby, we are going to go out for a full-on girls' night together.'

Shelley smiled. 'Sounds good to me.'

Lara threw the tissue in the bin. 'In the meantime, as someone who took up residence in a very dark tunnel for a while, we need to do what the book says. Both of us. Start making way for joy.'

CHAPTER THIRTY-TWO

Lara

Cooking Matt's favourite dinner was a sure sign that Lara was about to ask him for something. Tonight, as she pummelled the steaks with the tenderiser, she mentally rehearsed what she wanted to say.

However she phrased it, it mustn't sound like criticism. Matt had been a life raft for her these last two years. There was no doubt that without his calm, solid hold on her, she would have gone under. He had lost their babies too, and yet his first thought and concern had always been for her.

The last time had been the worst. They had cradled baby Aaron for a long time. If anything, it had been more painful when Matt had held him. He'd been so impossibly tiny in Matt's large, capable hands.

When Matt got in from work, she told him to take a shower while she finished preparing dinner: he liked his steak pretty rare, but even the well-done version she would have to have wouldn't take long.

Once they were sitting down to eat, she poured him a glass of red wine and told him about Shelley's revelation this afternoon.

Matt's eyes nearly bulged out of his head. 'Wow. Poor Shelley. That must have been a shock when she told you.'

Lara sipped at her sparkling water. 'I'm glad she felt able to tell me, to be honest. So, I was honest with her. About everything.'

Matt lowered his eyes, spent longer than necessary sawing a tiny slice of steak. 'That's good.'

Lara put down her knife and fork. She wanted to say this right. 'It did feel good. A relief. And it made me realise that we haven't been able to be honest recently, have we?'

'I don't know what you mean.' Matt still wasn't meeting her eye. All the proof she needed for what she was about to say.

'This baby, Matt. You don't think it's going to happen, do you? That's why you won't feel him move or talk about him or make any plans.'

Matt didn't move for a few moments. Was he deciding whether to tell her the truth? Much as she wanted honesty, if he was to tell her now that he didn't think this baby would make it either, it might be more than she could bear.

When he did speak, his voice was very quiet. 'It was so hard, Lara.'

Her throat tightened. 'I know, babe. It *was* hard. For both of us.'

He leaned forwards, placed his hand over hers. 'I don't know what was more difficult for me. Losing the baby or seeing you in so much pain and not being able to help. When you've got a problem, I like fixing it for you, making it better. But I couldn't fix that. I couldn't make it better.'

Lara squeezed her fist, encased in Matt's hand, wanting to throw her arms around him but knowing how important it was for her to say all that she wanted to say. 'You couldn't fix it because it had already happened. It was over. But we can try again. We are trying again. And I need you to believe it can work this time. We need to hope for this baby and believe he or she can make it. Because whatever has happened in the past, we need to give this baby the best chance.'

Matt's eyes filled. 'I can't pretend it didn't happen, Lara. I can't just clear everything away and act like those babies didn't exist.'

Lara froze as if he'd struck her. Is that what he thought? That she wanted to forget them? Something broke away in her chest and a moan grazed her throat. 'I'll never forget them. I'll never forget my babies. How could you even think that I wanted to forget them?'

'Hey, hey, don't get yourself worked up.' Matt looked genuinely frightened. 'I know that you haven't forgotten them, but the book, the decluttering – I just thought you didn't want me to talk about them, to be reminded.'

'Reminded?' Lara knew her voice was getting louder, but she couldn't hold it down. 'Every time this baby moves, I am reminded. Every time the midwife listens to the heartbeat. Every scan, every blood test…' She couldn't speak anymore. Having taken her hand away from the table, both fists were now clenched in her lap as she rocked backwards and forwards.

Matt pulled his chair until they were sitting beside each other, and he held her close as she cried, his own tears falling into her hair. 'Shush, honey. Shush. It's okay. It's okay.'

Once the storm had subsided, he pulled away and held her arms as he looked her in the eye. 'Wait there. I want to show you something.'

His feet on the stairs thudded away. How come they had never spoken like this? They'd always been tight and had been through so much together. Clearly they had hidden a lot too. Trying to spare one another, they had allowed a distance to grow. She was fearful of what he might be about to show her. What other secrets had been hidden?

She soon found out. The kitchen door creaked as he pushed it open. In his hands was a shoebox from a pair of his running shoes. He didn't normally keep the boxes. He only ever had one pair of shoes for running, which he would wear until they were beyond useable and then throw them away and buy replacements. How long had he had this box, and where had it been hidden?

Matt sat next to her so that their knees were touching. He took a deep breath and lifted the lid from the box. It took every ounce of self-control she possessed not to lean forwards and look in.

'So.' Matt put his hand inside the box, rested it there and took a deep breath. 'I'm not showing you these to upset you. I just need you to understand.'

'I understand. I know you would never hurt me.' She spoke the truth, but her heart thumped. What was he about to show her?

Matt's hand came out of the box closed. He turned his fist over and opened it. In the middle of his palm was a tiny hospital identity bracelet. Aaron's identity bracelet.

There were other mementos. A Babygro, which had to be from the first pregnancy. A hand-knitted blanket that a stillbirth charity had given them at the hospital for Aaron. And, lastly, a photograph of their tiny, beautiful boy.

Lara groaned again. It came from somewhere so deep within her chest that she could feel it. She could barely form the words she wanted to say. 'I knew we hadn't got rid of it but I didn't know where it was. I was so scared that I'd thrown it away by accident that I couldn't ask.'

Matt nodded. 'When you were... recovering, I hid it away. You couldn't cope with it. I knew. I understood. It was too painful. So, I kept it safe. With the other things. I knew someday that you might want to see them.'

Lara could barely speak. She stroked the photograph of her beautiful boy. Her Aaron. 'I do.' Her voice was barely a whisper. 'I do want to see him.'

Matt reached out for her other hand. 'And I want to see this baby, Lara. Oh God, I want to see this baby so much. But I'm scared. And not just about losing the baby. I'm even more scared of what another loss would do to you. To us.'

Lara nodded, tears dripped from her face. 'I know, but we have to take that chance. We have to hope.'

Matt breathed in deeply. 'We have to accept what happened too. We can't pretend this is a clean slate.'

'Yes. Yes, we do. But we need to make way for this baby. We need to open ourselves up and hope that we get to keep this one.'

Matt's eyes filled again. 'Okay. Yes. I can do that.' He looked down at her stomach and gently placed his hand onto it. For a few moments, they sat in silence. Then Matt spoke.

'Hey, baby.' He gulped. 'Daddy's waiting to meet you.'

CHAPTER THIRTY-THREE

Shelley

The Garden of Remembrance was empty. If you didn't know better, you could imagine you were in a really well-kept park. Bright bedding plants and shrubs had been thoughtfully arranged to provide private areas for grieving relatives. Remembrance plaques were the only indication of the purpose of the place. That and the multitude of benches positioned at tactful intervals.

It was strange being back here and taking it all in. The last time Shelley had been here, the surroundings had been a blur of hugs and handshakes and empty words of consolation. Not empty. That wasn't fair. The words were well meant; it was the hole inside of her that had been too cavernous to fill.

She found a bench underneath a tree and sat, not even sure why she was here. All she knew was that, after opening up to Lara, the one thing she really needed to do was talk to Greg.

She looked around again. Yes, she was still on her own. Would this have felt less strange if she had a headstone to talk to? A small plot to tend? She took a deep breath.

'I've come to talk to you, Greg.'

Why had she said his name? Surely if he could hear her, he would know that she was talking to him. And if he couldn't, then she was wasting her time anyway. She took another deep breath. *Stop overthinking it.*

'I'm sorry that I haven't come before. It was difficult, I…'

For God's sake, this was stupid. Why had she thought that this was a good idea? She closed her eyes. What did she want to say?

'I'm not doing this right.' Her throat constricted again. She closed her eyes and let the tightness pass. 'I don't even know how to do it. How to be a… a widow. I don't feel like a widow, I just don't feel like anything.'

She swallowed. It was painful over the lump in her throat. 'The thing is… it was a shock. It was sudden. And I didn't really take it in. That you were gone. Dee and your parents sorted everything out. The funeral, the paperwork for the bank, the endless forms that had to be filled in.'

Dee had been amazing. Who knew how it would all have happened if she hadn't been there? So why had Shelley been avoiding her ever since the funeral? Because it was painful?

Another deep breath.

'After the numbness wore off, and all the drugs they gave me at the hospital, I got angry. Really angry and I didn't know what to do with it. I wanted to shout at you. But you can't, can you? You can't shout at someone who has died because that would make you a really bad person. Especially if it was someone you loved.' Her voice croaked and she brought her fingers to her lips to steady them.

'So, I shouted at Dee instead. I yelled at her. Told her it was her fault that all this happened. That it was because of the baby and that I had only wanted to have the baby because of her. And I told her that I didn't want to see her because she reminded me of you but that wasn't the reason. I just couldn't bear to see her bump. Her baby bump.' She put her hands up to her face in shame. 'I can't believe how horrible I am.'

She sat there for a while. A bird called above her head and the wind whispered through a tree off to the right. Otherwise, there was total silence. She took a deep breath and sat up again.

'I've made a new friend. Ironically, she's pregnant, but she's been good for me. I've told her about you. We've talked about the last few months, the feeling sad and lonely and… angry.' She paused. How could she explain the anger? The feeling that he'd abandoned her? It wasn't logical; she knew he hadn't chosen to go but that was exactly how it felt.

At the back of the bench was a brass plaque: FOR GLADYS FROM ARTHUR. ALL MY LOVE ALWAYS. Maybe she should have a plaque engraved for Greg? Maybe that would make this all seem more real. Because it wasn't. A year on and she was still expecting him to appear from somewhere. That there had been an awful mistake.

'The thing is, I've got used to the fact you're not here. I had to. Going to work, getting the shopping, cooking for one – it's become normal. But I can't think about you *never* coming back. You were always there in my life. Always steady. Always kind and good and funny and I don't know how to be if you're not here.'

Her nose started to run and she rummaged in her bag for a tissue. She blew her nose loudly. The loud trumpet call that used to make him laugh. *How can such a big sound come from such a small nose?*

She pressed her lips together. 'Dee was right, you know. I did change. I changed the music I listened to and the books I read and even the colour paint I liked on the walls. It wasn't your fault. You didn't make me. I don't even think you were aware that I did it. For God's sake, even *I* wasn't aware that I was doing it.'

It was true. At no point did she decide that she was going to put his wants and desires before her own. It hadn't been like that.

'It didn't feel like I was making sacrifices. I *wanted* to like the things you liked. You knew so much more than I did about everything – wine, restaurants, music – and I was happy to learn. We were a team, right? A couple. A perfect fit. But then there was something I *did* want. Something I wanted very much.'

The sodden tissue was no match for the tears that came now. There was still no one in the garden but she had gone past the point of caring even if there was. 'I was so angry about the baby, Greg. I know this is crazy but it felt like I'd asked you for one thing in all our marriage and I was being punished for it. Losing a baby wasn't bad enough – I had to lose you, too? All the feelings got mixed up and it was just too much to bear. I pushed it down and shut the door and tried everything I could not to have to face it.'

She leaned forwards so that her elbows were on her knees and her face was in her palms, and she let the grief roll over her in waves. The anger, the pain, the disappointment. Over it rolled. She let all the feelings come, one after the other, her chest battered by them like a small boat in an angry ocean.

Eventually, the tempest calmed and she righted herself. It was a relief to let these feelings loose but the pain in her chest was still there. Greg was still gone. She was still alone. This was supposed to be cathartic; it was supposed to help her process her feelings, but there was no joy that could replace the loss of the most important person she had ever known.

Back in their religious studies class, she and Dee had been horrified when their mild-mannered teacher had explained the ancient Hindu custom of *suttee* where a widow would throw herself onto the funeral pyre of her husband. Right now, she felt she could understand how that might come about. It was exhausting and horrible and terrifying to think about living without him. Actual living, not the existing she had been doing.

Would it have been easier if they had had a child? That's what people said, wasn't it? What the women on the widow forums kept saying to each other: *You have to keep going for the children.* But if you don't have a child, then you have to keep going on your own. You do have to keep going though. Somehow, you have to.

'I know now that I have to face it. I have to start accepting that you're gone. I don't have a choice, do I? About living again, I mean. About finding out who I am without you. I need to make a start. Make some decisions for myself.'

Like the new job that Steve wanted her to apply for. She couldn't look to Greg for help anymore; only she could decide whether she wanted to go to the interview or not. Although at least she did have a friend who could help now. She'd call Lara as soon as she got home.

CHAPTER THIRTY-FOUR

Shelley

Maybe it was the gentleness, or the warmth, or the fact it was a long time since Shelley had been touched, but tears threatened at the backs of her eyes. She closed them firmly and tried to concentrate on something else. 'That's it,' said the girl. 'Just relax.'

It had been Lara's idea to have her hair restyled. It felt like such a cliché, but Lara had insisted that a new haircut might give her the confidence she needed to go for this new job. She hadn't had her hair cut since the funeral – it had felt like too much effort – and she was nervous about having anything too drastic.

Under normal conditions, it would have been nice to relax into the head massage, but things like this were fraught with danger for her; the unguarded moments were the most difficult. Times when something made her relax or smile or forget were actually cruel, because when she remembered again, grief punched her twice as hard.

As if she needed further punishment, 'Creep' by Radiohead started to play on the radio: one of Greg's favourites. Sitting with her head laid back on the basin, throat stretched, Shelley couldn't breathe. Her chest began to tighten and her lungs wouldn't expand. She couldn't just sit here listening to this. She couldn't.

'That's it, you're all washed and ready.'

Thank God. She sat up as Marie wrapped a thick towel around her head. *Just don't listen to the song.* 'Thank you,' she just about managed to croak through her tight throat.

'You're welcome. Would you like something to drink? Tea? Coffee? Glass of wine?'

A wine would definitely help. She tried not to drink during the day but this was an emergency. 'White wine would be great if you have one.'

'I'll pop you back over with your friend and I'll bring one over. Edward will be with you shortly.'

Lara put down the magazine she was reading and smiled as Shelley sat down next to her on the sofa. 'Did you get the head massage? Isn't it fabulous?' She tilted her head. 'Are you okay?'

Shelley waved a hand around in the air which was full of strident guitar chords. 'This song. Greg's favourite.' Her lips started to tremble. *Must not cry.*

'Oh, Shelley, I'm sorry – shall I ask them to change it?'

Shelley shook her head. The song was nearly finished anyway and she didn't want to make a fuss. She just wanted to get her hair cut and get out of here. 'No, just talk to me. At me. Whatever, just talk about anything.'

Lara sprang into action. She flipped open one of the magazines which she had marked by putting another inside it. 'Okay. Let's talk hair. I saw this and think it would look fabulous on you. What do you think?'

It's hard to think when you are trying to stop your ears from hearing, your eyes from leaking and your brain from remembering. Which picture was Lara even referring to? That one? 'It's quite short.'

Lara looked at it and shrugged. 'Not terribly. It's not shaved or anything. It's chic. And you have a great shape face to carry it off.'

Shelley put a hand to her jaw. Did she? It felt more angular than it had ever been. Like her bones were emerging. 'I don't know. It seems a bit dramatic.'

Lara raised an eyebrow. 'It's up to you, obviously, but I thought you wanted a change.'

Dee's comments about the length of her hair came to mind. That she had only kept it long because Greg liked it that way. 'You're right, I do. Maybe we can take it over with us and ask your hairdresser if he can do that but a longer version.'

Lara folded her arms. 'Do you mean just a trim of what you already have?'

Shelley could see her point. 'Am I being a coward?'

'A little bit. But I can forgive you. In the circumstances. Oh, look. There's Edward over there.' She pointed in the direction of a tall, thin man with a shaved head and a tattoo of a pair of scissors on his neck.

Was that trendy looking man the one who was going to cut her hair? This was beginning to feel like a terrible idea. Her fear must have shown on her face because Lara nudged her. 'It'll be fine. Honestly.'

Lara must wonder if she'd ever had her hair cut before. 'Sorry. I know it'll be fine. Thanks. For booking the appointment, I mean. And for coming with me to hold my hand.'

'Don't thank me. I'm enjoying myself. It's been a while since I've had a girly day out like this.' Lara leaned back in her seat and folded her arms over her bump; it had really grown this week. 'The women I used to go out with – shopping, drinks, pamper days – have all got young children now and it was just… difficult for me. And for them, I think.'

There was no need for any further explanation. 'Yeah, I think I pushed a lot of people away. And there were others who just kind of disappeared.'

Lara looked interested. 'Like who?'

Shelley could remember one in particular. 'There was one called Emily, a good friend of mine. Of Greg's and mine.' Saying his name out loud was still not easy. 'We used to go out for dinner with her and her husband sometimes.'

'So, why don't you want to see her?'

Shelley took a deep breath. 'She hasn't been in touch once since Greg… since he died. Actually, that's not true. She sent a card about a week after – *sorry for your loss, let us know if you need anything* – but nothing since.'

Lara frowned. 'Did they not come to the funeral?'

Shelley shook her head. 'Nope. I sent an email to everyone we knew saying that all were welcome, and her husband replied with apologies that they couldn't make it. Which is understandable, I mean, not everyone can get a day off work in the middle of the week.'

'I'm getting the feeling that there's more.'

Shelley nodded. 'About a month after the funeral, I was walking along the high street and I saw her coming towards me. I know that she saw me too. But just as I was about to put up a hand to wave, she crossed over the road and then started walking back in the opposite direction.'

Lara opened her mouth to speak and then closed it again. She screwed up her nose. 'I don't know what to say.'

'That's probably how she felt. Difference is, she didn't even try.'

Marie appeared with their drinks and showed them over to the stylist's chair. Moments later, the tall thin man with the scissors tattoo swept into their space. 'Good afternoon, ladies! Lara! So lovely to see you! You are positively blooming!'

Lara smiled. 'I know that means fat. Just say it.'

'Not at all. Your skin is radiant.' He turned to look at Shelley. 'Hi. I'm Edward. Sorry to keep you waiting, it's a really busy afternoon. Lara said that you are looking for a new style?'

That sounded scary. 'Uh, yes. Well, just a nice cut, really. I've had my hair like this for a long time. Lara thinks a change will do me good.'

Edward moved her chair so that he was standing behind her and they were both looking in the mirror. He started to pull on the strands of hair either side of her head. It was surprisingly long. 'So, you must have been growing your hair for a while. How brave are you willing to be?'

Lara held out the magazine. 'We liked this one.'

Shelley still wasn't sure. 'Maybe a longer version of it though.'

Edward shook his head. 'I think you'd need to have it short at the back, but we can maybe keep some of the length at the front. Will you trust me?'

He looked at her reflection intently. What could she say? His scissors and comb were poised like weapons. Lara was nodding at her. There was no way out. 'Okay.'

Edward spun her chair around to face him. 'You can't look until it's done.'

As his scissors flew over her scalp, Edward chatted to her and Lara. Well, more to Lara, really. Shelley seemed to have lost the use of her voice. Thankfully, the music had changed to something that she didn't recognise, but telling Lara about Emily had made her consider how few people she talked to these days. Apart from Lara, there was her mum, Flora and, strangely, Steve. When had her other friends given up on her and trickled away?

'Are you okay under there?' Edward leaned down towards her with an overly bright smile. 'You're awfully quiet.'

'I'm fine, thanks, just listening to you both.' There seemed to be an awful lot of hair on her gown and around her feet. 'It's not going to be too short, is it?'

'Wait and see.' Edward winked, clearly the kind of man used to getting his own way with women.

She tried to catch Lara's eye, but Lara was watching Edward's hands fly around Shelley's head and sipping her orange juice. Shelley took another gulp of her wine.

After about three weeks, no one had come. Well, her mother had been there, obviously, and Dee had tried, but Shelley hadn't wanted to see her. They hadn't spent time alone together since the pregnancy announcement when Dee had been so unpleasant, and then on the day Greg had died. She knew she would speak to her again, just not yet. As for everyone else, they must have returned to their normal lives. Towards the end of the third month, after a particularly terrible week in which she hadn't got out of her pyjamas until her mother had come to see her mid-afternoon, she had decided to return to work.

Another big chunk of hair fell onto her lap. Her heart sank with it. What was she going to look like?

Finally, the cutting was over and Edward picked up a hairdryer the size of a bazooka. Its volume was mercifully loud enough to make it impossible to hear what he and Lara were saying.

Her head was getting hotter and hotter. Should she mention it? Just as she opened her mouth to say something, he shut it off. Three more flicks of the comb and she was done.

Lara clapped her hands. 'You look amazing!'

Edward smiled at her. 'Ready?'

He spun the chair around and she saw his reflection beaming back at her from the top of the mirror. Below his face was a very sharp bob. She turned her head left, then right. Yes, it was definitely her underneath that. She put a hand to the back of her neck and swept it upwards until it made contact with her hair. She felt bare. Even her face seemed to have changed. This wasn't what she'd expected. Greg had loved her hair. Had told her many times how beautiful it was. And now it was gone. The very hair he had threaded through his fingers was on the floor around her feet.

Lara was of the opinion it suited her at least. 'You look fantastic, Shelley. Every inch the professional woman – perfect for the interview. What do *you* think?'

She couldn't think. The noise in her head was back. She wanted to get out of there.

'I love it. Thank you,' she lied.

CHAPTER THIRTY-FIVE

Lara

Shelley looked very different. Younger. Lighter, even. Her face had been opening up over the last few weeks and she had lost the dark, hooded look from when they'd first met. And the new hairstyle really did suit her.

But when she came over to Lara's house on Monday evening – Matt was going to be late again – Shelley didn't look so sure. As she walked through to the lounge, she kept touching the back of her head as if feeling for her missing hair. As soon as they sat down, she turned to Lara. 'I know I said I loved my new hair, but I don't. I absolutely hate it.'

Oh no. Was this Lara's fault? She was the one who'd recommended the hairdresser. The one who'd encouraged Shelley to be brave. 'But it looks really great on you. Maybe it'll take a bit of getting used to.'

Shelley shook her head. 'Nope. I might get over the shock of it, but I shouldn't have had it done. I should have said what I wanted.'

She did blame Lara. What could she say? 'I'm sorry, Shelley. I really am. I thought…' She tailed off as Shelley lifted a hand to stop her.

'You don't need to apologise. I should have spoken up. I don't blame you; I blame me.' Shelley sighed and collapsed back into the sofa. 'Why can't I make a decision for myself, Lara? What's wrong with me?'

So, Shelley wasn't angry with her? That was a relief. 'You need to give yourself a break. Old habits die hard. You'll get there.'

'Thanks.' Shelley smiled. 'How are *you* feeling, anyway?'

'Fine. I'm absolutely fine.' Now that Lara was sure Shelley wasn't about to yell at her, she sat down at the other end of the sofa. 'Matt and I are in a much better place since the talk, but I still couldn't persuade him to go out with his friends unless I promised I would have someone over to "keep me company".' She made inverted commas in the air with her fingers. 'Which is why I asked you over to babysit me.'

'Well, as we can't have alcohol, I brought some elderflower pressé which we can pretend is Prosecco.' Shelley slid a dark green bottle onto the table.

That was kind of her. 'Thanks, but you can have a proper drink if you want one.'

Shelley pretended to be shocked and shook her head. 'I take my babysitting duties very seriously.'

Lara laughed. Since Shelley had begun to defrost, she really was quite funny. 'I'll just go and get some glasses.'

Despite protesting to Matt that she was more than happy to spend the evening alone, it was nice to have Shelley here. Lack of alcohol aside, it felt like the kind of evening she might have had with a girlfriend in the old days before life got complicated. She was still thinking about this when she walked back into the lounge. There was something that had been itching at her since Shelley's haircut. 'I've been thinking about that woman you talked about in the hair salon – the one who didn't come to Greg's funeral.'

The pressé fizzed as Shelley filled their glasses. 'Emily?'

'Yes. Did she really cross the road when she saw you coming?' Imagining this had twisted something inside Lara; what a horrible thing to happen to her friend.

Shelley passed one of the glasses over. 'Yep. And she's not the only one. I'm sure they think they've got away with it. A quick glance in my direction and then suddenly they are staring into the middle distance, intent on getting somewhere, anywhere that is not facing up to me.'

'It made me think because,' Lara twisted the glass in her hands, 'because the same sort of thing happened to me. Not that anyone crossed over the road but they did kind of ignore me.'

Shelley tilted her head. 'Go on.'

'When I had the first miscarriage, not many people knew about it. But the second time, we made it past the twelve-week stage and we thought we were safe. I mean, we didn't take out a full-page ad in the local paper or anything, but we did tell our friends. And then, when we lost the baby, there were some people who just… I don't know, just kind of disappeared from our lives.'

Natalie had been one of those people. She'd sent a card, saying how sorry she was. Then a text to say she was 'there if you need me', and she had even popped round one evening with flowers. But Lara knew she'd had a group of mutual friends over for the evening more than once and not invited her. It had hurt.

Shelley was nodding. 'I think we bring the party down. Seeing us makes them realise how quickly things can change. It makes them uncomfortable.'

'Do you think that's what it is?' Lara hadn't made much effort to see Natalie either; too weighed down by sadness to pick up the phone and organise anything. But she'd needed company. Sitting in a room of women chatting about anything other than the thoughts circling her mind would have done her a world of good. 'I used to think it was because they wanted to talk about their children and they felt like they couldn't do that around me.'

Shelley shrugged. 'It could have been that too.' She sipped at her drink. 'For the first couple of months after Greg… after the funeral, I didn't want to see anyone really. Then, when I was ready, there was no one around. It was as if the world had moved on and I was still here. Stuck.'

'Yes. That's exactly how I felt. Everyone else was having children and meeting at baby clubs or soft play centres and I didn't fit into that world. It was like this great new club they'd all joined and I'd been refused membership.' Lara paused. Maybe Shelley had felt like that after her miscarriage too. She didn't want to rub salt in the wound.

But Shelley was nodding again. 'For me, I used to be in a club. The cosy married couples club. Then I wasn't a couple anymore. I was just a single and it felt like I was an inconvenience, someone that needed to be accommodated somehow.'

'Like an odd shoe?' That's how Lara had described it to Matt when she'd told him how upset she was about it.

'Yes. Exactly like an odd shoe.' Shelley smiled. 'Size six.'

'Me too!' Lara leaned forwards and clinked her glass onto Shelley's. She looked her in the eye. 'I'm glad we moved next to you. We've spoken in a way I haven't spoken to any other friends.'

Shelley looked uncomfortable. 'I still feel guilty that I lied to you. About Greg, I mean. That I let you think that he'd left me. And I've been feeling guilty about the things I've told you about him too.'

That was strange. She'd done nothing wrong as far as Lara could tell. 'What do you mean?'

Shelley put her drink down, turned to face Lara as if she'd been planning this speech for a while. 'I was so angry with him. About the baby. It wasn't his fault. He hadn't changed; I had. But I hated *him* for it.' When Shelley looked up, her bottom lip quivered and she bit down to keep it still, closing her eyes for a few moments. 'All the stories I've told you, my memories. They've been tainted by how angry I've felt. I was so mad at him for saying no to trying again for a baby and then, when he… when he *died*, I just got angrier.'

When she opened her eyes, they were so full of pain it almost hurt Lara to look at her. 'It's normal to feel angry when you've been bereaved. And you hadn't long lost your baby either.' If anyone knew how angry that injustice could make a person, Lara did.

Shelley hadn't finished. 'But it coloured every memory I had. I couldn't think of anything he'd said and done without blaming him somehow. The trouble is, when someone dies, everyone starts talking about them as if they were a saint. *He was so kind. So generous. So perfect.* But he wasn't. He was bossy and he liked things to be done his way and he thought he knew best about everything. When people – some of whom he hadn't seen in years – kept saying these things to me at the funeral, I just wanted to scream at them, *No, he bloody well wasn't!* Shelley's eyes flashed in anger and then seemed to burn themselves out. 'But I don't want you to think he was a bad husband, because he was a lovely husband in so many ways. Like leaving little messages in the cutlery drawer for me to find after he went to work. Or if he saw something funny when he was out, he would take a picture and send it to me. And I only had to mention that I wanted a new hairdryer or mobile or other random thing and he would be online researching it for me and finding what was best. He liked to look after me and I didn't ever tell him that I wanted otherwise.' She sighed. 'I guess what I'm saying is, he wasn't perfect, but he definitely wasn't the complete control freak I've made him out to be. And I did love him and I do miss him so very much. I don't even know who I am or what I am supposed to be without him here.'

The tears in Shelley's eyes spilled down her cheeks and Lara reached out for her hand. 'Oh, Shelley, of course you miss him.' She pushed a box of tissues across the table and Shelley ripped two from the top, wiped at her eyes roughly and blew her nose. Her hands were trembling. Lara gave her a few moments to compose herself before speaking. 'Like I said, anger is a common part of grief; there's no reason to feel guilty about it. And as for not knowing who you are? You need to give yourself some time.'

Shelley nodded; she was folding a tissue over and over. 'I was reading the joy book last night in bed. The chapter about your emotions: *In order to heal, you have to feel.*'

Lara remembered that one well. It had been a difficult lesson and, going by her conversation with Matt the other night, one she was still learning. 'What did you think of that idea?'

'Initially I hated it – I nearly threw the book across the room.' Shelley wiped at her nose again. 'But it's true, isn't it? I've been doing the opposite. Shoving everything of Greg's into that room. Trying not to remember. Or feel. Or think. And now…' She gulped down a sob. 'Now I am feeling *everything*. Anger. Shame. Guilt. Fear. They're coming at me like missiles and I just can't cope.'

Lara knew how that felt. To be assailed on every side and want to barricade yourself in. To hide away. But hiding was a dark place and she didn't want Shelley to spiral down into that pit. 'And love?' she said softly. 'What about love?'

Shelley moaned, tears falling freely. 'That's the most painful one of all,' she whispered. 'Oh, Lara. I loved him so much.'

Lara put a hand on Shelley's back and Shelley leaned inwards so that her head was on Lara's shoulder, and she sobbed. It was all Lara could do not to join in with her. The pain in her cries was so raw. Her grief so fresh. An observer might guess that her husband had died yesterday rather than a year ago. But grief doesn't have an expiry date. Had Shelley had *anyone* to hold her like this as she cried? Lara was so grateful for Matt; she couldn't have got through her loss without him by her side. But Shelley had been all alone.

As Shelley's cries calmed, she righted herself, not able to look Lara in the eye. 'I'm sorry. I just haven't had anyone to… to say all that to.'

Lara shook her head. 'Don't apologise. It must be so hard when the one person you're closest to is the one person you can't talk to. You can talk to me anytime, though.'

'Thanks.'

Something else occurred to Lara. Could she suggest it to Shelley? Or was it overstepping the mark? She had to try. 'Look, you can tell me to mind my own business if you want, but have you thought about getting in touch with Dee?'

Shelley looked a little guarded. 'I have thought about it, yes. But I'm not sure I can do it. It feels too hard.'

The rest of the evening was quiet but pleasant. They watched *The Wedding Date* on Netflix, ate the snacks that Matt had bought for them before he went out and progressed from the elderflower pressé to cups of tea. Before Shelley left, she followed Lara to the kitchen carrying the tray with the snack bowls, mugs and wine glasses. After laying it down on the counter, she turned to look at Lara. 'I'm really sorry about getting so upset and offloading all that onto you earlier. It must be the haircut. Maybe I'm like Samson – all my strength was in my hair.'

Lara nudged her. 'I hope that doesn't make me Delilah. Wasn't she a right cow? Anyway, that's what friends are for.' She paused. 'You've come a long way in the last few weeks, Shelley. You should give yourself some credit. And you've had a lot to think about with your job and everything too. Have you made a decision about that?'

Shelley shook her head. 'What do *you* think I should do?'

Was it because she was so used to pleasing Greg, or had Shelley always been this indecisive? Lara held up a hand. 'Oh, no you don't. I learned my lesson from the haircut. You need to do what you *want* to do. There is no *should*.' She had been thinking about Shelley and this promotion. It sounded like Greg had had a really good job, so wouldn't there be a chance Shelley had been left quite comfortably off? 'Also, I don't want to be insensitive, but I've had to deal with quite a few wills in my time. Do you *need* a job? Financially, I mean. When your company is taken over, do you need to go straight into another job?'

Shelley looked as if she was considering this for the first time. 'Well, I do need to get a job, but, no, I suppose it's not super urgent. I mean, Greg was very good with life insurances and things, so the mortgage has been paid in full. And we have savings…' She looked at Lara. 'You don't think I should go for the promotion, do you?'

Lara wanted to shake her. 'I'm not saying that. What *I* think is immaterial. What is it that *you* want to do?' When Shelley didn't answer, she continued. 'Do you even know for sure what the new job entails? Why don't you book a meeting with your manager and ask him? At least then you can make an informed decision.'

Shelley nodded. She didn't look certain but she nodded. 'Okay. I'll speak to him in the morning.'

CHAPTER THIRTY-SIX

Shelley

The passenger door of Steve's BMW 6 Series made an expensive thud as she closed it. When Shelley had called to ask him about the job, he'd insisted she join him for lunch to talk it through and her attempt to use an urgent visa application as an excuse had failed because Flora had offered to do it. Traitor.

However, Flora had immediately made it back into her good books by telling her how great she was looking. It wasn't just her outward appearance that had improved. On the inside too, she felt better than she had in months. The box room was nearly clear, she'd been back to Lara's gym to enrol as a member and was even getting used to her new, shorter hair. The promotion – and what to do about it – was the logical next piece of the puzzle. So why was she feeling so apprehensive?

There was nowhere decent to eat on the industrial estate where the office was situated, so Steve had driven ten minutes down the road to a pub, only a couple of miles from Shelley's house. Though it was surprisingly busy for a Wednesday lunchtime, they managed to get a table in the corner. Steve took off his jacket and draped it over the back of his chair, making it difficult not to notice through his shirt sleeves how toned his arms were. God, it was so strange being here with another man. When were these butterflies in her stomach going to stop? *It's just business.*

'I don't know what you fancy but their sandwiches are really good.' Steve squeezed himself in opposite and handed over a menu. She stared at it. Nothing appealed. Was it because the table between them was so small that this felt more intimate than it should?

Steve didn't seem to have the same problem deciding. 'Ham hock baguette for me. I'll go and get us a drink while you're looking. What would you like?'

Now they were in the pub together, her nerves were almost strangling her. 'I'll have a… erm… a…'

Steve smiled; his face kind. 'Wine? Coke? Water?'

She let out a long breath. 'A sparkling water would be great.'

While he was gone, she tried to compose herself. There was no need to be so anxious. This was just a lunch with her boss to talk about a possible new role. Lara had worked on her CV for her – deleting about thirty superlatives that Flora had added – but she still hadn't sent in her application. Indecisiveness had been permeating her life. What to wear. What to watch. Even what to eat for lunch. What had Lara said? *Just find out more.*

So, when Steve got back with the drinks, she put the menu down and got straight to business. 'I'm not sure that this job is right for me.'

Steven was mid gulp from what looked like a pint of shandy and he coughed in surprise at her directness. 'What is it you're not sure about?'

He was looking at her so intently that her stomach flipped over. 'I don't know. It's just a big change from what I've been doing. I know what I'm doing at the moment and I like that it's a small office; we all work well together here. A move to a huge company in town is just so… different.'

He looked ready for that argument. 'But different can be good.'

Different had not been working out tremendously well for her. 'Yes… I know…'

'You don't sound certain.'

How could she tell him without getting into a deep and meaningful explanation? 'It's just more change. And I'm not sure this is a good time for me.'

Steve took a deep breath and sat up as if he was about to deliver a prepared speech. 'Look, I know it's really soon for you to be making a decision like this. Ideally you wouldn't have to. But the company has been sold. So, I'm assuming it's either this or look for a whole new job altogether. At least you know our company. You know how the systems work. Surely going somewhere new would be a lot more difficult?'

She'd considered this too. 'Maybe.'

Steve started to get into his pitch. 'And it's not that you have to start work there for a while yet. We will wind down this office over the next three months. Your move to London can be as gradual as you want it to be.'

He was being so kind. She knew that. 'I haven't had a long commute into London since I was a student.'

'Well, that's something you'll just get used to again, I reckon. You never know, you might even like being in London. There's a lot more life up there than there is around here, that's for sure.'

Steve froze with his pint halfway to his mouth. She waited for what she knew was coming. 'I am so sorry. That was completely tactless of me. I didn't mean—'

She held up a hand to cut him off. 'Please. Don't apologise. I didn't take it that way at all.' This was what happened. People panicked every time they used the word 'life' or 'death' around her. It's what she had tried to explain to Lara. Why she hadn't told her from the beginning about Greg. She just wanted to be treated normally.

Steve still looked mortified. 'I know, but...'

'Please. You're right. There would be a lot more for me up there, it's just... I'm not sure I can cope with starting anything new right now. It's only been a year.'

Steve gulped a couple more mouthfuls of shandy. 'I understand that, I do. And I don't want to pressure you *at all*.' He emphasised the last two words. 'It's just such a great opportunity and I know that you'd be perfect for it. Look, let's order some food and we can talk through the practicalities of the role, and you can tell me which parts you're not sure about.'

Shelley still wasn't hungry but didn't want to make him think she wasn't eating because she was upset with his 'life' comment. 'A cheese sandwich would be great. Thanks.'

'Coming right up. Do you want another drink?'

'I'm fine.'

While he was at the bar, Shelley flicked through her phone. There was a message from her mum, checking in, and one from Flora:

Make sure you order something expensive!!!

Flora could always make her smile; Shelley really wouldn't have got through this last year without her. Or without this job. Maybe moving over to the new company, and taking the management role, would be a good idea; Steve certainly thought she was up to it which made her feel good. Being here with him – now that she'd got over the initial panic – was also more pleasant than she'd anticipated. He was easy company, no wonder he had so much luck meeting women.

'Hello, Shelley. Fancy seeing you here.'

Shelley jumped in surprise. Rachel, the wife of one of Greg's colleagues, was standing over her. They also lived around here and used to go out with them and a few of the other couples from the company. She had a vague memory of them being at the funeral but hadn't heard from them since. With Steve at the bar, this was definitely not great timing. Did she look as guilty as she felt? *Play it cool.* 'Oh, hi, Rachel. Just popped in for some lunch. How are you?'

'I'm fine.' Rachel put her head to one side. 'How are *you*? We were so sorry about Greg. So young. It must be so terrible for you.'

Shelley took a deep breath. 'I'm fine, thank you. It hasn't been easy. But I am getting there.'

She wasn't getting there at all. But the last thing she wanted to do was discuss it in public with a woman she barely knew. People fell into two categories: they either pretended that they hadn't seen her or they engaged her in lengthy, painful conversation.

'Really? Are you? Because you look terribly pale. And you've lost weight. You look positively gaunt.'

Shelley almost laughed: was this supposed to make her feel better? 'Oh, well, I guess there is an upside to loss then.'

Rachel shook her head slowly. 'So brave.'

Steve came back over and slid a bottle of water onto the table. 'I know you said you didn't need another drink but I thought I'd get us some water.'

Rachel's eyes nearly popped out of her head. Why did he have to say *us*? Now she would definitely think they were on a date. 'This is my *boss*, Steve.'

Rachel nodded hello but she didn't look convinced. It probably didn't help that Steve had loosened his tie. 'Okay, well, I'll let you get on with it.' She looked from Steve to Shelley and backed away to her table on the other side of the bar.

If Steve had noticed a change in atmosphere, he didn't show it. 'Okay. So. What is it about the job itself that most worries you?'

From the other side of the bar, Rachel was watching them, while talking to a friend. Shelley could feel her face getting warm. What was Rachel telling that woman? *Just keep going, get it over with.* 'Oh, er, I guess it's mainly the commute that is a concern. Getting stuck on a train on the way home. Being in a packed carriage.'

Steve considered this for a moment. 'Yes, I think that can be a pain. But I reckon you'd get used to it. A lot of people read or watch a film on their phone. What else?'

Rachel glanced over again. Did she assume that something was going on with Shelley and Steve? Why was it so damn hot in here? 'Running a team of people. They won't know me from Adam. What if they don't like the way I do things?'

Steve shrugged. 'I can't guarantee they'll all be like Flora. But you'll be the manager. They'll have to do things your way. Anyhow, you've been the supervisor of your team, so you've already managed members of staff without any issues.'

Rachel glanced again. Shelley was sure she could see her mouth the words, *So soon.*

Now Steve was looking at her with concern in his eyes. 'Are you okay, Shelley? I don't want to pressure you over this, I really don't. This is supposed to be a good thing. I'm looking out for you.'

He leaned forwards and put a hand on hers. She drew it back as if scalded. What if Rachel saw that? *He's just being nice.* 'Sorry, sorry.'

'No, I'm sorry. I shouldn't have touched you. I was just trying…'

This was excruciating. The back of her neck was damp with sweat. 'I know, I'm sorry. I'm just not really with it today.'

Before he could say anything else, Steve's phone rang and he glanced at the number. 'Sorry, I have to take this.' He shifted his knees from under the table. 'Hi, it's Steve.'

While he was speaking, Shelley tried to take another surreptitious look in Rachel's direction. Maybe she was just being paranoid. Maybe they weren't talking about her at all. She'd told Rachel that Steve was her boss. There was nothing suspicious about that. But what would she think if she had seen him touch her hand? Why had she come for lunch with him at all? It wasn't as if they were friends. They could have discussed this at the office. What had she been thinking accepting his offer of lunch? *Idiot.*

Steve was waving his mobile at her. 'Bad reception. I'm going to need to take this outside. I can't really understand what she's saying. I won't be long.'

Shelley poured some of the water after all, hoping it might help to shift this huge lump in her throat. As she poured, she glanced up and caught Rachel watching Steve go. When she noticed Shelley watching her, Rachel gave a little wave, her face a picture of suspicion. She *did* think something was going on between them.

From nowhere, a flash of anger burned in Shelley's chest. This wasn't a date but, even if it was, what business was it of Rachel's? Did she have any clue how it felt to come home every night to an empty house? An empty bed? To want more than anything to feel a strong pair of arms around her and be told everything was all right? Tears pricked the back of Shelley's eyes. She squeezed her hands together. *Don't cry in here. Don't.*

Steve slid back into his seat. 'Sorry. All sorted. I've tried to tell them not to call all the time but there seems to be something every ten minutes.'

'Them?' The injustice of Rachel's eyes bearing down on the two of them from across the bar had sparked something in Shelley that needed to be earthed. She turned on Steve. 'Maybe they wouldn't be calling you so often if you weren't three-timing them.'

Steve looked confused. 'Sorry?'

That innocent face wasn't going to wash either. 'Your girl-friends. They probably feel insecure. That's why you're getting calls every five minutes.'

He raised his eyebrows. 'My girlfr—' A light went on in his eyes and a smile started to spread across his face. 'They aren't calls from girlfriends. Crikey. Chance would be a fine thing. They're my mum's carers.'

Shelley froze; the heat of anger gone. 'Pardon?'

'My mum has dementia. I am caring for her at my house until I can find her a home that she likes. She has to have round-the-clock care because of her habit of escaping and getting lost. But the agency keeps changing the carers, which is why I get so many calls. Mum gets shirty with them and won't let them wash her or anything, and they have to call me so that I can speak to her and persuade her to let them touch her.'

She was the worst person in the world. 'I'm so sorry. I didn't realise.'

He waved her apology away. 'Please. It doesn't matter. I'm actually quite flattered you thought I could date three women at once. Truth be told, I haven't been out in months. That's why I was so keen to have this meeting at a pub. It's a lot easier to get out in the afternoon than in the evening.'

Now she felt even worse. She wasn't the only one who had been living the life of a hermit. 'I am sorry, though. It must be tough.'

'It has been. But I have a place for her in a home from next week, so life should get a lot easier. Just need to swallow down the guilt and then I'll be right as rain.' He laughed it off but she could tell he meant it.

'I'm sure it's not easy to make that decision but it sounds like it's the best thing for your mum if she needs constant care. And you are entitled to a life too, you know.' As she said the words, Shelley realised how much they could apply to her too. She'd spent the last year in suspended animation. It was time to do something different.

Steve took a swig of his beer. 'Thanks. I appreciate it. Anyway, where were we?'

It's your decision. 'I'll do it. I'll apply for the job.'

Steve coughed mid-gulp of beer. 'Really? What happened? What changed your mind?'

How could she explain it to him when she still didn't really understand it herself? Something had shifted in the last few days and she was ready to take a chance. 'It doesn't matter. I'll email my completed application form as soon as I get back.'

This might turn out to be the worst snap decision she'd ever made, but at least it was a decision. And she had been the one to make it.

CHAPTER THIRTY-SEVEN

Lara

'Have you heard of Suited and Booted?'

Lara had found them online, a charity that helped unemployed men in need of financial and practical support to find work. As well as cash, they took donations of good-quality suits and professional clothing: the perfect place for Shelley to donate some of Greg's designer clothes. Lara had been tentative about proposing it to her, but she had looked almost relieved at the suggestion. It was time to move them out.

Remembering how aggressively Shelley had thrown the clothes into the wardrobe the first time they'd been in that room together, Lara knew they should take it slowly today. She knew how she'd feel if they were baby clothes. Not that they'd bought any baby clothes for Baby Aaron; they'd learned their lesson the first time. So, when Shelley offered her a drink, Lara didn't accuse her of delaying tactics like she had in the past; she just accepted.

'I was so jealous of this kitchen when I first came in here, you know.' It felt a lot longer ago than six weeks. The Shelley of that day seemed a complete stranger compared to the woman in front of her. 'I was so miserable to be moving into our house. We'd worked so hard to get our old house exactly how we wanted it and I couldn't bear to leave.'

Shelley leaned against the counter, sipping her coffee. 'You weren't jealous of the mess in my box room though, were you?'

Lara smiled. 'No, I wasn't. And I think I still have the bump on my head.' She screwed up her nose and pretended to rub an imaginary injury.

'Good job I didn't know you were a solicitor that day. I would have panicked that you were going to sue me.'

Their relationship had become so easy in the last few weeks. Shelley was her friend. It felt good. 'How did the meeting with your boss go today?'

Shelley sipped at her coffee again. 'He explained the role and it all sounded straightforward and doable. He thinks I would be ideal for it, so I agreed to apply for the job.'

Her face didn't match this positive news so Lara wasn't sure how best to react. 'That's good. Isn't it?'

Shelley pulled at her ear lobe. 'I think so? It's still a bit scary, but I finished the application form at work this afternoon and sent it off before I could change my mind again. We'll see what happens. I've got the next two days off, anyway, HR have been nagging me again to use my holiday entitlement. They've got some sort of staff wellness drive.'

Lara wanted to make her feel more upbeat, especially as they were about to go through Greg's clothes. 'Well, why don't we go for a shopping trip tomorrow to buy you an interview suit? That way, even if you decide not to take the job, at least you got a new outfit out of it.'

Shelley wrinkled her nose. 'I'd love to, but my mum is coming up to spend the day with me tomorrow. I haven't seen her in weeks so I can't put her off.'

She seemed genuinely disappointed. It would be nice to have a shopping trip together. 'No problem. What about Friday?'

Shelley smiled. 'It's a deal. And while we're on the subject of suits, shall we get this over with?'

*

When Shelley slid the wardrobe door open, Greg's clothes came tumbling out of the section she'd stuffed them into. For a few moments, she stood there looking at them. Lara needed to say something to break the tension in the air. But what could she say? These clothes belonged to the husband Shelley had lost forever. What words could make this easier?

Shelley lowered herself down onto her knees. She started to pick up shirts: a blue one, a pink pinstriped one, a white one which still had cufflinks attached. She held them up to her face and breathed deeply. 'Calvin Klein. I'm not sure if I can actually smell it or if my mind is just adding it in.'

Scent and memory were so closely linked. The smell of hospital disinfectant was enough to make Lara feel physically sick. She could imagine the churning in Shelley's stomach right now. 'Greg was obviously a well-dressed man.'

Shelley rolled her eyes. 'He loved clothes. Much more than I ever have. That's why these suits are in such great condition. Some of them were only worn a handful of times.'

Lara picked up a pair of trousers which had come loose from their hanger and started to fold them. 'That will make them perfect to donate to Suited and Booted. Any man in one of these will have a head start on a new job, I reckon.' She wanted Shelley to feel positive about this. She wasn't clearing out Greg's suits; she was giving other men an opportunity.

Shelley nodded her agreement and found hangers for the shirts in the pile. 'Greg donated some of his organs, you know.' She spoke in a matter-of-fact tone but didn't look at Lara.

What was the correct response? 'That's very generous.'

Shelley nodded again. 'I had to sign the release papers or whatever you call them, but I knew it was what he wanted. The nurses were very kind. When they took him away...' She paused, breathed in and out a few times. 'When they took him away they said it was done just like an operation on a living person. That he was doing something amazing.'

Lara's heart was hurting; she reached out to comfort her but Shelley shook her head and kept folding. Lara understood: she didn't want sympathy right now. Instead, she started on the polo shirts: Hugo Boss, Ralph Lauren – there was a small fortune in menswear in the pile. 'Do they tell you who gets them?'

Shelley stood to lay some suits on the bed. She had her back to Lara. 'They gave me some information but I couldn't read it. I put it away.'

It must have been so hard to make the decision about organ donation when she was at her weakest point. But what a wonderful thing to do – literally saving the lives of others. Maybe it would bring Shelley some comfort. Would it help to see it now, a year later? 'Have you…'

Shelley turned to look at her. 'You're going to suggest we look at it, aren't you?'

'Only if you want to.'

Shelley didn't answer but turned towards the box of papers excavated from under the bed which was still in the corner of the room. While Shelley leafed through it, Lara tried to suck in the tears that were threatening her own eyes. She was here to be strong for Shelley, and that meant not letting her own feelings get the better of her. Shelley pulled out an official-looking envelope. 'They sent this through a few weeks after Greg died. My mum opened it for me and tried to get me to read it, but I couldn't. She said it might help but it just made it all seem so… real. So final.'

Sitting beside Lara on the floor, she stared at the envelope for a few moments. Then she opened it, slipped out the folded letter, hand trembling and shaking the paper. The anxiety creeping over her was palpable. How could Lara make it easier for her? 'Do you want me to hold your hand?'

Shelley turned, her face close enough for Lara to see the sadness in her eyes and hear her when she whispered, 'Yes, please.'

Shelley unfolded the letter and then Lara gripped her hand tightly as Shelley read aloud. 'Dear Mrs Thomas. On behalf of Surrey Transplant Services, we would like to offer our condolences on the recent loss of your husband, Greg Thomas.'

A large tear fell onto the page. Shelley wiped her cheek with the back of the hand that was holding the letter; Lara squeezed her other hand even tighter.

Her voice wobbled as she continued to read. 'We hope that you can take consolation in the knowledge that five people are alive today because of his gift of life.

'Because of your generous agreement to donate on Greg's behalf, one person with lung failure received a double lung transplant, one—' She coughed out a sob and held the letter out to Lara. 'I can't. Please. Can you?'

Lara didn't know if she could trust her own voice but she had to. She had suggested Shelley do this and she couldn't let her down now. She took the letter, not letting go of Shelley's hand. 'One person with failing sight received a cornea transplant, two people with kidney failure received kidney transplants and one person with diabetes received a pancreas transplant.' She had to pause and regain her breath before reading the final paragraph. 'We understand the great loss to you and your family. We are truly grateful for his donation and can only hope that the knowledge that he has helped others regain their health will bring some comfort in your time of grief.' She passed the letter back to Shelley.

'Thank you.'

Lara squeezed her hand. 'You did a wonderful thing. Greg did a wonderful thing.'

Shelley nodded. 'He was always a very generous man. I know I've made it sound like he took over my life, but he was very kind.

Very generous.' She looked around at his clothes on the floor. 'He would be glad we're doing this.'

It had been easy to think of Greg as being controlling or bossy. But Lara could see how much Shelley had loved him. 'He sounds like a good man.'

'He was. Just like Matt. He wanted to look after me, I suppose.'

Lara was struggling with that right now. 'Even when you didn't want to be looked after?'

Shelley smiled. 'Even then. Is Matt still driving you crazy?'

It felt selfish to be talking about her own husband after the letter they'd just read, but maybe Shelley needed to think about something else for a minute or two. 'After our conversation about Aaron, things were better. But he's back to being a bit claustrophobic. I'm hardly getting out of the house, he calls me ten times a day, I don't see anyone all day long. If I didn't have you, I'm not sure I wouldn't be throwing things at the TV again.'

Shelley put the letter back into its envelope but kept hold of it. 'Well, let's get you out somewhere for the day, then. Suit shopping on Friday is a date.'

'That would be great.' Lara followed Shelley when she stood up. As she did, there was a twinge across the underside of her stomach. It was probably because she'd been sitting awkwardly on the floor, but she'd get the baby heartbeat app out when she got home, just to reassure herself.

CHAPTER THIRTY-EIGHT

Shelley

Every time her mum came to visit from Kent – where she now lived with a lovely man who she'd met online not long after Shelley's wedding – she would insist on going to the supermarket so that she could return home satisfied that Shelley had cupboards full of 'proper' food. Other than that, Shelley had been living on ready meals or takeaways or not bothering with dinner at all. Greg had always been the chef. He would pore over recipe books and make a list of ingredients for her to add to the shopping list.

'They've changed it around since I was last here.' Mum had been like this since she'd picked her up this morning. Keeping up a steady patter of conversation, not letting it slip into anything dangerous or upsetting. It had been like this between them since the funeral when Shelley had told her – in no uncertain terms – that she didn't want to talk about Greg's death.

Now her mother just asked how she was and she would say she was fine and then they'd keep to safe topics like her mother's neighbours or what they'd seen on TV. 'I think you're right. I haven't been in here either.'

Her mother frowned. 'You have been eating though? I've put another lot of dinners in the freezer for you. I can always make some more.'

That was the other topic of conversation. She had become obsessed with making sure that Shelley was eating. As if she would get through this awful period in her life as long as she was getting daily servings of fresh fruit and vegetables. Every visit, her mum would also turn up with ten or twelve individual portions of homemade lasagne and bolognese and macaroni cheese. It was the one-person portions which Shelley found most depressing.

The last lot of dinners were still in the freezer; the previous delivery in landfill somewhere by now. Somehow, she never remembered to get them out in the morning to defrost. 'Yes, I've been eating well, Mum,' she lied.

They pushed their trolleys out of the fresh veg section and towards the fridges.

Her mum scrutinised the range of sausages: picking them up, reading the ingredients, putting them down again. 'Have you seen much of those new neighbours you mentioned?'

'Yes, actually. I've been spending quite a bit of time with Lara.' Shelley paused. 'She's helped me to sort out that box room.'

Shelley's mum froze then turned her head to look at her. She had been there the day that Shelley had torn everything that reminded her of Greg from each room and thrown it in there. That had been one of the dark days. One of the days after she had stopped taking the medication. 'I see. That's good?'

It was a question, and Shelley felt bad that her mum was trying so hard to be tactful. How had they got to this point? 'Yes. It's done me good. She's introduced me to the joys of decluttering. There's a book. *Make Way for Joy.*'

'A book?' Now her mother had turned and stood in front of her. 'Who's Joy?'

Shelley laughed. 'I'll show you when we get back. Come on, get your sausages and let's move on.' Slowly, she pushed her trolley forwards to carry on with their shopping. Once her mother was following, she glanced back at her. 'And I went to the Garden of Remembrance.'

'What?' Her mother stopped still in the middle of the aisle. 'And you're telling me this here? When?'

Her mum had tried to suggest a couple of times that she might like to visit the place where Greg had been laid to rest. Shelley had practically bitten her head off. 'I thought you'd be pleased.'

'I am pleased!' She lowered her voice and pushed her trolley closer to Shelley's. 'I'd just rather talk to you about it when we're sitting down. Not next to five shelves of bacon.'

It was a fair request. 'Okay, then. Shall we put the trolleys back for now and go to the café?'

Tea was the go-to for everyone in times of trouble. Every visitor Shelley had had in the days after Greg's death had insisted on making one for her. Most of them had been left to go cold, but they did have the benefit of giving her something to do when faced with the same conversation on a loop. *Yes, it was very sudden. No, I don't need anything, thank you. Yes, he was a very good man.*

Shelley insisted on queuing for the tea while her mum found a seat. In front of her was a young mother with a baby in one of those papoose carriers. She must have been very young: tiny fingers curled around the fabric, eyes closed, mouth twitching as if it was suckling. Would this be easier with a baby to love? Or more difficult? A familiar feeling rose in her chest and she looked away. Then stopped. *In order to heal, you have to feel.* She looked at the baby again and thought of Dee. And Dee's baby. The child she'd never met.

'What would you like, love?' The woman behind the counter broke into her thoughts.

Shelley could barely get the words out. 'Two teas, please.'

By the time she had the teas on a tray and had paid, she'd regained control of her throat. Her mum was sitting in the far corner, probably to give them maximum privacy. Shelley slid the tray onto the table.

Her mother picked up one of the sachets of sugar and shook it before tearing it open. 'So, then?'

'So, I went to the garden and I sat on a bench and I… I spoke to Greg. I told him how I felt. It didn't feel as weird as it sounds. I might go again.'

Her mother stirred her drink, watching the spoon as she did so. She looked like she was choosing her words carefully. 'And did it help?'

Did it help? Help with what? The anger? The guilt? The loss? 'I don't know. But it made me face a few things. I've been re-evaluating some things lately.' She watched as her mother tapped the spoon on the side of her cup. Once. Twice. 'Mum, were you disappointed in me?'

Her mother nearly dropped the spoon in her surprise. 'Whatever gave you that idea? Of course not. How could I be disappointed in you?'

She had been considering this for the last couple of days. 'When I didn't stay at university. I know how proud you were when I got the place.'

Her mum smiled. 'Of course I was proud. No one in my family had ever been to university. I particularly enjoyed telling my Aunt Pat. Perfect revenge for eighteen years of "single mother" comments, that was.' Her mum laughed, trying to lighten the mood, but she'd just made Shelley feel worse.

'But then I didn't stay. Were you very disappointed?'

'No. Not disappointed. I only wanted you to be happy. I was confused a bit, I guess. You had set your heart on that course, and when you decided to give it up, I was a little worried that you might regret it.'

'But you never said anything!'

'You were so happy with Greg, I thought that was more important. It wasn't down to me to decide what you did with your life. That was always your choice.'

It *had* been her choice. She couldn't blame anyone else. Greg hadn't told her to leave – she'd just missed him so much. And university had felt so lonely. No Dee. No Greg. It had been too scary.

Now her mum looked nervous. 'Should I have persuaded you to stay? *Are* you regretting it now?'

Did she regret it? No. How could she regret the years she'd had with Greg? If she'd stayed at university, they might not have made it. Long-distance relationships weren't known to be easy.

Dee had always been full of stories when she'd come home during the holidays. Big nights out, student productions she'd got involved with, interesting people she'd met. But Shelley hadn't been envious; she'd been happy with her local travel course and then the job. 'No, Mum. I'm not regretting it. Just wondering, that's all.'

'Is that what you've been talking to your new friend Lara about? I'm not prying, I'm just glad you've got someone to talk to. Since the funeral, I've been so worried about you.'

'I'm okay, Mum. You don't need to worry.'

Her mum shook her head. 'I could see you were bottling it all up. You've been like that since you were a small child. If you hurt yourself, you wouldn't cry. I used to say to you, "Let it all out," but you wouldn't.'

'I think I was still in shock, to be honest. It all felt a little bit surreal.'

'And now?'

Shelley tried to smile. 'Still pretty surreal, but I'm dealing with it better. I think. Trying not to bottle it all up.'

'Well, I'm pleased about that.' Her mum paused. Looked at her. 'I haven't told you before now, but I spoke to Dione at the funeral.'

It took Shelley a few moments to realise who her mum was talking about. It had been so long since she'd heard someone use Dee's full name. 'Oh, yes?'

'She was trying to speak with you but there seemed to be a constant flow of people. She said that she hadn't seen much of you or Greg in the weeks before he… before it happened.'

Why was it so difficult to talk about death? Everyone spoke in euphemisms. She hadn't *lost* her husband; he hadn't *passed*. He had died, but no one wanted to say the word. Maybe that was why it was so difficult for her to get her head around it. 'Yes, we had a, er, a disagreement. It was complicated.'

Her mother patted her hand. 'All I know is, you two were inseparable as youngsters. Way before you met her brother.'

Something occurred to Shelley that she'd never considered before. 'Mum, did you like Greg?'

'Oh, Shelley. What an awful thing to say. Of course I liked him.'

'It's just, I've been thinking a lot lately and I'm seeing things a little differently. Was I a bad daughter?'

'A bad daughter? Of course not! What gave you that idea?'

'I don't know. Maybe I didn't visit enough or take you out enough or something. Did I change when I met Greg?'

'Everyone changes when they settle down. It's natural. It's not like I expected to see as much of you once you were a married woman.'

'How did I change?'

'Oh, I don't know, Shelley. What's this all about? You're not all right, are you?'

'It's nothing like that, Mum, honestly. It's just, the argument with Dee – she said that I changed after I met Greg. That I wasn't me anymore. Do you think that's true?'

Her mother looked decidedly uncomfortable. 'Like I said, everyone changes a bit when they get married. It's inevitable.'

'Mum.'

Her mother sighed. 'Maybe. A little. You started to dress differently. None of your crazy clothes you wore when you were travelling with Dee, your funny tie-dye stuff. And you started wearing shoes that you used to call 'too grown up'. Actually, that's what it was. You just kind of grew up overnight. Became more sophisticated. Your clothes, the restaurants you went to. Everything.'

Shelley almost winced at a sudden memory of refusing to use the local Chinese restaurant – which she and her mother had ordered takeaway from for years – because it wasn't 'authentic'. That had been one of Greg's favourite words at the time, and she had also adopted it. She felt a pang of guilt. Maybe none of this was Greg's fault.

She had changed. Dee had been right about that. But Greg hadn't asked her to. She'd done it on her own. So, who was she now?

CHAPTER THIRTY-NINE

Lara

At every midwife appointment, listening to the baby's heartbeat was Lara's favourite part: the galloping horse sound reassured her that everything was okay. On one of her many trawls online, she'd found out about an app for her phone which would let her listen to it at home, and she had persuaded a reluctant Matt that this would help. He was reluctant because their midwife had cautioned against it. 'If the baby is in the wrong position or you hold it at the wrong angle, you won't be able to detect the heartbeat and then you're going to make yourself feel worse.' Lara had persisted. She wouldn't listen every day. Just when she needed to. And so far, it *had* helped. Until today.

The whooshing underwater sound was coming through the speaker clearly, but there was no galloping. She wasn't concerned, she just needed to move it around until she found the baby's heart. She moved lower. Nothing. To the right. Nothing. Left. Nothing. 'Come on, baby,' she whispered. 'Where are you?'

As she moved the phone around her belly, her own heartbeat was pulsing loudly in her ears. She tried to talk her anxiety down. *There's nothing to worry about. Stay calm. You'll find it in a minute.*

But she didn't. Her brain started to race ahead. Had she felt the baby move today? Yes. This morning in bed, she had lain there for twenty minutes with her hand on her stomach, enjoying the fluttering movements. But that was four hours ago. Anything could have happened.

She called her midwife. Voicemail. Matt was in Liverpool today. No point calling him and stressing him out. Shelley? She'd had a text from Shelley last night with an email screenshot of her interview date next week. She'd also mentioned that her mother was staying over and wasn't leaving until lunchtime; it wouldn't be fair to interrupt their time together. They'd see each other this afternoon anyway when they went to Guildford to find Shelley an interview suit. Lara had promised Matt faithfully that she would rest all day today in preparation. This wasn't resting: it was panic.

Another check with the Doppler and still nothing. She had to do something. She didn't feel ill so she should have been able to drive to the hospital, but she felt too trembly to get behind the wheel. She called a cab.

The cab driver was very nice but she could really have done without his jokes about towels and hot water. Eventually, her terse replies got through and he left her to her own thoughts. She stared blindly out of the window. *Please, God, don't let this be happening again.*

Should she call Matt and let him know what was happening? There was no point until she knew something: he was hours away. No point putting him through it if she didn't have to. Oh God, she hoped she was worrying for no reason. This was their last chance. If it happened again, there was no way Matt would want to try for another baby. No way he would let her put them both through this again. *One last time and then we have to accept it.* He had made her promise.

The maternity ward entrance was achingly familiar. She blocked out the happy couple carrying a baby in a car seat to their car and made straight for the ultrasound department.

She must have looked terrified because – though it was totally against protocol – the receptionist managed to get her in front of a midwife. She prayed in her head as the gel squeaked onto her stomach and then…

It was there. The heartbeat. Thank God.

A warmth washed over her from head to toe as the midwife smiled. 'All okay. Heartbeat is lovely and strong.'

Lara burst into tears. 'Thank you. Oh, thank you so much.'

After a brief lecture from the midwife about home use of Doppler apps, Lara called a taxi and returned home. This time she did as she'd promised Matt and went to bed for a nap before she knocked for Shelley.

Waiting until they were a good fifteen minutes into their journey before she told Shelley about the events of the morning was intentional; that way she was less likely to turn around and take her back home for a rest.

However, Shelley was still concerned even after they arrived in the High Street. 'Are you sure you should be here?'

'I'm fine. The baby is fine. Matt isn't due back until late this evening, and if I sit at home, I'll end up using the damn heartbeat app again.' It was becoming an addiction – an unhealthy addiction if the stress of this afternoon was replicated.

Shelley didn't look convinced. 'Okay. But we'll take it slowly. And if you feel *anything*, you have to tell me. Deal?'

Lara felt more foolish than anything else. Today had been a whole lot of fuss over nothing. 'Deal. Now, where do you want to go?'

They were stood outside a café. Shelley peered down the row of shops to their right. 'I don't really mind. Where's good? Where did you go to buy your work clothes?'

It had been a while since Lara had bought any new clothes. Apart from the maternity ones she'd picked up in the charity shop. 'All different places. House of Fraser has a lot of choice. Shall we start there?'

Shelley gave her a thumbs up. 'Perfect. But we'll walk slowly. There's no huge rush.'

Lara gave her a mock salute. 'Right. No more worrying about each other. We should be enjoying ourselves. When was the last time you bought yourself some new clothes?'

'Probably the dress for Greg's funeral.'

Lara put her hand to her head. She'd put her foot in it again. 'Oh, crikey, Shelley. Sorry.'

Shelley shook her head and smiled. 'Don't be silly. Strictly speaking, my mum bought that one, anyway. Actually, she bought three and brought them home for me to try on. At that stage, I couldn't have cared less if she'd made me a dress from bin bags, but she insisted that it would be easier to deal with the day if I felt comfortable and suitably dressed.'

'There you go then.' It must be a good sign that Shelley was starting to talk about Greg and what happened more freely in everyday conversation. 'A new outfit can make a difference. We just need to find one that screams, "Give me that job!"'

House of Fraser's women's department was huge. As soon as they got there, Shelley began to flick through summer dresses, holding them away from the rail with both hands to appraise them. They looked nice enough but were definitely not what she should have been looking for, so Lara kept walking until Shelley's voice called her back. 'What do you think of this one?'

Lara turned and saw Shelley holding up a yellow floral dress from Coast. 'It's nice. I mean, it's pretty and I'm sure it would look great on you, but if someone came to me for an interview and they were wearing a flowery dress, I wouldn't think efficient and proactive. Your clothes say a lot about you. You need to make this work *for* you. Come with me. Let's look at the office wear over there. If you don't like it, we can come back here.'

Shelley had the kind of slim build that would look great in a tailored jacket. Why did she seem intent on hiding herself under floaty fabric or long, shapeless clothes like the striped tunic and leggings she was wearing today?

The women's suit section was small but there were still a few options. Lara held out her right hand while her left rested on her belly. 'So, what colour do you prefer?'

Shelley picked up the sleeve of a beige skirt suit and let it fall again. 'How about this?'

'Mmm.' Lara looked at it and then her. 'I'm not sure it goes with your colouring. How about this navy one?' She picked a hanger from the rail and held it up.

Shelley's arms were crossed. She shook her head. 'No.'

Lara liked it, but fair enough. 'The colour or the style?'

Shelley pressed her lips together, then took a deep breath. 'Both. Look, I know you are trying to help me and I appreciate it, but this is *my* job interview. *I* need to choose the outfit I want to wear.'

Lara could have kicked herself. This was exactly what they'd talked about. How had she been so insensitive? 'I'm sorry. I'm being so bossy! You're completely right. I won't say another word.' She mimed locking her lips and throwing away the key.

Shelley looked relieved; it had obviously made her uncomfortable. 'Don't apologise. I was letting you do it. Old habits die hard. But it's time for me to make some decisions for myself, right?'

Lara nodded. 'Absolutely right. Do you want to go back and pick up that dress you liked? What size do you need?'

'Sixteen, please.'

Was she being serious? There was nothing of her. 'You are *not* a size sixteen.'

Shelley put her hands on her hips. 'Yes, I am. I've been a size sixteen for about the last six years.'

Lara shook her head. 'Maybe you *were*, but I'd guess you were a twelve now. Maybe even a generous ten.'

'It's very kind of you to flatter me but—'

Lara held up her hands. 'Okay. I'm not going to argue.'

Five minutes later, she tried not to gloat when Shelley stuck her head out of the changing rooms. 'Okay, you win. Can you get me a smaller size?'

Losing weight was another side effect of grief. Lara had had to force herself to eat so she could maintain a healthy weight for the fertility treatment. It would have been far easier to just not bother. Shelley had obviously been the same. 'Did you not realise that everything you wear is baggy? You were right about the dress though; that style looks great on you. I'd definitely give you the job. Do you want me to get anything else while I'm picking up the smaller size?'

'Yes, please. Can you grab the jacket that was next to it? The cream one?'

Cream? She had to be joking. Lara opened her mouth to suggest she went for something brighter and then closed it again. This was Shelley's choice. 'I'll be back in two minutes.'

Once she had on the right size, and the cream jacket, Shelley stood in front of Lara and gave her a twirl. 'So, what do you think?'

Lara stood back and looked at Shelley. It wasn't what she would have chosen for a job interview but that really wasn't important. Shelley had picked the dress that she wanted. That's what mattered. 'You look really great.'

Shelley was looking in the mirror again, and Lara stood behind her. Their smiling faces reflected back at them. Then another face appeared alongside them. A woman. She was speaking. 'Shelley?'

Lara watched as Shelley's smile froze on her face and her skin paled. They both turned. The woman stepped forwards with her arms outstretched. 'Oh, Shelley, it is you. I've wanted to see you so much. How are you?'

Lara had no idea who this was, but she had the urge to move closer to Shelley to protect her. Was this another friend who

Shelley had seen nothing of since Greg's death? She didn't want anyone to upset her friend, especially when she was just beginning to have a little more confidence in herself.

But Shelley allowed this woman to hug her, and after a few seconds, she put her arms around the woman and hugged her back. Lara moved away slightly to give them some space. When they pulled apart, still holding each other's hands, Shelley turned to explain.

'Lara, this is Dee.'

CHAPTER FORTY

Shelley

Chinking china, clinking cutlery and burbled conversation: John Lewis's café was noisy and busy and possibly not the best place for an attempted reconciliation with your estranged best friend. Dee insisted that Shelley find a seat while she queued for coffee and Shelley was grateful for the opportunity to collect her thoughts and slow her heart rate down. She should have been getting used to this; there had been more big conversations in cafés in the last few weeks than she'd had in her whole life.

After they'd met Dee by the changing rooms, Lara had made an excuse about wanting to look in the baby department and left them to it. Shelley had slipped out of the dress as quickly as she could, heart beating at the thought of Dee waiting for her outside. Despite that hug, what would she think of her? New haircut, clothes shopping, *laughing*? Would she be angry that Shelley seemed to be happily getting on with her life? Not that she was, but she could see how that might look. What was Dee going to say?

But when she'd emerged from the changing rooms, Dee had just looked overjoyed to see her. Practically ecstatic when she'd agreed to go for a drink. And now she was coming over with two mugs of coffee and what looked like some kind of biscuits.

She started speaking as soon as she slid the tray onto the table. 'I'm so happy to see you. I was getting to the point of just turning up at your house, but I know how much you'd hate that. How have you been?'

Actually, Shelley didn't mind; it had been Greg who wasn't keen on unexpected guests. 'I should be asking you that. How is it being a mum? Congratulations on the baby.'

'Your nephew, you mean? He's great. He's called Jacob and he's with Jamie today. I'm having a couple of hours to myself, although I must admit, I'm missing him already. What a saddo, eh?' Dee pulled a self-mocking face but Shelley could see the shine in her eyes at the mention of her son.

'Did you get my card? And the gift?' Shelley's mother had bought a blanket for her to send and had even picked out the congratulations card. Jacob had been born during the early days with the antidepressants where Shelley had been moving through treacle. Her mum had laid the card out in front of her and handed her a pen as if she were a small child who had just learned to write.

Dee nodded. 'I did. Thanks. I would rather have seen you though.'

Guilt flooded in. She had been so selfish. Dee had had her first child and Shelley hadn't even been to visit her. She stared down into the latte that Dee had bought. 'I know. I'm sorry, Dee. I really am so sorry. I just couldn't handle it. It was too much.'

Dee reached over and placed a hand on Shelley's. She lowered her voice. 'I get it, Shelley. I do. But shutting me out won't change anything. I'm grieving too. Greg was my brother. Losing him is like losing half of my childhood. Who am I going to laugh about crazy Nanny Weena with? Who will remember the time Dad took us to the cinema and fell asleep and had to be woken up by the attendant because he was snoring? Who will understand the particular brand of emotional blackmail our mother employed to make us do what she wanted?' A sob took her breath and she put a hand over her mouth.

'Oh, Dee. I have been so selfish. I just locked down. It was too painful, and seeing you... It would have been unbearable. And the baby...'

Dee was crying openly and Shelley was barely keeping it together herself. People were glancing over at them. Should she stop her? Maybe they could go somewhere else? No. She'd spent too much time worrying what other people thought. And where had that got her? This was Dee. Her best friend. Breaking her heart in front of her.

'Shelley, I've been desperate to see you. I wanted to cry with you. I just wanted to check that you are okay. I've been so worried about you. And guilty. I've been so absorbed with caring for Jacob and crying about Greg that I gave up trying to get through to you. I convinced myself that you weren't my problem right now – I couldn't make you accept my help. But I look at you now and I feel so guilty that I didn't try harder.'

For all these months, Shelley had been telling herself that she couldn't face this. That it would be too much, too painful. But this was Dee. Her Dee. Her funny, kind, passionate friend. Inseparable from the age of eleven, they'd practically lived at one another's homes. Dee had always been the outgoing one, the one with the plans, the one with the confidence. Shelley wouldn't have done half the things she had if it weren't for Dee. But Dee had needed Shelley just as much. Shelley had talked her down from the crazier ideas, had listened to her rant when Dee felt misunderstood. If Dee had been the wind that blew Shelley onwards, then Shelley had been the calm to Dee's storm. Greg's death had been the worst thing that had ever happened to either of them. They should have grieved together, not apart. And that was Shelley's fault for pushing her away.

So much guilt. So much useless emotion. So much wasted time. 'Oh, Dee, you don't need to feel guilty. I am the one who was wrong. You tried to talk to me but I didn't want to listen. I should be the one saying sorry, not you.'

Dee shook her head. 'No. You've lost your husband. Your whole world has been…'

Shelley interrupted her. She owed Dee this apology, whatever she said. 'I don't just mean this last year. Before that. You were right about me but I didn't want to hear it at the time.'

Dee looked confused. 'What do you mean? Right about what?'

Shelley sighed. 'That night at your parents' house. When you told me you were pregnant. What you said.'

Dee closed her eyes for a moment and opened them again. 'I thought we'd made our peace with that. It was the hormones; I was out of order.'

Now Shelley shook her head. 'No. You were right. About me doing everything that Greg wanted, living my life the way he lived his. It wasn't his fault though. It was me. I just kind of… morphed into this other person.' Shelley broke eye contact and started moving her mug around on the table. 'I know we agreed to forget it, but if I'm honest, I was still carrying it all when Greg died. I was so angry with you. It felt like you'd attacked me and I couldn't work out where it had come from. I'd always known that you weren't happy about me and Greg getting together. I knew that I was never good enough for your brother. But that night in your old bedroom seemed like an all-out assault.'

Dee's eyes widened. 'Good enough? Good enough? Of course you were good enough. What do you mean?'

Shelley sighed. 'Your family. We both know that our families were worlds apart. I suppose it didn't matter when we were kids, but when I started dating your brother, I could see how uncomfortable you were.'

Dee laughed in disbelief. 'It wasn't that, Shel.'

'And I know your parents weren't happy. I know they would rather he married someone of their "type". Not the girl from around the corner who didn't even finish university.'

'Well, that was Greg's fault. He wanted you back home with him.'

'No, it wasn't. It was me. I wasn't confident enough to be there on my own, and when I came home, you weren't there and I just started seeing a lot more of him.'

'A lot more of him? You moved in together.'

'Not straight away.'

'And when I came home that first Christmas, I barely saw you. Either of you.'

'That first Christmas all you wanted to talk about was how wonderful university life was and how I was missing out. You kept talking about all your new friends and what you were planning to do when you went back.'

'That's because I wanted to persuade you to try again. I didn't want you to miss out because you were shacking up with my brother.'

'And that's how you seemed to feel about it. I was "shacking up" with him. You hated it. You were jealous because I was spending time with him.'

Dee gave a hollow laugh. 'What do you mean? It was never him I was afraid of losing. It was you.'

Shelley had no idea what she was talking about. 'What do you mean, losing me? Surely if I married your brother, you were guaranteed to see me for the rest of my life?'

Dee sighed. 'See you, yes. But not spend time with you. Not on my own. You became part of the family. Every time we were together, Greg was there too.' She sighed again. 'I loved my brother, of course I did. But you were my best friend, and when you married Greg, I lost you.'

How could Shelley have read the situation so badly? How could she not have realised this? 'Oh, Dee. I got so much wrong. It wasn't just that you lost me. I lost myself along the way too. Greg was so confident, so clever, so… I don't know, worldly? He just seemed to know how everything should be done, and it was easy to follow his lead.'

Dee nodded; her eyes sad. 'I get that. He was a pretty great guy. I did love him too, you know. For all that he drove me crazy.'

Why had she left it so long before speaking to Dee? She was the one other person who would miss Greg as much as she did. Maybe that was why. Putting a mirror up to her own grief meant she was forced to face it. She reached across the table for Dee's hand and squeezed it. They sat there for a few moments until Shelley could trust her voice again. 'I'm so sorry I shut you out after the miscarriage. That we didn't see you the week before... before Greg died.'

Dee tilted her head to the side. 'But I did see him. He came to visit the day before... before his heart attack.'

That was strange; why hadn't he mentioned that to Shelley? Although, when she thought back, he had got in late the night before and she had been in bed. She had pretended to be asleep when he'd crept upstairs so that she wouldn't have to speak to him. Another stick she'd used to beat herself with in those early days after he'd died. 'Why didn't you tell me this before?'

Dee held her hands out. 'When? At the hospital when you refused to speak to me? At the funeral when you shook my hand then shook your head when I tried to hug you? On one of the many phone calls you've refused to take? It's not the kind of thing you can text or email.' Dee softened her voice and tentatively put a hand on Shelley's shoulder. 'I wasn't even sure whether I should tell you. I wasn't sure if it would make it worse.'

Shelley's face must have shown all the pain she was in. 'Worse? How could it ever be worse? My husband had just died, Dee. It doesn't actually get worse.'

Dee bit her lip then took a deep breath. 'He wanted to talk to me about you. That you were still adamant that you wanted to try for another baby and that you'd been arguing about it.' She paused and looked up at Shelley, as if she was weighing something up in her mind.

'Go on.' Shelley wanted to hear it, whatever it was. Like pulling off a plaster, she wanted it over as quickly as possible.

Dee nodded and continued. 'He really couldn't understand why you were talking about trying again. I honestly think he regarded it as some kind of hormonal reaction to the miscarriage, that you didn't really want a child. He even said he'd booked a consultation for a vasectomy.'

Shelley's stomach was flipping over and over, reliving those feelings of disappointment. Of loss. She could barely get her words out. 'And?'

'And I know that you didn't want me to say anything to him, but my brother was sitting there on my couch with his head in his hands, not knowing what to do. So, I tried to explain to him what it was like when you wanted a child that much. That need. I said I could see it in you and I also said that he needed to really consider what was stopping him from wanting a baby. And whether that was as strong a conviction as the one you had. He told me he was going to take some time and think about it. He was going to talk to you.'

Shelley felt as if someone had punched her in the stomach. Greg had been considering whether to have a baby? And she had lain there that night and pretended to be asleep. And the next day, there was no conversation to be had anymore.

She'd been wrong before. The pain could definitely get worse.

CHAPTER FORTY-ONE

Lara

Tiny pairs of trousers, mini T-shirts, a doll-sized floral dress: it was the first time that Lara had allowed herself inside the children's section of a shop since the first pregnancy. It was only one physical step over the threshold from womenswear, but it felt like a big leap. There were other mothers flicking through the hangers. Some with babies or toddlers in tow, some pregnant like her. She couldn't shake off the feeling of being an interloper. When would she feel as if she belonged here at last?

She picked up a tiny pair of socks, held them to her bump and whispered, 'What do you think of these, little one?'

A larger bump appeared beside hers; its owner smiled. 'Fun, isn't it? Do you know what you're having?'

Lara dropped the socks as if she'd been caught stealing them. 'No. We want a surprise.'

The woman picked up the socks from where they'd caught on the handle of her buggy and passed them back to her. 'Good for you. I'm having another boy so we'll mainly be recycling my two-year-old's clothes, but I wanted to get him a few new things. Seems only fair.'

Fairness wasn't something that Lara equated with pregnancy. This friendly woman looked ready to pop. 'How long until your due date?'

She did the reflexive bump-rub. 'Next week. Although I'm not sure I'll make it that far. I've had a terrible backache for the last two days and I'm wondering if he's on his way.'

Lara's back had been aching too, but she'd tried not to read anything into that. It was probably because she was starting to stand differently as her bump grew. The same with the twinges she'd had. Everything was okay. The hospital had confirmed it.

The little boy in the buggy started to cry, so the woman grabbed hold of the handles and turned it around. 'Uh-oh. That's my time up. Good luck. Hope everything goes well.'

'You too.' *From your lips to the ears of God*, she wanted to add.

Lara's phone pinged. A text from Shelley. Maybe she'd finished chatting to Dee and was ready to carry on shopping. No, she wasn't texting to suggest getting back to trying on suits.

No rush, but I'll meet you at the car whenever you're done.

What had happened?

It didn't take long for Lara to get back to the car, but Shelley was already there, in the driver's seat. Tears were streaming down her face.

Lara opened the door and practically jumped in. 'What happened?'

Shelley turned to look at her. 'He told Dee he would think about having another baby. The night before he died. He told her he would think about it.'

Lara's hands went to her face. No wonder Shelley looked so upset. 'How? What? Where?'

Shelley told her what Dee had said. Greg's visit to Dee, their conversation, the fact that she had pretended to be asleep that night when he'd got home from work. The more she spoke, the more worked up she seemed to get until she hit the steering wheel hard with both hands and yelled, 'I'm so bloody angry!'

Lara's head whirled trying to think of the right thing to say. 'At Dee?'

Shelley's eyes were on fire. 'Yes, at Dee. And Greg. And God. And myself. I'm angry at my stupid. Bloody. Self.'

She punctuated the last few words with more strikes on the steering wheel. Lara tried to say something soothing. 'It's not your fault, Shelley. None of this is your fault.'

But there was no placating her. 'Yes, it is. If I had been pushier. If I had made him realise how much I wanted a baby. If I hadn't just gone along with everything he wanted.' She covered her face with her hands and leaned forwards onto the steering wheel. Lara could barely hear the next sentence. 'I might have had a baby.'

Lara knew how the 'if' game worked. She was a professional player. *If I had started trying for a baby earlier. If I had looked after my body better. If Matt had married someone else.* But that game was bad news. It took its player on a downward spiral that was hard to climb back up. She put a hand on Shelley's back and rubbed gently. 'It might not have changed anything. You can't let your mind go there. You can only deal with what is, not what might have been.'

Shelley's face was almost haunted. 'I've been feeling a little better recently. Clearing out the room. Spending time with you. But now I feel like I'm right back at the beginning. Standing in the crematorium. Staring at the coffin with no idea what to do or how to feel.'

Lara couldn't stop the tears falling down her own face. 'Oh, Shelley, it's a lot to take in and you don't have to do that all at once. You can take your time. Grief isn't linear. You will be up and down and back and forth. Especially when you get a curveball like this.'

Shelley leaned back in her seat and closed her eyes. 'I miss him so much, Lara. Even right now when I am so angry with him for leaving me that I can barely breathe. I want him to hold me. To make me smile. To tell me it is all going to be all right.' Her face crumpled like a tissue and she leaned sideways into Lara's arms.

Once Shelley had composed herself enough to be able to drive, they headed for home. When they pulled up outside, Lara invited Shelley to come in. They had planned to eat out, but that had been forgotten after meeting up with Dee. 'I could make you an omelette if you like? That's about all I've got in, unless you fancy ordering a takeaway?'

Shelley shook her head. 'Just a cup of tea will be fine. I don't feel like eating, really.'

That was a relief because neither did Lara. Maybe it was the twisting around in her car seat in the car park, but she was feeling a little nauseous. A ginger biscuit with her tea would sort that out.

Once Lara had made the tea, they sat in the lounge. Shelley sighed. 'I feel exhausted.'

So did Lara. 'It's the emotion. It knocks it out of you.'

Shelley nodded thoughtfully. 'I've been angry for a long time. But tonight it just bubbled out of me. I'm sorry you had to see that.'

'Don't apologise. It needed to come out.'

Shelley sipped at her tea. 'I don't have a new outfit for my interview now. Maybe it's a sign that the job is not for me.'

Sometimes she was exasperating. 'It's not a *sign* of anything. But you don't have to take that job if you don't want it. Even if you go to the interview, you can still change your mind. You need to do what you want to do, Shelley.'

Shelley reached out and patted her hand. 'I know. Thank you. I just need to work out what that is first. And when I do, you'll be the first to know.'

'When is the interview again?'

'Tuesday. I'll go online and order that dress and jacket I tried on. I did like it. Thanks for your help.'

'No problem.' Lara yawned then quickly put her hand over her mouth. 'Sorry.'

Shelley scrutinised her. 'You look exhausted. I'm so sorry that I've worn you out with all my drama. I'll drink this and then go in. I want to get *Make Way for Joy* out tonight and reread the chapter on emotions. Sounds like I need it.'

'Good plan.' Lara didn't want to mention it to Shelley but she wasn't actually feeling that well. She'd overdone it walking through the shops, and her back was aching again. An early night would do her good.

CHAPTER FORTY-TWO

Shelley

Tourists, suits and students: the Underground train was packed. The mainline train to Waterloo had been busy too, but at least Shelley had been able to get a seat. She only had to go a couple of stops; if she got the job, she would work out a way to walk it. There was no way she wanted to do this every day.

As the doors beeped to close, a woman of around fifty jumped on the train at the last minute, almost colliding with Shelley. 'I'm so sorry, do you mind if I swap places with you so that I can lean my bag against there? It's full of textbooks and it weighs a ton.'

'Of course.' Shelley shuffled to the other side of the standing area so that the woman could drop her bag where she'd been standing. It landed with a thunk. 'Crikey. You weren't joking about the weight.'

The woman laughed. Despite her greying hair and fine lines, there was something youthful about her. Maybe it was her brightly coloured clothes or the way she had her hair tied back. 'It's my induction day at university and I wanted to look super prepared by bringing all the course books. My darling twenty-year-old daughter tells me I'm going to look like a try-hard mature student. But I told her at least I'll be a *prepared* try-hard mature student.'

The pride with which she said 'university' made Shelley smile. She remembered Dee complaining about the mature students all those years ago. That they would do all the required reading and sit at the front of lectures and hand all their essays in a week before the deadline. 'What are you studying?'

'History. It's a bit of a passion of mine. I didn't get the chance to go to university when I was younger – just wasn't expected for someone like me. But now my youngest son has gone off to Durham to study French, and my husband has retired so that he can spend his time chasing birds and cats off our front lawn, and I thought, why not?'

History? It seemed another life since Shelley had been in this woman's position. Her textbooks had long since been given away, and the closest she got to studying past civilisations was Simon Schama documentaries on BBC Four. 'Good for you.'

The woman put her hand on the rucksack, which was in danger of toppling over. 'Thanks. It's never too late, that's what I think. It's never too late to do what you want to do.'

The train slowed into Shelley's station. She needed to move nearer to the door, ready to get out. 'Absolutely. Good luck with your induction day.'

The Travel Express office was less than a five-minute walk from the station but Shelley was half an hour early so she stopped at a coffee shop. While she waited in line, she thought about the woman on the train. University courses were expensive these days. She didn't know the woman's circumstances but it was a big investment to become a full-time student. Could she even get a loan to pay her fees at her age? *It's never too late*, she'd said. *It's never too late to do what you want.*

'Hi, Shelley. We really must stop meeting in a hot drinks queue.'

She turned to face Steve, who was holding a takeaway cup. 'Oh, hi. Yes. Although I hope this coffee tastes a lot better than the one at the table top sale.' Seeing him made the butterflies in her stomach worse. Why did she always feel like this around him?

His laugh sounded as nervous as she felt. 'I'm actually on my way to see a prospective client. I'm not part of the interview process but I've told them how capable you are.'

'Thanks. I appreciate that.' Something had been prickling at the back of her mind during all this talk of a new job, and if she didn't ask now, she might never know. 'Actually, Steve, I don't want to sound ungrateful, but I'm just wondering why you have been recommending me for this position.'

Steve reddened and scratched his ear. 'I just think you'd be good at it.'

She narrowed her eyes. 'Yes, but so would other people in the team.'

His face grew even redder and he shuffled from foot to foot. When he finally spoke, he addressed half of his conversation to the lid on his takeaway cup. 'Okay. This is totally unprofessional and probably way out of line but... I like you.' He practically winced as he looked up.

What did he mean? 'I don't understand.'

Steve looked as if he regretted walking into this café in the first place. 'I know this is not a good time and I would never have said anything... yet. But... I like you, Shelley, and I know that if you don't join the new company, then we'll lose touch, and if, at some point in the distant future, you find yourself ready to start dating again, I wouldn't be around to... ask you out.'

He winced again. It was excruciating.

It was also her turn to blush. 'I... I had no idea... I, er...'

Steve shook his head. 'Please don't say anything. I am mortified that we are even having this conversation. Especially as I am still your boss at the moment until you move to another role. And, anyway, it's not the only reason I've been talking to you about the job. You would be really good at it. I wouldn't have recommended you otherwise.' He glanced down at his watch, looking relieved to see the time. 'I'm really sorry but I have to go. You would be great at this job. I know you would. Please ignore what I just said. It has nothing to do with this. Good luck.'

After Steve dashed away, Shelley was in such a state of shock that the barista had to ask her three times what she wanted to drink. Steve was *interested* in her? How had she not picked up on that? Or maybe she had? Was that where the constant butterflies in her stomach came from whenever she spent time with him? *Oh, God.* Did she like him too?

The hiss of the coffee machine brought her back out of her head. Collecting her cup from the end of the counter, she pushed the thoughts of Steve from her mind. There was the interview to cope with right now – the lorry load of Greg guilt that was about to hit would have to wait a while.

The reception desk of Travel Express was in a huge atrium. Glass, chrome and bold colours – a modern, vibrant workplace. She gave her name to the receptionist and sat down to wait. Wearing the bright yellow dress that had arrived yesterday – and in which she'd twirled around in front of Lara last night – she looked as if she would fit right in.

But she had a sudden, overwhelming feeling that she didn't want to.

These feelings had started last night, talking to Lara, when she'd repeated her advice. *Do what you want to do.* Then there was the woman on the train, starting a university course. *It's never too late.* And now Steve's revelation. *If you find yourself ready.*

She stood up to speak to the receptionist and cancel her interview. And then she headed straight home to tell Lara what she wanted to do. What she really, really wanted to do.

CHAPTER FORTY-THREE

Shelley

This point in her pregnancy should still be the blooming period, but when Lara opened the door, she looked pale and tired. Shelley began to doubt whether she should have dropped by like this, especially when Lara yawned. 'Sorry, were you getting some rest? Shall I come back later?'

Lara opened the door wide. 'No, I want to hear all about your interview. Come in.'

Shelley followed Lara to the back of the house where her kitchen was. Was she walking slower than usual? 'Are you sure you're feeling okay?'

Lara disconnected the kettle from its base and took it to the sink to fill it. 'I'm fine. Just didn't sleep very well and I must have been lying in a funny position because I've got an ache in my lower back.'

'Why don't you sit down? I can make the drinks.' She began to get a strange feeling in the pit of her stomach, the announcement she'd planned to make forgotten in her concern for her friend.

Lara ignored her offer and flicked the switch on the kettle. 'Stop stalling. Come on, how did it go?' Lara rubbed the underside of her belly as if she had a cramp. Was her face getting paler? It was almost grey.

Shelley pulled out a seat. 'Lara, I really think you should sit d—'

Lara took a sharp breath in and doubled over suddenly as if she was going to vomit.

Shelley sprang forward. 'Are you going to throw up? I'll get a bowl.'

Lara righted herself. Now Shelley was closer to her, she could see a film of sweat on her forehead. 'No. I'm not going to be sick. I think it might be Braxton Hicks – false contractions. Although I didn't realise they would be this painful.'

Shelley's pregnancy hadn't lasted long enough for her to have experienced these, but she'd been through the pregnancies of friends and she didn't remember them saying that Braxton Hicks contractions were painful. More just a tightening feeling. All pregnancies were different, but she didn't like the look of Lara's face.

'Do you want to lie down?'

Lara shook her head. 'No. I want to—' A spasm of pain creased her face and she doubled over again. This time, when she straightened up, her eyes were full of fear. She was finding it hard to breathe.

A chill trickled down Shelley's spine. She knelt in front of Lara and took both her hands. 'You are not fine. Let me take you to the hospital.'

Lara's face seemed to melt, mouth slackened, eyes pleading. 'Oh my God, Shelley, I can feel something. It feels like blood. It can't be blood. Not again. Not now. No, please don't let it be blood. No. Shelley, please help me. Help me.'

Shelley squeezed Lara's hands tightly. 'Can you get to my car or shall I call an ambulance?'

'I think I can walk.' Hesitantly, she began to move upwards and then fell back again. 'I can't. I can't move. Oh God, I can't move.' Sobs gave way to moans. 'Help me. Please help me.'

Shelley grabbed Lara's mobile phone which was on the table. Thank God she didn't have a lock on it. She tapped 999 with a trembling finger. 'Hello? I need an ambulance. Urgently. I have a pregnant woman in a lot of pain.'

Lara reached for her hand with both of hers like she was drowning. As soon as Shelley had given the address to the call handler, she knelt down beside her. 'Keep breathing, my darling. It's going to be okay. The ambulance will come and they will take you to the hospital and everything is going to be okay.'

Lara winced again. Were the pains coming quicker now? 'I'm scared, Shelley, I'm so scared. Matt said… Oh God, can you call Matt? His number is in my—'

Another spasm cut her off.

'Of course, I'll ask him to meet us at the hospital.'

Shelley was trying to keep her voice calm but she was terrified. Lara did not look good. Her palms were cold and clammy as they clutched at Shelley's hand. Shelley managed to find Matt in Lara's favourites. *Please let him answer.* Voicemail.

She didn't want to frighten him into dashing full pelt to the hospital in case he ended up crashing the car but she also needed to make sure he came. 'Hi, Matt. It's Shelley from next door. Lara needs to go to the hospital because she's not feeling well. Can you head straight there? I have Lara's phone so please call on that and I will let you know where we are.'

'Why the hell isn't he answering his phone?' Lara was roaring. 'I need him! I need him here now!'

Shelley had thought the same thing. Where the hell was he? But she didn't want to worry Lara further.

The phone rang. Matt.

His voice was heartbreakingly jovial. 'Hi, love, just got a missed call from you. I was on the other phone. What's up? More emergency chocolate needed?'

He hadn't listened to the voicemail. Shelley took a deep breath. 'Sorry, Matt. It's Shelley. I called you on Lara's phone.'

The panic in his voice almost came out and hit her. 'What is it? Is she okay? What happened?'

'She's not feeling great. I've called an ambulance and…' There was a knock on the door. She needed to get off the phone. 'Meet us at the hospital.'

Lara released her hand and Shelley raced to open the door. A man of about forty walked in, the personification of calm. 'Hi, I'm Phil. I'm a first responder. The ambulance is on its way.'

It was such a relief to have someone there who knew what they were doing. Surely, he would make everything all right. His voice was soothing as he spoke to Lara, telling her what he was doing as he checked her over.

'I think I'll take you straight in if you can walk? Might be quicker than waiting for the ambulance. I can put a blue light on and get us there quicker.'

He was still talking calmly but this didn't sound good. Lara and Shelley locked eyes. If Shelley could have picked Lara up like a baby right then and carried her to the car, she would have done. She heard her own voice as if it were down a long tunnel. 'Okay, Lara, my darling. Let's get you there and make sure you and this baby are okay.'

CHAPTER FORTY-FOUR

Shelley

The hospital canteen had a coffee bar in the centre. Shelley was on her third cup because buying, stirring and drinking coffee gave her something to do. Something other than compulsively checking her phone to see if there was any word from Matt.

The first responder had driven them to the hospital under a blue light and Shelley had had to watch helplessly as they'd wheeled Lara inside in a wheelchair. She had hung around the entrance so that she could tell Matt where to go when he'd arrived, breathless and terrified, thirty minutes later. A friend had driven him from London; she didn't want to think about how many speed limits they had broken.

He'd been allowed further into the hospital but not into the operating theatre, where their tiny baby was being delivered by Caesarean section. He'd sent her a message to thank her and let her know that they were delivering the baby, and that was the last she'd heard.

Of course, she should have just gone home. But she couldn't bear to leave until she knew the outcome. *Please let the baby be okay.*

The coffee was cold, but still she sat. An older couple was walking towards the table next to hers. He carried the tray and she removed a couple of stray cups which hadn't been cleared away.

He rested the tray on the table, holding onto it with his left hand as he picked up their cups and saucers and put them on the table along with two metal teapots, a metal jug of milk and a plate with two small packets of biscuits. He returned the tray to the coffee bar and then sat opposite his wife, who smiled at him. 'Are you feeling a bit better now, love?'

He nodded. 'Fine now. Nothing a nice cuppa won't fix.'

Shelley watched them from over the rim of her paper cup. The woman poured the tea – milk first – and he opened the biscuits and laid them out on the plate. She chattered at him – the grandkids, the garden, when they'd be able to get down to their caravan next – and he just nodded, gave the occasional answer. They were so settled in each other's company. Must be what years of marriage can bring.

Tears burned at the backs of Shelley's eyes. This was what they were supposed to have: her and Greg. They were supposed to grow old together; they'd even joked of a future where they'd buy a little place in a village with a nice café by the sea. Every time they went on holiday to a quaint English town, they would press their noses up against the estate agents' window, looking to see which house they would buy one day.

But this was never going to happen for them. They wouldn't be going for long walks in the countryside, or signing up for that Italian cooking course they'd always talked about, or even just sitting either side of the log burner that Greg had coveted. He was gone. Any growing older, she'd be doing on her own. It was so bloody unfair.

She couldn't sit there any longer. Couldn't think about the future she wasn't going to have.

Outside the hospital was a small garden with a bench. It was empty and the ideal place to sit so no one would see her cry. Worry about Lara, the smell of the hospital and now the old couple – it was all too much to take. With her face in her palms, Shelley sobbed. 'I can't do this on my own, Greg. I can't. I need you here.'

What would he do if he were here? He'd put his arms around her and tell her that everything was going to be okay. Like he had when she'd lost the baby. He'd looked after her and comforted her. That's what he did. But he couldn't do it now. She was on her own.

'It's just not fair!' She said the words aloud. Pushing them out of her felt like a relief. It wasn't bloody fair. It wasn't fair that there were nasty people, violent people, cruel people who got to carry on living and Greg had been taken. 'It's not fair.'

And it wasn't fair about Lara either. She would be a wonderful mother. Why was her body making it so difficult? Why were there neglectful parents out there able to have several children easily while Lara and Matt had to go through all of this to have one tiny baby? Who was running this show?

It was impossible not to think about the last time she'd been at this hospital. Sitting in that small room. Listening to the doctor's attempt at comforting words, which she couldn't take in. The day her life had changed.

There had been that moment. The moment she had felt him. He had held her before he'd left, she was sure of it. She'd never told anyone because she knew it would make her sound crazy, but he had said goodbye.

She checked her mobile again. There was still no news from Matt. Maybe she should go home. But the thought of going back to her empty house – with Lara and Matt's house empty next door – was more than she could bear.

Lara had looked so frightened, haunted even. Shelley knew that look. She'd seen it in the mirror enough times in those first few months. Loss could hollow you out, leave you with nothing.

'Oh, Greg. Wherever you are. Please make Lara's baby okay. Please don't let her lose another one.'

And then her phone rang. Matt.

CHAPTER FORTY-FIVE

Lara

Waking up from a general anaesthetic is very strange. It's not like waking up from a night's sleep because at least then you are aware that time has passed. A general anaesthetic is more like closing your eyes and then opening them to find that the world has moved on a few hours. When Lara first came round, she saw a man in a nurse's uniform smiling at her. When he spoke, she heard his strong Spanish accent. 'Hi, Lara. How are you feeling?'

How was she feeling? Her mind was foggy and she couldn't quite work out where she was. She was lying down on a bed. The man had hold of her arm and was wrapping a blood pressure cuff around… Suddenly, her memory caught up in a rush. The cramps. The first responder. The operating theatre. *Oh no.* She tried to push herself up from the bed, but a pain seared across her stomach and she fell back. 'Where's Matt?'

The nurse was smiling at her. 'Please, just give yourself a minute. He has gone to NICU. With your daughter. He didn't know whether he should stay with you or go with her. Then I think his exact words were, "She'll bloody kill me if I don't go with the baby."'

My daughter? The baby? Dare I hope? 'Did she make it? Is she okay?'

It was one second and one lifetime before he replied. 'She's doing okay. A very respectable weight for a premature baby, and her colour was good. Congratulations, Mummy.'

A well of emotion rose up through Lara's chest and threatened to overwhelm her. She was okay. Her baby was okay. 'Can I see her? Can I go to her now?'

The nurse was about to reply when the door opened and Matt came into the recovery room. She could barely see his face for the size of his smile. 'You're awake.'

She thought he was up in the special care baby unit. 'What are you doing here? You should have stayed with the baby.'

The nurse chuckled to himself as he finished checking Lara's obs. He winked at Matt. 'You said she'd say that.'

Matt held his hands up. 'I did go with her. But they need to get her equipment sorted out and they said it was a good time for me to pop back down and check on you.'

Lara's heart started to race. Was there something wrong? What were they keeping from her? 'What equipment? What is it? Tell me.'

Matt took her hand. 'Hey, hey, shush. She's fine. It's all standard stuff for a prem baby, they said. Just some oxygen and monitors.'

Lara looked at the nurse for confirmation, and he nodded. 'I'll give you two a minute while I find some orderlies to take you up to the ward.'

Matt leaned down beside Lara and kissed her on the cheek, brushed a few hairs from her forehead. His own eyes were full. 'Wait until you meet her, Lara. She's the most beautiful baby you've ever seen.'

She tried to speak but she could only sob. All these years. All the loss. The pain. The ache. Everything tumbled out of her. Matt wrapped himself around her and his sobs joined hers.

Once Lara had persuaded the nurse on the ward that she was up to it, Matt took her in a wheelchair up to the neonatal intensive care unit to meet their daughter. It was strange to think that so many people had seen her before Lara could. The doctors, the nurses, Matt. Lara hadn't even been awake to see her born. How would it feel when she saw her for the first time? Would it even feel real?

Security was very tight to get into NICU and Lara couldn't bear how long it took to go through to the right ward. Didn't they know how desperate she was to see her baby? It was so quiet in there, just the beeps of a few machines and the squeak of the nurses' shoes on the floor. Matt pushed her wheelchair after the nurse who was showing them to their daughter's incubator. Their daughter. That was never going to get old.

'Here she is.' The nurse smiled and pointed at the plastic box in front of them.

And there she was.

How could she put into words that moment when she saw her child for the first time? A tiny, perfect human being. A living, breathing baby. It didn't matter how much she had tried to imagine it, nothing could have prepared her for the reality of that moment. Lara and Matt had waited so long for this, had been disappointed so many times, had endured such terrible loss. But in that moment, everything was worth it. Every injection, every medication, every ache.

Matt pushed her chair closer and Lara placed a hand on the top of the incubator. She couldn't stop looking at her. She was so incredibly perfect. Her hands, her feet, her mouth. Matt was right, she was the most beautiful baby she had ever seen.

The nurse leaned forwards and opened a circular flap in the side of the incubator. 'You can touch her.'

Lara held her breath. Her hand shook as she reached inside the hole and placed her fingertip into her daughter's palm. 'Hello, baby. I'm your mummy. And I've waited so long to meet you.'

CHAPTER FORTY-SIX

Shelley

Hospital corridors were always anonymous and echoing. This one had paintings of various exotic birds in homage to its name: Nightingale Ward. Which sounded a lot nicer than special care baby unit. Shelley had been itching all week to come in and see Lara for herself. Although Lara had texted her a picture of Baby Girl Simpson in her incubator, she wanted to hear it from her lips that both she and her new daughter were healthy and happy.

Lara's face was difficult to read. Exhaustion, anxiety and... relief?

Shelley hugged her gently; Lara's hands across the bottom of her stomach suggested that she was still tender from the emergency C-section. 'How is she?'

Lara's face lifted as she spoke. 'Perfect. Tiny, helpless. And so incredibly beautiful.'

It was wonderful to see the pride in Lara's face as she spoke. It was worth the week's wait. 'Oh, Lara. I'm so pleased she's okay. And you? How are you feeling?'

They shuffled along the corridor towards the hospital canteen. Matt was in the ward with their baby girl; Lara had originally said that she couldn't leave her to see Shelley, but Matt had assured her that it would do her good to go and get a coffee and see the world outside the ward in daylight.

'I'm okay. My stomach feels really tender and you can see I'm a bit slow getting about, but I'm just so relieved that she is okay. It's a bit tough being on the ward with the other mums because they have their babies right there next to them. But I've had a word with myself about feeling jealous.' She wiped away a fat tear; her voice croaked as she finished. 'I don't ever need to be jealous of anyone ever again. I'm a mum, Shelley. I'm an actual mum.'

There was something so pure and real in the way she spoke that it squeezed at Shelley's heart. She held out her elbow for Lara to link her arm for support. 'And you will be the best mum in the world.'

As they continued down the corridor, Lara filled her in on the last few days. The baby had weighed a surprisingly robust 4lbs 2oz and had only needed a couple of days' breathing assistance. This was said with an air of pride totally appropriate for a new mother. She also described how the nurses had shown her how to change a nappy by putting her hands through the port holes.

'When I got to hold her, oh Shelley, I just can't describe how wonderful it was. They lifted her from the incubator – naked apart from her nappy – and put her inside my pyjama top with a blanket over the both of us. I could feel her body, warm against my skin. Her tiny movements. Her breath like a little bird fluttering at the bottom of my neck.' She held her hands up to her chest as she spoke, as if the baby was there.

The ward wasn't far from the canteen, so even at Lara's pace it wasn't long before they were sitting in the same area Shelley had occupied a week earlier. It felt a lot sunnier seven days on. She made sure Lara was settled comfortably before buying them coffees and cake.

Lara picked at the lemon muffin she'd chosen, focusing on it rather than looking at Shelley. 'I am so glad you were there, Shelley. I keep going over and over it in my head while I'm sitting in there. If I had been on my own, I don't know… I just can't bear to think…' When she looked up again, her eyes were fearful at the thought of it.

Shelley reached over and put her hands around Lara's. 'Don't think about that anymore. I *was* there and we got you here and everything is fine. You're both okay.'

Lara gave her a watery smile. 'And what about you? You were going to tell me about your plans. I know you aren't taking the job, so what now?'

In the last couple of days, they had texted back and forth a few times. Shelley had told her that she wasn't going for the job but had said she'd explain everything when she saw her. Since losing Greg, she'd lost touch with a lot of people. Some of the friends she would have assumed would be there had taken a step away. She got it. It couldn't have been easy to be around her, and she'd been so unresponsive – she could understand why some people had stopped checking in. But Lara had been there for her. 'It can wait. Once you're back home, we can sit down and talk about it properly.'

'Okay, but you have to promise that you will come straight over and tell me. That is, if I haven't turned into a complete baby bore. She is my one topic of conversation at the moment, I'm afraid.'

'I think I can allow you that. At least for another week.' Shelley winked at her.

Lara grinned. 'You know, I never actually thought of her as a real live baby. I know that sounds crazy but it was just too… terrifying. I didn't dare to picture her because I didn't want to jinx it. I didn't want to risk the fact that she wouldn't actually come.'

Shelley smiled. 'Well, that's completely understandable. After everything that you've been through.'

Now she had started to talk about her daughter, Lara didn't seem to want to stop. 'It's the weirdest thing though. She looks *exactly* as she should. Exactly as I would have imagined her if I had let myself do it.' She screwed up her nose. 'I really do sound like one of those parent bores, don't I?'

Shelley laughed; it felt good. 'You do. But it's great to hear. You bore away.'

'Thank you. And I really do appreciate you coming in. But… do you mind if I take the rest of that coffee to go so that I can get back to them? I can't bear being away yet.' Lara pulled a self-mocking face but she was already pushing herself up out of her chair.

Shelley moved furniture out of the way to make it easier for Lara to leave the table. 'Of course, I'll walk you back to the ward and leave you to your girl. I don't suppose you know yet how long you will be in here?'

They started their slow walk out of the canteen, Lara's steps still tentative. 'I can't pin anyone down to a time frame but one of the nurses said that if she continues to make good progress, she might be home in three weeks.'

Shelley smiled at the thought of Lara cross-examining the staff. 'Well, that doesn't sound too long. If you need me to bring anything to the hospital for you or Matt, just text me a list.'

'Thanks. They want to discharge me soon anyway but I'm not thinking about that right now. Just the idea of going home and leaving her here makes me feel a bit sick.'

Shelley rubbed her arm. 'Don't think about that yet. Oh, Lara, I'm just so happy for you, I really am. And I can't wait to meet her. Does she have a name yet?'

A smile spread across Lara's face. 'She certainly does. As soon as I knew I had a daughter, there was only one possible name we could give her.' She stopped and turned for dramatic effect.

'Her name is Joy.'

CHAPTER FORTY-SEVEN

Shelley

The Garden of Remembrance looked even brighter today with the vibrant colours of the blooms. Shelley found the bench which she was beginning to think of as her own.

There was another family here today. A mother and her two adult sons. The sons looked older than Shelley, and the mother was elderly. She watched as one of the men gave his mother an arm and she leaned against him. It was hard to lose a partner at any age.

They were far enough away that they wouldn't hear her talking aloud if she kept it quiet. It was always the getting started which felt odd. 'Hi, Greg. I'm here again, come for a chat.'

She always paused as if he was going to reply. It felt the right thing to do. 'I've been at Dee's again today. Cuddling our nephew, Dee's little boy Jacob. Oh, Greg, he looks so much like you. I know that sounds crazy. I know how we used to mock people who said that their baby looked like them. All babies look the same, right? But he does look like you. I cried again when I held him today. I cried for you and for our baby who didn't make it. Dee cried too. She misses you so dreadfully. She keeps saying that she wants Jacob to have a brother just like you; or a sister he can boss around, like you did.'

She paused again and let the tears come. No good came from suppressing her feelings. She watched the family as they said their goodbyes to their father and husband. The mother kissed her fingertips and pressed them against the brass plaque. The taller of her sons put an arm around her and did the same.

'I'm surrounded by babies these days. Lara and Matt have asked me to be godmother for baby Joy. I was worried it was out of sympathy, but Matt said he wanted to thank me for looking after Lara the day she went into labour. She's a beautiful little baby. Makes me want one of my own. That's what I wanted to talk to you about.'

Lara had finally brought baby Joy home, three weeks after she was born. After they were settled into a routine, Shelley had kept her promise and explained to Lara what she wanted. And now she wanted to tell Greg too.

'When Lara first asked me what I wanted, all I could think of was you. And it's still true. The thing I want most in the whole world is to have you back. I want you sitting in your chair, moaning about the England cricket team, planning where we are going to go for dinner. To have you beside me in bed tonight so that I can put my cold feet on your legs. To ask you what I should do about work or holidays or which electric company we can switch to. But I can't.'

Her voice cracked. That was when she felt his absence the most: when she had to make a big decision or wanted to talk through her options. Now she had to rely on herself and her own intuition; it was difficult to get used to.

'Lara gave me this book, *Make Way for Joy*. It's how we got started clearing out that room. But it wasn't just the room that was full of things I needed to get rid of. I'd pushed something else down and not faced it. I tried pretending it wasn't real.'

She closed her eyes for a few moments. When she opened them again, the mother and her sons had been joined by other members of their family. One of the younger children was holding a small kite which was flapping in the air. That was how she felt, like a kite that had had its string cut. There was nothing anchoring her anymore, nothing holding her to the earth. It was scary and strange but she also felt free.

'I've had to be honest with myself. There was so much about our marriage that was wonderful, but I had to make sacrifices too. Some big sacrifices. And, the thing is, now you aren't here, I can admit that there is something else I want. I want a family, Greg. I want a baby.'

Saying the words out loud was liberating. She should have said them a long time ago, when they might have changed things. 'I love you, Greg. I love you and miss you so very much. But I wish things had been different. I wish that *I* had been different.'

Losing Greg had been the worst thing that had ever happened to her. Over the last year she had hidden herself away and tried to keep going, but she couldn't do that anymore. She didn't want to do that anymore. It was time to start living her life, her way. And though it made her feel guilty to think it, that meant she might be a mother after all.

It's never too late, the woman on the train had said. Shelley was only thirty-three. Steve's face flashed up in her mind. After telling Lara about their conversation, she'd grudgingly admitted that she did find him attractive. Whatever did, or didn't, happen between the two of them, it was possible that she might be ready for another relationship someday. Even if she wasn't, though, there were other ways she could have the family she wanted so very much.

At the entrance to the Garden of Remembrance, Lara stood waiting for her with Joy in her pram. Losing Greg had been devastating. His loss had opened up a gaping hole that she'd thought could never be filled. She had been so frightened of facing the void he'd left because she was scared she might fall in and never climb out. But she wouldn't fall, because her wonderful new friend wouldn't let her.

'I hope you understand, Greg. I do love you and miss you so very much. I'm going to go now. I'll be back soon.'

Just as she had seen the older lady do, Shelley touched her fingers to her lips and then pressed them to the brass plaque with Greg's name.

EPILOGUE

Clear carpet, half-empty wardrobes and a new cot which had taken nearly an hour to put together. Shelley had been left with two extra screws, but it seemed sturdy enough for her small house guest. Dee and Jamie were spending the night in a hotel for their wedding anniversary and baby Jacob was coming to stay with Auntie Shelley.

On the bedside table, a black-and-white photograph: Greg and her on that first weekend away in Southwold. She ran a finger around the edge of the frame. It still hurt to look at his smiling face but she needed to do it. She kissed the photograph and put it back.

She'd been for a drink with Steve, too. It had been purely platonic – they'd stayed in touch after the local office had closed – but it had been nice. Maybe she would try a proper date in the near future. Also on the table were the leaflets she had been reading: fostering, adoption, respite care. There had been a fostering open evening in Guildford last weekend, and she had gone along to find out what was involved. She wasn't sure if she was ready for that yet, but it was a definite possibility.

Underneath the leaflets was a now-familiar smiling face. *Make Way for Joy*. It felt a lifetime ago since Lara had pressed this book onto her and they'd begun the clear-out of this room. Of her mind. Her soul.

In the last few months, she had been able to talk about Greg several times without crying and had even laughed with Dee about the time he'd made a fool of himself during charades one Christmas. It was still painful to think about him but it wasn't unbearable. She was getting there. She wasn't hiding anymore.

It wouldn't be easy, but it was time to start the next chapter. She'd made way for joy.

A LETTER FROM EMMA

I want to say a huge thank you for choosing to read *The Forgotten Wife*. If you enjoyed it, and want to be kept up-to-date with my future releases, just sign up at the following link. Your email address will never be shared and you can unsubscribe at any time.

www.bookouture.com/emma-robinson

Most people have experienced loss in their lives, and sometimes, the people who are there for you most are the ones you least expect. Bereavement hits people in different ways, and Shelley's approach – to push it down and not think about it – is not uncommon. For years after losing my dad, I couldn't listen to his beloved Beatles songs because it was just too painful. I believe wholeheartedly in the power of friendship and am extremely fortunate to have wonderful girlfriends who get me through any bad times. In *The Forgotten Wife*, I wanted to explore the idea of two broken women helping one another to heal. Giving them the space to do that in this novel comes via the fictitious book *Make Way for Joy* which was itself inspired by books like Marie Kondo's *The Life Changing Magic of Tidying*, *Hinch Yourself Happy* by Mrs Hinch, and *The Year of Less* by Cait Flanders – all of which I know have changed the lives of many of their readers.

If you have enjoyed *The Forgotten Wife*, please help me to reach other readers by writing a quick review. I'd also love to hear what you thought of it. Reviews make a huge difference in helping other people find my book and I am grateful for every single one.

I also love hearing from my readers. Come and join me on my Facebook page Motherhood for Slackers. You can also find me on Twitter or my website.

Stay in touch!
Emma

motherhoodforslackers

@emmarobinsonuk

www.motherhoodforslackers.com

ACKNOWLEDGEMENTS

Thank you to my very clever publisher Isobel Akenhead for her fantastic editing skills. Also, to Kim Nash for going above and beyond in PR, author care and general all-round fantasticness, and to everyone at Bookouture who has worked on this novel including DeAndra Lupu for insightful copy editing, proofreaders, cover designers and the marketing team. I feel so lucky to be working with you all. Another shout-out to the growing family of Bookouture authors who are the most supportive, funny and wonderful people to hang out with: online and off.

Publishing a book can be a scary business and the book bloggers and reviewers who support authors are more loved than they probably realise. Thanks to everyone who has reviewed this and my other books and talked about them online. I want to say a special thanks to the members of The Fiction Café Book Club for writing generous things about my books and for giving me a fun and supportive place to hang out online. Particularly Wendy Clarke and Emma Bunting for inviting me to do an author live and to Michaela Balfour, Ellie Bell, Lorna Corbin and Chloe Jordan for (virtually) holding my hand and for being the fastest readers in the West. Your support is hugely appreciated.

A huge debt of gratitude goes to my friend Jane Hunt for sharing her experiences of losing her wonderful husband Mark at such a young age. This story is very different from yours, but your generosity and honesty have helped so much and I hope I have done well with everything you told me.

Grateful thanks to my eagle-eyed pal Carrie Harvey for proof-reading help. Thanks to my lovely friend/dance partner/caravan buddy Nina Barnard for talking me through the corporate travel industry. Thank you to Sarah Martin for letting me steal some of your hilarious conversations with your clothes, and to Yasmin Youssaf for advising me on the yoga scene, which unfortunately didn't survive the edit – I will use it elsewhere!

Anyone who follows me online will know that I have a group of girlfriends who buy me the most amazing publication day gifts. What you may not know is how supportive and wonderful they are, and how they have believed in me from the beginning. Thank you to Louise Hoskins, Theresa Allen, Ashlie Hughes, Kerry Enever, Tracy Harper, Hayley Lill, Anita Hole and the 'Queen of Gifts' Felicity Squire. I love you all.

Thanks to William and Scarlett for playing Pokémon for about eight hours straight so that I could finish my edits, and to my mum for reminding me to speak slowly at my book launch. Even though I am forty-six.

And to Dan. For everything else.

Made in United States
North Haven, CT
08 March 2024

49688490R00168